W9-BNG-234

OLDER BROTHER

Mahir Guven

OLDER BROTHER

*Translated from the French
by Tina Kover*

Europa
editions

Europa Editions
214 West 29th Street
New York, N.Y. 10001
www.europaeditions.com
info@europaeditions.com

Copyright © Editions Philippe Rey, 2017
Published by special arrangement with Editions Philippe Rey, France,
in conjunction with their duly appointed agents L'autre agence
and 2 Seas Literary Agency
First Publication 2019 by Europa Editions

Translation by Tina Kover
Original title: *Grand frère*
Translation copyright © 2019 by Europa Editions

Library of Congress Cataloging in Publication Data is available
ISBN 978-1-60945-549-1

Guven, Mahir
Older Brother

Book design and cover illustration by Emanuele Ragnisco
www.mekkanografici.com

Prepress by Grafica Punto Print – Rome

Printed in the USA

For my mother, my sister Dodi, my bro Philippe,
Fotto and Greilsi, Natalie, Martina, Pierre, and Maïmiti.
For André.
For my family, and friends both past and present.

OLDER BROTHER

1
OLDER BROTHER

Death is the only true thing. Everything else is just a list of details. Whatever happens to you in life, all roads lead to the grave. Once you figure that out, all you have to do is find a reason to live. Life? Getting closer to death has put me and life on a first-name basis. I flirt with one while thinking of the other. All the time, since the other dog, my flesh, my blood, my brother, went away, back there, to the land of psychos and lunatics, to a place where they'll cut your head off for a half-smoked cigarette. The Holy Land. *Cham*, we call it in the hood. A lot of people say that word with fear; others— well, a few of them, anyway—with ecstasy. In the world of normal people, they call it Syria, with whispers and dark looks, as if they were talking about hell.

It destroyed the old man when the kid brother left. All you have to do is count the new wrinkles above his unibrow to see that. He spent his whole life slaving to make sure we'd choose the right path. Every morning, he dragged his ass into the driver's seat of that taxi to go up to Guantanamo, or down into the mines. In taxi-speak that means driving up to Roissy or down to Paris, taking customers into the citadel, the one we'll never conquer. And night after night, he brought back bags crammed with cash, to fill up the fridge. Starvation, hunger, an empty belly? We never felt it. Always had butter, and sometimes even cream in our spinach.

But no matter what Pop did, nothing around here is a perfect circle except the earth. Sometimes I'd like to be God, so I could save the world. And sometimes I just want to end it all. Including myself. If it were that easy, I'd just jump out a window—or maybe off the bridge at the Bondy RER station, right in front of an oncoming train; slower that way, and messier. But really, I haven't got a clue about any of it and I don't give a shit anyway, because today is the eighth, and that's the day God chose for his plan.

September 8th is the day the Virgin Mary was born. Not the seventh, not the ninth. The eighth was chosen for her birth, and, years later, it was on that day that she was entrusted with the mission of giving birth to Jesus. Eight is a number without end, the only one, a double circle. A perfect thing. Once you start thinking about it, you can't stop. Eight: a trick, a swagger, a swindler, the dodgy story a guy from Marseilles tries to feed you. And it's also the day when the woman in the picture hanging on the wall above our sideboard, the one smiling next to my dad, went home to be with Him. End of mission. Dead.

They quiver every time. My lips. So, I try to do without her. Her arms, her hands, her scent, her voice. And her face, and her smile, and the gentle way she'd stroke our hair. It's not easy to live. Sounds pathetic, but I'm not ashamed. I'd rather live without this thing lodged in my heart. Get up early, before the sun comes up, even; not a care in the world, and drink my coffee in some café on the boulevard de Belleville, reading the sports page, listening to the sounds of dishes clattering and waiters bustling around. It sucks to die in September, on the eighth. Because that's the Virgin Mary's birthday, and Mary didn't ask anyone for anything; she just got Jesus put in her belly, and then, out of necessity, she became a saint. Nobody really understood it. Nobody. Not the prophets, not the caliphs, not the priests, not the popes. It wasn't Jesus that God chose; it was Mary. The one he chose to *make* Jesus. She was the only one to receive his favor. She was the divine choice.

In the picture on the wall, my dad is still young. Skinny as fishing-line. No mustache, but he's already got the bushy uni-brow, taped right above that big foreign honker of his. Zahié, my dad's mother, my *jidda*, used to say that unibrow was like the highway from Damascus to Aleppo. As if the angel Gabriel had stuck a black bar in the middle of his forehead to make him stand out, so he'd never lose sight of him. So my dad got one eyebrow, and Mary got called home to be with Him. How many years has she been gone? At least ten or fifteen . . . ? Twenty, maybe? She loved Zidane, thought he was so hand-some. The French national team. *Les bleus*. Thuram and his two goals. The World Cup. Eighteen years! It's been eighteen years, and I've managed to survive all that time. Longer with-out her than with her, and yet it's still raw. It still burns. Like a hole filled with hot coals in the middle of my chest. Why us? Everything was going so well back then—I mean, I think it was. I can't really remember anymore, but I feel like it was. But maybe it wasn't. You never know. And why has Pop stayed sin-gle all these years? You should see him, so bitter and grumpy. Anyone who gets a smile out of him deserves a medal. What does he do, other than watch TV, soccer, political news? Or talk about his taxi? I don't even know if it's the job or life with-out my mom that's done it, but he's about as lively as an oyster on weed. Both, probably. But eighteen years alone! With just his taxi and his dick. Christ. One hand on the steering wheel, the other on his cock. And I'm not positive he does jerk off, even just to make sure the machinery still works. Maybe the old man uses hookers? He's always been kind of like a cowboy; a taxi for a horse and his tongue for a gun, cheeks loaded with words to spit at assholes, and two sons for sidekicks. One gone off to the Far East, and the other at the kitchen table, slurping his soup and listening to his fish stories. No, man, really, it would have been simpler another way.

He is stuck in solitary confinement. In a prison of doubts and fears. All you have to do is zoom in on the rock he's living under and watch how carefully he sets the table to wonder what the hell he's doing in this shitty building, in this slum neighborhood, with these punk kids, this Pashtun face and these gypsy teeth and this *gadjo* job that'll end up driving him around the bend. People think we're Jewish, I swear to Allah, because every Friday he puts out these fancy table settings like it's the fucking president's house or something. But it's meaningless, and anyway, my old man says he's a Communist, not a Muslim, and according to him that's not a religion, so . . .

Whether there are two or twenty people at dinner, he leaves nothing to chance; the arrangement of the food, the assortment of colors, the dishes, the silverware. *Appetite begins with the eyes first, and then the nose*, the old man says to me in Arabic, sprinkling spices on a dish of eggplant caviar. The table itself could raise its right hand and swear, *Yeah, your dad's basically a woman*. Well, half the time, anyway. Tonight I think he used up his feminine side cooking dinner, because all these beautiful *mezze* are spread out on a plastic tablecloth. Every time he gets that thing out—*to protect the table*, he says—I can hardly keep from screaming at him. Why buy a cherrywood table if you're going to drape a cheap, crappy piece of plastic over it? He's such a goddamned bumpkin, I swear on my mother's . . . !

Five girls were born before him, and he was raised as if he were the sixth. Housework, cooking, even sewing with minute attention to detail. Drudgery, sweaty forehead, dry hands, aching back. Not a man like other men, no. He can't be, the ancient customs and education given to women in his country have made him a unique specimen. His mom and sisters trained him like a Syrian girl coached from infancy to marry some asshole from the next village—and that's the best-case scenario, because it's usually a cousin instead, to keep a promise made between fathers over their cribs.

That's what he is half the time. The other half, he's just an almost ordinary guy with a mustache and a croaky voice who chews with his mouth open while coming up with his umpteenth theory about the war back in the old country. With every word, he spews out tiny pieces of spit-soaked food that end up getting caught in his mustache. Then, his big hairy hand wads up a napkin like a toilet-sponge, and he wipes his mouth like a construction worker sandpapering paint off a wall. My old man is practically a work of art. He never shuts up and talks about the same things over and over: Assad, ISIS, the Americans, Merkel, Hollande, Israel, Damascus, Aleppo, the Kurds, and Tadmor, his native village, blah, blah, blah, grunting at every comma and swearing at every period. Goddamn, he's a pain in the ass, but he's my pop, and you've just got to live with it, you know? Family, man. Ordinary.

So the table's all laid out like a photo in a cookbook. A banquet for ten, but there's only two of us left. His wife? Taken away by the grim reaper. His mother? Nursing home. His older son? Right there at the table, as expected. The other son? Disappeared, gone away, far, far away, supposedly to help the needy. But he's most likely right there with the lunatics, at war, on his way to death, maybe in the desert, maybe in a cemetery, cut down with a Kalashnikov in his hand, or still alive in his old man's village. The place from the Bible and TV and the Internet; the place with the religious nuts, the one everyone's horrified by, without really understanding what's going on there. To Cham, as the guys around here call it. Syria, get it? He's fucked off to the middle of the desert, west of the Tigris, east of the Euphrates and the Mediterranean, where life's worth less than a sideways glance or a half-smoked cigarette or a wrongly wrapped headscarf. That son of a bitch. Sorry, Mom.

2
YOUNGER BROTHER

You know, bro, deep down, I'm just like you. There are two *me*s. The one at the hospital who worked hard and kept his head down but was really just going around in circles, and the other one, who wanted to save the world. Because the world was calling out to me for help. At night I could hear them crying, the Palestinian and Malian and Sudanese and Somalian and Syrian children, and all the others too. Bombs were raining down on innocent people, and I was helpless to stop it, and it was driving me insane. We were supposed to be living in the land of liberty and human rights, but the government itself was sponsoring the bombardments. I've wondered for a long time why I left. Life's complicated. The choices we make, the paths we take, they depend on the little boy tucked away in our brains—on the way he develops, the way he grows, day by day. And on our state of mind at the time. There are some roads you can go down and turn around halfway, and others where, the moment you take the first step, it's all over. And others, too, where you don't know what you'll find at the end. The fear of missing out on something draws you like a magnet. When in doubt, you go.

It all started one afternoon in September. The eighth. The same day Mom died. At the hospital, I had two friends. One was a Turk, a real one, with Asian features, the back of his head so flat it was as if someone had ironed it. An immigrant's son, and a nurse, like me. My other friend an old Indonesian doctor who should have already retired. His name was Naeem, but people called him Guendou. At first they thought he was Indian and they nicknamed him Hindu, and then somehow that got twisted into Guendou. Twenty-five years, he'd been a doctor. He definitely had more surgeries under his belt than almost anyone in the world. He was a true engineer of the flesh. The guy could jury-rig just about anything in the thoracic cage: ventricles, aortas, lungs. He wasn't a butcher; he was an artist. He would open up chests with slow, calm movements, plunge his hands and his instruments inside, snip, cut, clean, sew, repair, close up. He was like a couturier of living tissue. I'd stand next to him when he operated, like his squire, handing him his weapons. Other than the interns, he was the only one who talked to me. It went even beyond that; he'd explain to me what he was doing. Where he came from, that was how you learned. You started out as a nurse, but you didn't have to stay one. If you studied part-time, you could aspire to better things. It might take years, but semester by semester you'd earn those doctor's stripes on your shoulder, and then you could wield a scalpel.

September eighth was my first transplant. I'll never forget it. Because it was the day Mom died, and the day we gave some poor guy his life back. It was an opportunity I'd been given, but I didn't feel totally ready. Transplants take concentration, endurance, experience. They take a long time, sometimes ten or fifteen hours. One day, during bypass surgery, Guendou asked me if I wanted to do a transplant with him. Switching out somebody's heart is a huge deal; you've got to show up in a big way. That's how it is at the hospital; you're in a department, and you gain confidence, and little by little you find your place.

So, on one September eighth at around six o'clock in the morning, I got a call to get to the hospital as fast as I could. I'd trained for this operation. Guendou had been badgering me for weeks to brush up on my nursing protocol. Usually, the patient who's receiving the transplant comes in first, and the nurses start "preparing" him for the donor organ's arrival. Then we, the surgical team, get the patient once he's under anesthesia. Lying there in a smock on the gurney, under the white neon light, the patient looks dead. It's up to us to fix him, to get the machine up and running again. The patient waiting for a new heart that day was a North African man. Big head, big lips, short kinky hair. Not old; forty-five, maybe. My colleagues were acting as if it were just another day, but I kept thinking about the guy's life—his wife and kids, his job, his apartment, his mom and dad, his neighbors. His face was pale. I thought to myself. *Holy shit*. When we close this guy's chest and he wakes up, he's going to have a new heart. With some scars, maybe, but brand new. A second chance, man. He'd better spend the rest of his life thanking God.

Guendou told me to focus. He knew the first transplant causes a sort of emotional freak-out in your head. Surgeons always act as if everything's fine, you know, calm as a butcher slicing steaks. Work with precision, be quick without rushing, and eliminate any unnecessary movements, because from the time a donor organ is harvested and assigned to a recipient, you've only got a matter of hours to get everything done. Otherwise, it all goes in the trash.

Guendou sliced him open from the neck to the middle of his abdomen, and then it was Mr. Fix It all the way. I handed him a saw, and he cut through the sternum and then pried the chest open with a pair of surgical pliers. Every single time we crack a chest, I want to punch the patient in the face. Always full of fat. They eat too much. You lose time taking out all that shit. Anyway, then we put him on a heart-lung bypass machine. I love that thing. That day, I kept thinking about how God had even managed to make us invent a machine that could replace the human heart. It collects the blood at the entrance to the cardiac muscle and reinjects it, full of oxygen, at the exit. It does what the heart and lungs do. It was so crazy: this Maghrebi's life depended on a machine that looks just like a gas pump. At the controls, a kind of DJ regulates oxygenation, outflow, and whatever else it takes to keep the patient alive. So now we'd prepared this guy, and we left him there with his chest wide open, with his old heart beating while it waited for its replacement, and we went off to the break room. Guendou gave me all the hospital scoop. He was a hell of a busybody, that guy. So there he was, chattering about all the departmental gossip, but I couldn't stop thinking about the patient alone in the operating room, and his family, waiting anxiously outside. The slightest screw-up and the patient would be a goner. And we were just sitting there, calmly drinking coffee, like everything was normal. Life is insane, man.

As usual, Naeem wouldn't stop bugging me about medical school. I told him it wasn't my fault, that where I came from, a nursing job was already the top. He laughed and said he was tired of answering my questions that I had a lot of the qualities it took to be a good doctor. That I had the right mentality for it, asked the right questions, that I could go far. I didn't know, then, that going far would mean leaving for the old country. With my nursing diploma, I could skip the first year of medical school, but after that it would take me at least four or five years before I could operate, and ten to be a surgeon. And I couldn't see myself doing a shorter version of med school just to end up an idiot behind a GP's desk. Not for me. I would have had to open a practice close to home and spend my time patching up all the freaks and losers in the neighborhood. More than anything, the problem wasn't my abilities; it was my lack of technique and, especially, the right education. College wasn't my thing. It freaked me out. Every time the interns talked to me, I'd think to myself that I could never have friends there, that they'd hate me. I knew I grasped things more quickly than the young doctors my age, and it made me crazy to receive orders from people who were less intelligent than me but who had the degree. In this country, people like me don't belong in the ivory tower. They don't want us there. No one tells us how to get there. And the worst part is that when we talk, people look right through us; they laugh at us, our hairstyles and clothes, our religion, what we watch on TV, the music we listen to. But I didn't say any of this to Guendou. He wouldn't have gotten it. He would just have thought I was a loser with a chip on my shoulder.

He made me sad. He made me think of Dad. The guy had come over from Indonesia when he was thirty-five and had worked in this hospital for twenty-five years. He'd done the most complex surgeries. The hospital bigwigs used to sub-contract procedures out to him, and he'd slave away with his scalpels in return for a salary on par with that of a taxi driver, like a kind of medical Cyrano de Bergerac. The worst part of the whole thing was that he'd recently asked for permission to retire, and the management said they couldn't let him do it because of some bullshit regulation. Totally ridiculous. I mean, okay, he didn't look like he was going to starve to death or anything, but when I thought about everyone who'd stepped on him on their way up the ladder, I wanted to hit them all. It's that kind of stuff that makes people fucking lose it in France. Because all through school, they talk us to death about justice and injustice. Of course, everyone's in agreement about justice. Everyone's for it. Once we've been thoroughly educated, we learn how to revolt, fists raised, against anything that's unjust. And then one day it's right there in front of you, and everything you believed in comes to nothing. You want to blow everything up. Especially when it's that kind of people, the respectable, well-educated, good French citizens, who'll blather on until the cows come home about right and wrong, and then turn around and swindle a poor

Indonesian immigrant. The very same people you'd thought were defenders of justice.

So anyway, he was telling me about his retirement problems, and we heard sirens blaring. Out the window, we could see flashing lights and an ambulance, escorted by two police motorcycles, like when a prisoner was being transported. It was the donor organ, arriving from Avicenne Hospital. When we got back to the operating room, Naeem was stressed. We'd taken out almost all of the bad heart. That piece of rotten muscle was lying in the waste container like a corpse.

Guendou didn't show it, but he was angry at himself for losing the few minutes it had taken to drink a coffee. Beside him, in an iron bowl, the new heart was floating in some cold liquid. The first thing to do is to graft it onto the auricle of the old heart. Then you suture the veins and the aortas. It seems easy, but it takes quite a bit of time and it's stressful—you have to stay focused. Next to Guendou, I followed his actions to the letter; I tried to think ahead. As soon as he needed something, I reacted quickly so we wouldn't lose a second. But even when you do everything perfectly, there's always some damn thing that doesn't cooperate and you have to improvise, like cheating on the suture when the size of the donor aorta doesn't match the size of the recipient's, and they don't fit together. And I mean, you're up to your elbows in a living being, so of course it's not like in math; you have to tinker around, think fast and fix it. Gently, bit by bit, he closed up the chest.

We went out to eat with Naeem next door to the hospital, to debrief after the eight-hour operation. He had to go back, after that, to monitor the patient. The new heart was in the process of adapting. With a transplant, there's a significant risk of rejection, especially in the first few days. Naeem was a kind of hero, my role model. The perfect immigrant: highly trained, educated, calm, willing. But instead of putting him on a pedestal, they'd used him and bled him dry. I told him I wanted to leave France. I'd been thinking about it for six months. I wanted to go and care for people who really needed it. Brothers and sisters who hadn't been as lucky as I was to grow up in a country at peace. And here we have all the resources we need, and enough people to provide medical care. And diseases of decay weren't my thing. When I said that, Naeem's face turned serious, like an "I'm proud of you" kind of look. An encouraging look. He wanted to introduce me to somebody who could help me with my plans, because he knew a lot of people in humanitarian work. When he spoke, it was as if Gandhi were speaking through him. He chose each word carefully. His eyes shone. I wished Dad had been like him: a mentor, not a dictator. So Naeem went back to the hospital and I followed him. The bastard was still alive. Yeah, bro, the truth is that a guy who you've just given a new heart is a bastard saved by God. The new heart was beating and the bastard was breathing. And the other truth is that He took Mom away because the old man was a sinner. A blasphemer, no less. And not even Mom's death taught him to keep his mouth shut. That day, I told myself I'd had enough. I wanted to be like Guendou. To operate. To do real things, not just to hand over surgical instruments and compresses. Ideas had to become plans now, and plans had to become reality. As the priest of our other grandmother—our mom's mother, who was from Brittany—used to say, "Help yourself, and heaven will help you."

On the metro on the way home, everyone was dull and gray as usual, but the divine ambience I felt myself surrounded by made all of them beautiful. We had saved a man! Holy shit! We'd given him back his life, the desire to keep going a little longer before taking off for heaven or hell. It was bizarre. Putting a stranger's heart in some dude changed everything. Bodies could be repaired. God had even guided us to invent heaven on Earth; eternal life. After your first transplant, that's it: you're on God's side once and for all. Life is too amazing to happen all by itself. It's beyond our understanding. I didn't sleep that night. I tossed and turned under the covers; the minutes ticked by as I glanced at my phone, and sleep didn't come. I kept thinking about the guy we'd given the new heart. About his life afterward. A second chance—that must make you want to change everything, to enjoy every second. Life's too short to spend twenty-five years in scrubs, in a hospital in Paris. I wanted adventure, the real thing. God was holding out a hand, and it was up to me to grab it.

The next morning, even before starting my shift, I told Guendou that I'd given it a lot of thought and I really wanted to leave. During our lunch hour, he arranged for me to meet with a guy from the NGO Doctors Without Borders. One of his friends. They went all over the world and were highly respected.

Three days later, I was in their offices next to the Place de la Bastille. A male nurse and a doctor greeted me in a dreary room overlooking the courtyard. I introduced myself and talked a little bit about my motivations and who I was. The doctor asked me where I was from and if I spoke Arabic. When I said Syria and yes, he smiled. He said he'd have a look at my application and call me shortly. Now it was just a matter of waiting. I was confident. I looked up, palms turned skyward, and whispered a prayer that a new day might be dawning for me.

3
OLDER BROTHER

A voice as rough as if it came from the center of the earth. The air leaves his lungs, rattles his thick, tobacco-caked vocal cords to kidnap some sound, which rises up into his throat, dodging pieces of barely-chewed food, slides beneath his mustache, and flies out into the room to punch my eardrums. The nerves receive it, transform it, and carry the information up there between my forehead and the back of my neck. Between Mars and Saturn. All my parts work, but I can't understand what he's saying. It's like an old AM radio. Impossible to tune, no matter how much you fiddle with the dial; it's staticky. You can catch snippets here and there, but more than anything else, it just hurts your ears. Elbows on the table, mustache wet with tea, he's sweaty with the effort it takes to eat as much as he eats. His forehead gleams with sweat that streams along his unibrow before rolling down his cheek, which is shaven close. Always. Every morning, otherwise it itches. The man is impressively hairy. It's all over him, and it grows back with amazing speed. My dad's the hairiest man I've ever known. Thank God I don't look like him. He's covered from head to toe. An endless forest, a sort of eight.

He puts down his knife. It's almost over. My dad's meals are always kind of like a marathon; once he starts, there's no stopping. He goes at it like a dingo. Then at some point, eventually, he puts down his knife, gives a sour little burp, swallows the bile back down, and realizes that he's got to stop, that he's eaten too much. The fork is still in his other hand, ready to stab something. One last olive? A piece of cheese? He considers it for a second, but the doc said no, otherwise he might end up six feet under. The fork lowers to his plate. He's done. And now I know I'm really in for it; I can feel it. There's been a taxi strike the last few days, and he's not going to be able to talk about anything else.

"You still working for the traitors?"

He can't wrap his head around it. His ass has basically grown roots in the seat of his taxi, and his brain is stuck on his 240,000 euro medallion.

"Why don't you just sell your license and retire?"

He mutters something in Arabic; I don't quite catch it all. Something like, *You've grown up to be an ass in a land of lions.* "You thirty years old soon, no? You moron. You idiot. I can't sell my license now. Retirement in two years. But you are going to kill us all with your Uber. More than twenty years, I've worked. All alone. Aren't you ashamed, betraying your father, working for the competition?"

I've never quite been able to figure out how somebody who hates French so much managed to earn a doctorate in France. Charity?

When he talks about my work, his eyes pop out and bulge with little red blood vessels. He goes into a sort of trance, even worse than when he hears Bashar al-Assad's name.

"Stupid. Stupid. Stupid! Idiot! This is all because you've been hanging out with those punk Arab friends of yours!"

"And you're not an Arab?"

"I'm a *human*, yeah? You'll say *yeah* to anything, but you're still an idiot! Human is more important than anything. Even God, he doesn't say *Arab* or *not Arab*; he tells you what's important five times a day. But that's for assholes who believe in God—like it's *God* who fills up your cart at the supermarket."

"*Astaghfirullah!* Come on, Dad, are you Syrian or aren't you?"

"*Astaghfirullah! Astaghfirullah!* Bah! What the hell you know about religion? Get your head out of your ass! *Syrian* doesn't mean *Arabic.* It's nationality, not ethnicity. I'm half Arabic, half Kurdish, but, above all, Communist."

Communist. That might be his favorite word. He says it with passion, his hand over his heart. And he only came up with the Kurdish part after the Siege of Kobanî. It gives him style, like white people who make up their own ancestry. We used to just be Syrians. Well, he was Syrian, and we were Maghrebis, Syrians, sometimes French, occasionally Breton; it depended on who we were hanging out with. In real life, until the war in Syria, we were all more just *banlieusards* than anything else. But since the war, everyone's been calling themselves Muslim.

"If you don't help your family, it's normal for problems after. If I didn't keep you busy, like the others you prison or scum or extreme Islamist now, go and cut heads off in Syria. Bobigny shit, anyway."

He doesn't even know what he's talking about. He always speaks like that, says the same things, like a broken record playing over and over. Blah blah blah. When he gets angry, his French turns broken, and French people can't understand him anymore. It's fine for us, because that kind of French is our native language. We've tried everything to correct him. Don't try to figure out why immigrants talk the way they do. Their tongues never assimilate as well as they do.

"You drink Syrian coffee?"

"Why don't you call it Turkish coffee?"

He waves the question away. More of his old-man gibberish. Don't say this; say that instead. Stupid stuff that just wastes time. It's my dad. You've just got to live with it.

"You know how to make coffee like back home?"

Pop's been nicer lately than he used to be. He just turned sixty; every breath brings him a little closer to death, and he's taking stock of his life, which, for him, means doling out little flashes of kindness, like a croupier of love. I think he's got nothing left to prove. To anyone. Maybe it's finally time for him to come out of his cage and live his life.

"You put one spoonful of coffee per cup you want to make. Then water. For one cup of coffee, you put one cup of water."

The mixture has begun boiling in the little copper saucepan on the stove. He skims the froth off the top with a spoon and divides it between the cups. His bullshit lightens up gradually, as it always does when he comes home. Because of the political problems in Syria, he's never been able to go back, so with food, coffee, and music, it's as if he were back in his village; he nurses his memories of the old country. Exile has never been his thing. He knows the history and politics and economics of this country like the back of his hand, but he doesn't really understand anything about France. He thinks it's a perfect country where everyone is intelligent. Except that bullshit is the most equitably distributed wealth in the world, and God hasn't left France out. So suddenly, it's as if a computer virus invades my dad's brain, and he can't make sense of it; the bullshit trips him up and infects him, and he starts spewing it himself. His hairy hand puts the coffee pot back on the burner so it will foam up a second time.

"Life's like Turkish coffee, or Syrian, or Greek; name meaningless not serious. Life's like coffee from home, okay?"

Meaningless not serious means *doesn't matter*, in real French.

"For success at all, you have to measure things out. Then watch, be patient, wait. You take froth off once, you make it foam twice, and you divide. At the end, you have nice, quiet cup of coffee. Gently. Take advantage. Turkish coffee is work and patience, then pleasure. Smell the aromas. You see? Like life. Work, then pleasure, fun. So important. You see?"

I didn't get a word of it. Grandiose theories about anything and everything; that's his thing. They could make a whole TV series out of it, like "Thingamajigs for Idiots." "Grand Theories and Turkish Coffee by my Old Man." "Grand Theories, Bashar al-Assad, Work, Taxis, and Uber by My Old Man." "Exile, Immigration, Geopolitics, and Bobigny by My Old Man." "Sarkozy, Qaddafi, Karl Marx, and Mohammed by My Old Man." We'd make money faster than by driving people around, both of us, that's for sure. Well, I say that, but I've got a customer who works for Éditions Nathan who says books are fucked, that they aren't selling well. When I see guys who are killing themselves studying and still can't put food on the table, I tell myself being a driver's not a bad gig at all. You don't need to have a head full of useless crap to drive a heap of junk and follow a GPS.

We drink our coffee, quietly, without speaking, glancing at each other now and then. His skin's getting lighter with age. When he was younger, they used to call him the Maharajah because he was so dark. His wrinkles are getting deeper, especially the one he's had in the middle of his forehead since my brother disappeared. Even his thick communist mustache has lost some of its style; it takes years of effort and careful grooming to get a scrub brush like that under your nose. It's old-fashioned, maybe, but you have to respect it as an art handed down from father to son. As for my generation, though, I'd prefer to be left out of it. Sorry, Dad, but thousands of kilometers of sea and distance have transformed customs into memories. When we finish our coffees, he insists on reading the grounds. Another ancient belief from the village, an old wives' tale, but whatever, it's my dad, so . . . You turn the cup upside down on the saucer and wait for it to cool, and then you turn it over again. In the coffee grounds there are all kinds of shapes: rivers, birds, men and women, camels, horses. It's like a comic book, and our *marabouts*, our holy men, tell us what the shapes say—I mean, they make up stories. Grandma Zahié was really good at it; people used to come to the house, some-times traveling a long way, just to listen to her stories. And even though she couldn't see much because of her cataracts, every-one believed what she said. Some people would slip her fifty or a hundred francs to thank her. And no matter what she said, they'd think, Muslim, *Astaghfirullah.*

With the same kind of wise insanity his mother had, my dad pushes the cup away so he can see it better, because he's as short-sighted as she is. And you can only get the kind of glasses he wears, crazy old-fashioned ones, in Marrakesh. With his checked shirts and corduroy trousers, he looks like a Soviet spy. He starts telling me what he sees in the cup, his other hand gesticulating wildly to illustrate the story. We speak with our hands as much as our mouths around here. He lets a sentence drop: I'm going to find somebody important, a man about as tall as I am, same age, who looks like me, and there will be fire all around us. I find all this crap absolutely hilarious, but I hold in my laughter so as not to disturb him in his delirium. He's old, you know. It wouldn't be right. I used to not give a fuck; I'd say anything that popped into my head and end up hurting him. Once I even told him he was being a fool. He didn't say anything, just squared his shoulders like a boxer and took it. It killed him, I think. His eyes glistened and he muttered some-thing like, "You'll understand. You'll see when you have chil-dren. It's hard." I was already too old to tease my dad for a couple of cookies, and I felt like an idiot. He treated me like a junkyard dog for a long time after that, kept his distance until my brother went down the wrong path, and since then I've become the prodigal son again, especially since I've been tak-ing care of my grandmother.

Old Zahié came here from Syria because of the war. She's pretty much lost her mind since then; she mixes everything up. The bombing of Aleppo, the fighting, the death, all of it drove her over the edge, poor thing. Pop's put her in a nice nursing home; we had no choice, but we didn't tell anyone in the neighborhood because they would have given us hell. They don't know what it is to be old and sick. They left their grandmothers and grandfathers to die back in the old country, in their villages rotten and crawling with Maghrebis, and now they act high and mighty. Anyway, people are like that about everything. An old person is harder to take care of than a baby. You don't mind feeding a baby, or wiping its ass; it's even a pleasure. You can decide to have a baby if that's what you want. But an old person, especially a member of your family, your mother or father, that's hard. It's a question of dignity. Honor, even. Given the choice, I'd rather know that my relative is being taken care of by pros than leave her to rot like a vegetable right beside me with shit crusted all over her ass. I know it might seem heartless to say that, but life is hard, so there. We didn't just sit there and suffer; we found a good solution for the old lady. The aides take really good care of her, thank God. And by some stroke of luck, there are even a couple of Arabs who can talk with her. They say they're Jordanian, because my grandma is a little bit racist, which isn't great, but that's the way it is. People from Syria don't like Maghrebis. Mesopotamians think they're the princes of the Arab people. *Jordan*, they told her, and she smiled. In France, a racist Arab is where people draw the line.

My father takes a deep breath, as if he's getting ready to launch into another half-hour monologue.

"Listen, *ibni*."

Ibni means *son* in my old man's Arab-Syrian dialect.

"I'm going to get the car fixed. Give me the address of that Portuguese garage in Bondy."

Until recently, my dad always got his immortal gray Mercedes with big headlights serviced at a brand dealership. His car is his mistress; he's always taken her to five-star restaurants only. It cost him an arm and a leg, he knew, but he took a sort of pride in leaving the keys at reception and then signing a big fat check. It's a weird interpretation of Communism, but there you go. Money's been tight for a while now, though, and there aren't as many *mezze* on the Friday-night dinner table, and the Mercedes is going to have to visit the Portuguese. He doesn't say it, but it's because of the competition from Uber. I admire him for it, because if I were in his place and my son started working for the competition, I would disown him. But I'm young, and I've figured out that people calm down with age, get wiser.

I take out my wallet to give him Pinto's number. When I open it, a piece of folded paper falls onto the table. His features twitch slightly. It's the summons to the police station I got the day before yesterday. I don't know if he has time to read what's written on it, or if it's the way I grab it and stuff it in my trouser pocket that makes him suspicious, but I'll have to be careful; it'll be easier with him that way. I can remember bad years, hard years, times when he threw me out. If he sees that I've gotten a summons from the cops, he won't even try to understand; he'll think I've gotten mixed up in some bad stuff again, and then it'll be another battle royal.

He lights a cigarette. I'm dying to smoke too, but . . . well, I've never dared to do it in front of Pop. It's a question of respect. He fills his lungs with smoke, as if he's going to expel all the world's wisdom in a single breath. I'm afraid he's going to mention the summons—but then he exhales, blowing a series of smoke rings. This is a changed man. Maybe he doesn't give a fuck anymore.

"Life's not complicated. Okay, you work with Uber application, telephone, and so, and so. But who is owner of Uber? You participate in destroying a profession, taxi, for others. If tomorrow, one day, no more taxi, Uber monopoly, not good . . ."

Ten minutes to explain the simplest things to me. My dad is

ferociously opposed to Uber. He's well-placed in one of the taxi drivers' unions. Since Uber and other platforms like it started, they have lost a lot of fares and a lot of customers. Too bad for them. I understand that they're angry, but it's partly their own fault. They've always refused to take card payments and they're never polite. But at the same time, it isn't that simple. Driving a taxi is damn hard work and you don't earn shit, but people still want you to be friendly and nice—they want to have their cake and eat it, too. You can't have it both ways. Simple. Uber gets all that. It's easy to be a customer, and it's easy to be a driver. Sitting like pashas at their computers, they invented the app and then let other people do the work. If I'd known you could get rich off IT like that, I'd have spent more time behind a keyboard than behind a steering wheel.

My old man thinks the whole thing's disgusting. It's way over his head. The day I told him I was driving for them, I thought he was going to disown me. I wasn't trying to be an asshole by doing it, I swear; I just didn't think. The worst part for him was thinking that everything he had built was caving in; he'd staked everything he had on the taxi driver's permit he was going to sell for his retirement, and what made him livid was that Uber doesn't require a special permit. So that meant, according to the law of supply and demand, that the price of his good was getting screwed over. But there's some weird stuff about that, too, because in the beginning, the government gave out permits free of charge. That was part of the law of 1947 voted in after the war. I heard that on the radio once. But the law was poorly written, because it didn't have any provision against reselling taxi permits. So drivers started doing it, and, of course, like with real estate, prices changed according to the market. Little by little, people started taking out loans to buy their permits, and then they paid those back, and then sold their permits before retiring. It wasn't working too badly, actually, until Uber. Now the easy ride is over for taxi drivers. They're freaking out, protesting, and they want to blow everything up.

To be honest, if I were one of the Uber guys, I'd have kept my mouth shut instead of screaming back at taxi drivers and calling them idiots. They hide in their fancy offices, out in Silicon Valley, being clever, dressing all "sloppy" on purpose, in those jeans that look all beat-up but are brand new, and those T-shirts with dumb sayings nobody understands, and those stupid lumberjack beards, but with no muscles and no balls, acting like rebels, like "we don't play by the rules" and all that, but really, they're only against taxis, and they're fucking them over, fast. Taxi drivers are their own worst enemies; they're guys from the street, bitter and worn out by life. Eleven hours a day in the car, watching for fares, will drive a guy out of his mind. Once, I was listening to a radio show about suicide, and they had a psychologist listing the professions most at risk, and I swear taxi driver was one of them. Suffering leads to violence. This isn't just hot air; I know what I'm talking about, because I have an example right in front of me. It's no accident that they all keep a baseball bat or a collapsible truncheon or a crowbar under the driver's seat. Nothing to lose. Violence makes them feel better. Fortunately, there are unions to calm them down. I guess the Uber bosses actually know what they're doing, because the taxi drivers attack us, the private hires, and not the guys who created and maintain the system. It's like with the protests. The hooligans go after the cops, but the cops aren't the ones who make the laws. Logic = 0. What they should really do is storm the Assemblée Nationale and go after the ministers, the Assemblée members and their teams; they're the ones in charge. Protesters could actually threaten the decision-makers there. There was a journalist on the radio talking about politics and sports, like, the prime minister and the minister of economics like to box. Ha ha ha! I'd like to see them show us if they can throw right hooks and handle shivs like the street rats.

For my dad, if I were intelligent and had used my head, I could have inherited his taxi permit, which I'd have to pay him only half-price for. This is how he was thinking: This little punk didn't go to school, and at least taxi driving is a profession that pays. I was about to be thirty fucking years old; I didn't want to lock myself into spending the next thirty years hating my life. He didn't get it at all.

"You and your brother, you don't understand anything about life. It's true. If you were intelligent, both of you, you'd start a little taxi company with me, with a permit. We'd be open seven days a week, twenty-four hours a day, and you'd save money. We'd buy two more permits and your brother would do some work for us and then go work for the hospital. Secure, see? Money going in both pockets, right and left."

"Why are you talking to me about my brother? Why are you talking about him? He's not here anymore. He's gone. Maybe he's dead. Maybe he's killed people. Where is he, that son of a bitch? Syria? Dubai? Mali? Libya? Nobody knows. He slipped away like a shadow, like a whore before the sun comes up. He left us. You don't want to see it. And anyway, it's . . . "

I don't say it to him. I hold it in. It's all his fault. My mom. My grandma. My brother. The old man has always done everything wrong. He didn't take care of us. He's spent all his time surviving, not living. Always thinking about the future and never really being in the present.

"Don't talk about your brother like that. Humanitarian mission him, at least; not like you, crappy thief driver. I know better than you; I've done twenty-five years. And you, stupider than your father, do the same thing. Your brother. He's my son; he'll come back. I know it. I feel."

He says it coldly, pointing his finger at me, his eyes calm but convinced. He means *accept it, or get out*. I don't know what to do. I'm still too young to stand up to my father. Where is that bastard! My fucking brother! One day I'll end up in prison with the old man because of him. Some kind of joint offense. My dad's still standing there, incensed but silent. He's waiting for me to say something. I turn the knob, murmur a goodbye, and close the door behind me.

4
Older Brother

It's nighttime, and I love it when it rains at night. The drops stream down my windshield, and the city lights in the distance are faint through the mist, and there's the swishing sound of water flying up under the car, and the red reflections of taillights on the wet asphalt. Sometimes, above Les Lilas, near the Fort de Romainville, I stop the car to roll a joint. You can see all of Paris from there, from the Philharmonie to the Eiffel Tower. But no one knows this spot. This is the ghetto, Seine-Saint-Denis, and nobody gives a flying fuck here. I don't know why it has to be so shitty. Deep down, it makes me sick that they use this as the dump of France. We didn't ask for it to be so fucked up; we just grew up with it that way. The adults just let everything go to hell, and we kids imitated them. And the little ones growing up now will imitate us. It's a culture of self-destruction. We don't respect anything, because people don't respect us. When you become an adult, you understand, and you regret it, and you have the ability to fight back with words, not just by lashing out or destroying things. But a lot of the time, it's too late.

Here, everything only just barely works. Schools, buildings, cars, supermarkets, doctors, pharmacies. You can always leave if you want, but that doesn't mean things are going to go right for you. And when you're not in it, it's not so easy to really understand it. You can't just adjust the antenna or rotate the satellite dish to capture the ambience. You have to feel the vibe, all the way deep in your gut, to really understand the ins and outs of life here. Sometimes I hear debates about our hood on the radio, not between politicians or journalists but decent guys, like university professors. But even they just say useless stuff; it's like someone talking about the jungle—the lions and the underbrush—without having been there. Any brother from around here who heard them would immediately call bullshit. You don't become a *banlieusard* on the benches of a lecture hall. You get your bachelor's degree by wearing out the soles of your shoes on concrete, and then your master's by busting your ass for a few pennies, and possibly a doctorate the day you take your first hundred paces around a prison exercise yard.

It goes the other way, too. Guys from around here are always saying ridiculous shit about the rich areas, Neuilly, the sixteenth, and all that. Nothing they know anything about. Not to blow my own horn, but my head is full of what I see and hear. A driver goes everywhere, you know? He meets people. The whole day, shut inside his ride, listening to customers and the radio, he thinks and compares, and, suddenly, he's over-flowing with stories to tell.

When I left my dad's place, the moon was almost at its highest point. I opened the Uber app on my phone and hardly had time to light a cigarette before I was sent to the avenue de Flandre, in the Grands Boulevards area of the city.

The rider's name popped up on my phone screen: Irmah Haddad. In that neighborhood, with that name, it had to be a Jew or an Arab. Who cares, as long as they pay. Money has no color; it's the best defense against racism.

Traffic is usually bad when it rains, but it's pretty calm is tonight. I'm going to be early. That's good, though, because right when I get there, the customer comes out of his house. No time lost. He gets in, and we're off.

I love looking at customers' faces in the rearview mirror. This guy isn't an Arab or a Jew; he might be a Kabyle, or maybe French or Turkish.

It's pretty much always the same thing with customers. Either they ask questions about your day, or they talk about their lives, or they gently steer the conversation toward politics or religion. Just like on the radio. And then there are the silent ones. Luckily, there aren't too many of those, or it would be the end of the job—guaranteed to kill you. I can imagine the funeral, some old friend whispering, *How did he die?* And someone answering, with tight lips and wet eyes, *Of boredom, at the wheel of his car. He died of boredom.* What a lousy way to go.

When a customer gets in the car, one of my games is to guess which kind of passenger he's going to be. You have to give it a minute, cast out the line a few times and then wait, to see what he reveals. Tonight we've already made it pretty far; the car has just passed the *rotonde* by the Stalingrad metro station, and my dude's lips are still sealed. He's lost in thought. Poor guy, he doesn't look too good. What must his life be like? Rich or poor? Plucked eyebrows; maybe he's a fruit and his boy toy just broke up with him. But it's not so easy to know who's who these days, and, deep down, nobody gives a fuck anyway, no one thinks about what's between the next person's legs before they shove their hand down their pants.

"Would you prefer a particular radio station?"

A small smile. That's his answer. I push the power button on the radio, and since he hasn't said anything, I flip through the stations. Oldies, French pop, it's not bad. We'll see what he thinks. The broadcaster announces France Gall. Perfect; that'll get a reaction out of him. She starts singing. It's damned annoying, like a cat yowling. Meow, meow. Once I heard on the radio that she took the name Hamburger after marriage. Her husband's last name.

"Did you know France Gall is her married name?" I ask.

"Pardon?"

"Her married name. The singer. It's France Gall."

"Sorry? What are you talking about?"

"The woman singing. It's France Gall. But when she got married, her name changed to Hamburger."

"You just said the opposite. That her married name is France Gall. Why are you talking to me about Hamburger?"

My head's spinning because of the joint. But I get things wrong sometimes even when I'm sober. As if the remnants of the weed detach themselves from my lungs and flow through my veins up to the control tower.

It's hard to get more than four sentences out of him. He gets out of the car the same way he got in; without a glance in my direction, just *goodnight* politely murmured from between barely parted lips. But whatever; no big deal. The customers are the first ones to complain when you aren't friendly enough. They're paying for smiles, for *hello*s and *thank you*s and *good-bye*s. But what about the drivers? Are we supposed to pay the customers to be friendly? *How are you*s and *Hang in there*s don't cost anything, and they don't hurt anybody. Quite the opposite. They should be standard procedure.

Rain, more rain, always rain, falling lightly now on the dark streets. The streetlights, guardians of the night, soldiers of light, fight against the darkness. A luminous halo over there, with people in front of it, standing in line. My customer's gotten in line for the Rex, a legendary dance club among people who live in central Paris. The rest of us never set foot inside. We'd never pass the physical. *Soirée automatic.* No need to ask; it's all right there in the name. A human anthill with techno playing on an endless loop.

Because life is hard, a lot of stuff gets swallowed in there, right at the bar, a pill in your cocktail to get your hips swaying. In the corners of the room and the VIP booths, a whole lot of blow gets snorted. And in the bathrooms, there are the rare, poor fuckers trying to find a vein in their forearm that'll still take a needle. Sucks for them. The rest of us, we can't afford any of that. The slickest of us earn our livings from their misery: sell them the shit and count the cash. I don't like to think it, but the truth is that brings a shred of equality back to society. They toss us in jail, they splatter us all over the TV, they lock us up and throw away the key. But we're far from being the only ones who live off other people's misfortune.

I was inside the Rex once. The bouncer must have been color-blind, because he didn't notice my immigrant face. In the club, I scanned the room until my eyes landed on a big black guy who was standing at the edge of the dance floor, wearing a hat and tugging his coat down like he was hiding a hot chick in there. And then the girl's head popped up out of the coat and she had her back to him. You could see that she was moving her ass, her tits bouncing a little every time. When she whipped around and then got down on her knees to swallow, it hit me what a genius this guy was. An artist, a secret agent of lust. Crazy. At twenty years old, everyone wishes they could get away with that kind of thing, but no one has the balls. It doesn't accomplish anything, or get you anything except personal pride. And if the chick enjoys it, well, that's the peak of happiness. Temporary as a hard-on at a red light.

I'm not the only one dropping people off at the Rex, or in Grands Boulevards in general. It's almost midnight, and the sidewalks are crammed with people, like at the Belleville market on a Saturday morning. There's a long line of dark sedans with Private Hire stickers on their windshields. There's time for a cigarette; another driver gives me a discreet wave and a nod. Black suit, black tie, black shoes, white shirt. In this rain, any more than five meters away and you'd think it was me. They don't ask us to be creative, just to follow the rules, look neat and "pro," as they say in the office.

I've got to quit smoking, man. My gums are bleeding, and I don't like the salty taste of blood. I sit in the car and take out the folded piece of paper I'd hidden so hastily from Pop. On the upper left is the police logo, and below it: SUMMONS FOR A MATTER CONCERNING YOU. We're used to getting these kinds of documents, for hold-ups, drug deals, fights, vandalism, breaking and entering, stolen cars.

The first time I got one, it was for some stupid thing with a guy who owed forty euros to a friend of mine. I buzzed the front door of his apartment building, and when his mom answered, I pretended the guy and I were friends. Since he didn't know me, I waited for him while my buddy hid behind a bush. He came out of his building, and once the heavy front door closed behind him, my buddy jumped out and hit him, yelling, "Where's my money, you son of a bitch?" The dude hollered for help. He got down on his knees, lurching around, and my friend landed an uppercut on his chin. "Well, you son of a bitch?" The poor guy went down, and the neighbors started leaning out their windows. So then my buddy screamed, "What are you waiting for?" and I ran over like an idiot and kicked the guy, in the head, just like you would a soccer ball. I can still hear the hollow sound of his skull and the way his neck crunched. We went through his pockets, took his phone and his wallet, and ran like hell. I couldn't sleep for weeks after that; my foot turned purple and swelled up to three times its normal size. I could hardly walk for days. I smoked joint after joint and bought *Le Parisien* every morning to make sure the guy hadn't died. That's how I got addicted to reading newspapers.

Then one day I got a letter marked FOR A MATTER CONCERNING YOU. I denied everything to the cops, and that was the end of it. We know how to handle summons and detainments. Years of experience. But since *Charlie Hebdo* and November 13th, they mostly call us in for terrorism. Like we've all become terrorists. When it's hot, the pigs lock you up without waiting for answers. Questions are for the second half of the game. I don't know what they want from me this time; my conscience is as clear as spring water, and my dad didn't see anything in the coffee grounds. Maybe it's because of my brother. Maybe he's dead.

My phone vibrates. An H. Melville has hailed a ride from me. Seat belt, key in the ignition, pedal to the floor. Under a streetlight, the rain falls on a couple with a little kid. They're waiting for me with a big suitcase. Melville hugs his wife tightly, kisses the toddler, and jumps into the car like a fugitive, leaving the suitcase behind. A shadow in the middle of the night. I think of my brother; it's his kind of thing.

Sometimes I make up people's life stories in my head while I'm driving them. Why did the man in the back seat get into the car without his suitcase, and why is he going to the Porte de Bagnolet bus station? That's a hideout for poor people and students, jammed beneath the highway, and this guy looks like a businessman in his suit and tie. I can see his fatigue in the rearview mirror. Eyes closed, head leaning against the window. Even swerving the car a few times and jostling over a few speed bumps doesn't wake him. We get there, and he thanks me in an Eastern European accent before boarding a bus that reads "Krakow."

I park the car, get out, and jam a cigarette between my lips. This spot beneath a shopping center on the side of a beltway has the same stale, lukewarm air as the bus station. The rain, the night, the crackling of the streetlights, the noise of cars on the highway, and hundreds of people, luggage in hand, lining up in the middle of the night. It feels like the end of the world. Some catastrophe that the radio and newspapers and TV aren't showing. People don't have any money. It's not complicated; it's right there, visible to the naked eye. There never used to be anyone here at midnight, in this rough station. But the journalists are blind to it—I'm not making this up, by the way; a customer, the editor of a paper, told me that. They don't leave their offices anymore. Asses firmly glued to their seats, they type away at their keyboards, filling up websites. And the ones on the radio just repeat what the newspapers say, and the ones on TV copy the radio. A permanent 69, where each one kisses the other's ass. Gives them terrible breath afterward, of course.

A bus arrives from Cologne, and a dozen guys get out. They look like *banlieusards*, like us, only restyled as members of the Taliban. Tracksuits under traditional Muslim *kamis*, Air Max sneakers on their feet. Islamopunks with little hats that look like foreskins on their heads. Kind of like those FEMEN activists that go around topless, but it's like they're pronouncing something like, "Free the foreskins!" Ha ha ha! I've still got mine. My parents didn't care, so my brother and I still have dicks like white Europeans. Sometimes when I'm getting it on with an Arab chick, I make sure she doesn't see it, or if she does, I make up some medical reason; otherwise she'll keep asking about it and act all disgusted. Sexual racism, man.

The smoke from my cigarette stings my eyes. My gums are bleeding again. The pack of Islamists from the bus are heading in my direction. I'm sure they're going to lecture me for the sin of smoking, and they do. But they don't insist, because it's late, and after a certain time of night, everyone just wants to find his bed more than he wants to find God.

One last guy gets off the bus. A ghost. He keeps his head down and doesn't follow the others. Hooded sweatshirt. Beat-up blue jeans. Hair cut like mine. Tall as me. Same skin color. Everything about him is familiar. He even walks like the guys from our hood. One hand in his pocket, the other carrying an American-style backpack slung over his shoulder. A car slows down; he opens the door, asks a couple of questions, and gets in. The tires squeal through a puddle, and he disappears into the night.

Stoic, brother. I stay stoic. I can't even breathe. This time there's no life story to make up; my own is flashing before my eyes. I wasn't even quick enough to call out to him. A second after he vanishes, I throw away my cigarette, jerk open the car door, plant my ass in the seat, jam my key in the ignition, shift into gear, floor the gas pedal, do a screeching U-turn, and pound on the horn with my left hand, speeding after them. Three hundred meters in front of me, I can see their car turning toward Montreuil. A black Citroën.

Good luck: it's raining, and there isn't much traffic. Bad luck: it's raining, and it's hard to keep track of the right car. My nickname is Pilot. I don't like it, because it's stupid, but it's true. No one can drive like me. I'm a chauffeur, a deliveryman, a conductor. Today I'm transporting people; yesterday I was transporting merchandise. Only grass, never blow. One day I'll have work out the number of joints that have been smoked thanks to my little errands. One gram is three joints, so a kilo is three thousand joints. So two hundred kilos is . . . six hundred thousand, right? Anyway, the steering wheel and the gas pedal are what I do. It's not the dealing drugs as much as it is the speed and the risk that appeal to me, because money's not really my thing.

Smooth, relaxed, going with the flow, keeping my gaze in the distance to anticipate the car's movements. A refrigerated truck with a Polish license plate gets between us, blocking my view, and two or three times I almost lose them. On the avenue de la Résistance in Montreuil, the Polish asshole slows down for a red light, while they keep going. I floor it into a smooth fishtail and say salaam to the traffic light and the Pole. Now it's working; they're only a hundred meters ahead of me. My heart's thumping out of my chest. Tssh, tssh, tssh, like a tambourine. My hands are vibrating with the steering wheel. A drop of sweat pops out on my temple and rolls down my cheek. My fingers are buzzing and I almost want to cry.

For about three seconds, I really think I might catch him, but in this black night, this thick, dark night, a siren holds me back. I see a flashing light overtaking me in the rearview mirror.

A Ford Focus gets in front of me, blocking the way, and a guy in an orange POLICE armband jumps out of it like Batman. The other car has sped away ahead. A redheaded cop with a face like a bulldog screams at me, "Didn't you see that red light? Cut the ignition! Out of the car!" The rest isn't even important, because it's just the usual: spread-eagled against the hood, frisked, mocked, insulted, and even humiliated, before being let go without a fine for the red light and with a kick to the rear fender of the car because they can see it's a private hire. The sons of bitches. Worse than the worst assholes in our neighborhood, godless and lawless. Nothing but pirates.

5
OLDER BROTHER

T he car vanished into the night, its ghost passenger with it. The cops took off, leaving me with my doubts. I was still on the avenue de la Résistance in Montreuil. I parked the car on the side of the road, reclined the seat back, rolled down the window, lit a cigarette, and turned on the radio. Nighttime programming, a deep-voiced host talking about the 1998 soccer World Cup.

June 10, 1998. I remember it like it was yesterday. Brazil narrowly beat Scotland in the opening match. It was a different time. We lived in Paris. Life was good. There were people everywhere in the streets. Foreign tourists. Pop was a supporter of the French team; to him, they were the team of the future. The color of their skin didn't matter; the game was what mattered. Mom just thought Zidane and Thuram were good-looking, which drove Dad crazy, because he said the first one was a dirty Arab—not dirty like racist French people say, but dirty the way Syrians say it, meaning not a real Arab. According to the old man, only Arabs from the Middle East count; the rest are only photocopies. As for Thuram, Pop just hated him. My dad would bark at him, and we didn't understand why. Years later, I realized it was racism. And that made *me* crazy. Parents, man. You start out loving them, and as you grow up, you judge them, and sometimes you forgive them. But I could never stay quiet about racism, even in front of Pop. So . . .

We were a normal family. The old man came to France in

the mid-80s to study. Mom was learning Arabic at the Institut des Langues Orientales, and he was teaching classes there, despite his terrible French. She was his student, and things just worked between them. They figured out solutions for everything—a place to live, the wedding, even the rings. Dad didn't have any money, but somehow they managed it. The only thing was that he didn't have a wedding finger to wear his ring on. They'd cut it off when he was in prison. He was putting up posters in the street when old Bashar's men nabbed him—and he got off lightly. His older brother, our uncle, had vanished from the face of the earth, and his cousin had his dick and balls fried with electric shocks. Luckily for Dad, it was only his finger. So I was born, and my brother two years later. The ring is still around Pop's neck on a chain. Next to his heart. A life of hardships. But it was a beautiful life, honestly. We lived near the Bois de Vincennes, and Mom and Dad used to take us there to play. In the summers we'd visit my maternal grandma in Saint-Malo, driving there in Dad's Renault 25. It was classy. Fuck, now that my brother's not around, it's weird to remember these things. If Mom had been around to see him leave, it might have killed her a second time.

On June 11, 1998, after breakfast, we all drove to the airport. My grandmother was in the air, on a plane whose landing had been delayed because of heavy clouds in the sky. We didn't know her yet then, this old lady who would teach us everything. In the arrival hall, at the baggage carousel, we watched through the windows as Grandma waited in line at customs. She was tiny, wearing a white scarf with a mauve pattern on her head. It looked like a curtain, man. A long beige overcoat reached her ankles, like a mini gestapo agent.

Then she came out, accompanied by a young man who was carrying her suitcase. She must have charmed him into helping her with her, toothless smile. Seven teeth, bro. But it was enough for her to tell you a million stories. She pressed us to her breasts, which hung down to her belly button. I recognized my dad's scent, only older and unwashed. Pop acted like none of it was a big deal, but when she took him in her arms, his eyes shone with tears. Fifteen years without his mother; I know what that means. He used to call her once a month. Then she turned to my mom, took her hand, and kissed it, like you'd do with a king or a queen.

At home, she put her suitcase down in our bedroom. Mom brought her some blankets. Grandma put two of them down on the floor as a mattress, and used the third one to cover herself. Our beds were on either side of the room, and my grandmother was in the middle. We loved it. And she'd brought amazing things with her. Dates, apricots, almond paste. She'd even swiped the jam they gave her with the breakfast they served on the plane. Such a crazy old hick. Snored like an orchestra at night. A chorus. And during the day, in the kitchen, like a musician with her drum kit, she created symphonies of flavors. Mom tried to learn. She asked questions in Arabic, and when my grandmother didn't understand, she'd make this sound, *heeee!* She was kind of deaf. So my mom would repeat it until she understood, and then Grandma would shake her head and give us a big smile, a panoramic view of her seven teeth. She loved Mom like crazy. Too proud of her daughter-in-law. A European, *and* she spoke Arabic. The old lady was always gazing at Mom, stroking her hair, kissing her hands. She loved her to death, so much that Pop was jealous. He spent his time snapping at Grandma. I don't know what his problem was. He should have been happy. He hadn't seen her in fifteen years.

Peace lasted just a few days. Pop went after the old girl, talking about his older brother who disappeared, and his father. The story was that my grandfather had died pointlessly, of the flu. The village imam had convinced my grandma that she couldn't allow a Christian, even a doctor, to take care of him, because it would keep him out of heaven. I can understand why Dad was angry.

Grandma tried to teach us Arabic by telling us stories about religion and the old country. That drove Dad nuts, too. Mom told us to listen; she said one day we'd be glad to know all this stuff. Pop told us it was all nothing but witchcraft. And we, caught in the middle, didn't know what to do; we loved our grandmother, and we knew our dad was an abuser. We learned to pray, and about the prophets and the holy book.

Everything changed on September 8th. Grandma had been with us for three months. In the summer, when the university was closed, Dad drove a taxi at night. He'd leave at around eight o'clock and come home at seven in the morning, when Mom was getting up. Sometimes my brother and I were already awake, watching TV, starting the day with cartoons. Every day, Pop brought something home for us: a candy bar he bought from a vending machine, a magazine, a soccer card, a balloon. That day we'd gotten up around nine, and Dad was already asleep. On the coffee table in the living room he'd left a Paris Saint-Germain scarf signed by Patrice Loko. I still have it in a dresser drawer. Well, my half of it, because when I wouldn't share it with my kid brother, the old man cut it in half. So we put on our half-scarves and went down to the square with our FC Nantes soccer ball. All the other kids went nuts. It was late summer and, with that wool around our necks, we got so hot running around after the ball, we were dying. But having class is worth any sacrifice. Around noon, Grandma yelled for us out the window. Like a hick, she called in Arabic for us to come in and eat. So embarrassing in that neighborhood; here everyone was French and civilized. Anyway. When she saw us come in all sweaty and muddy and grimy, the old lady's mouth twisted. "Take your clothes off," she ordered. Then she tossed us in the tub and scrubbed us with scalding hot water and a scratchy exfoliating glove until it felt like our skin was going to come off. After that she shampooed our hair with her peasant's hands, rough as sandpaper. All we needed were some feathers on our heads and we'd have looked like American Indians, our skin was so red. And we were starving, but she made us do the noon prayer with her before we ate. The Dhuhr. I'll skip the details. You start with the *salat*, the call to prayer.

> *God is great, God is great*
> *There is no God but Allah*
> *I testify that Mohammed is the messenger of God*
> *Come to Prayer, come to Happiness*
> *It is time to pray, it is time to pray*
> *God is great, God is great*
> *There is no God but Allah*

We'd had plenty of time to learn that in the past three months, but sometimes I still made mistakes. Especially on the third line; I'd repeat the second instead. My brother glanced at me from the corner of his eye like I was an idiot. But I was always thinking about something else; I had to force myself to not get distracted. For example, on that day, I remember that a guy had just come out onto the balcony across from ours, totally naked. My grandma saw him too, but she looked away fast enough that her prayer wasn't ruined. Suddenly, there was an enormous farting noise, crazy loud, like a machine gun. I couldn't keep from laughing, and then my brother laughed, too. The old lady didn't budge. It was one o'clock in the afternoon, and that was the signal that Pop had just gotten up. We knew the sound. Every day he let out a huge fart while he was pissing. We moved on to the *rakats*, movements and prayers you repeat several times. For the noon prayer, you have to do four *rakats*. I concentrated on imitating my grandmother. You start out standing up, and then bow your torso until it's parallel to the ground, with your hands on your knees. Then you straighten up and sit on your heels and press your forehead to the floor. Pop's deep voice rang through the apartment; he was looking for us. We could hear his heavy steps. The sound got closer to our bedroom. We'd just finished the *rakats*, and we were starting the first *tashahhud*, the prayer of the Prophet. Just then, the bedroom door opened.

"What are you doing?"

My dad went out again, slamming the door behind him so hard that the walls shook. We could hear him whispering with my mom: *You don't understand . . . It's religion . . . that isn't culture . . . Why are you allowing it?* And Mom, answering: *You're exhausting me. Do what you want. I'm going for a cigarette.* Pop paced around the apartment. We went through the salutations, the *salams*. First you turn your head to the right and say, "Assalamu alaikum wa rahmatullah" and then to the left, repeating the same phrase. "May the peace and mercy of Allah be upon you."

The bedroom door opened again.

"You old witch!" screamed my dad.

He stormed into the room in a rage and kicked my grandmother in the back with all his strength. His eyes were blood-red. "You can't keep yourself from teaching them this garbage! Do you know why my father died? Do you know?"

She started crying like a child. We pressed ourselves against her. Dad got even more furious. He called his mother every filthy name in the book. I prayed for Mom to come in and calm things down. Suddenly, my brother stood up and screamed at my dad in Arabic: "You're the son of a bitch! Why are you hitting our grandmother?"

The old man froze for a few seconds, just long enough for my brother to leap on him and bite his hand, hard. I screamed for him to let go, but the kid sunk his teeth in like a piranha. Dad howled in pain.

"Let go of my hand, or I'll kill you!"

He smacked my brother hard with his other hand once, and then again, and then a third time, and a fourth. The kid let go.

My father picked him up by the hair and hurled him down on the bed. Then he threw himself on top of him.

My brother was crying so hard he couldn't breathe. He was going to die. I ran into the living room. My mother was on the balcony. I begged her to come right away. She set her cigarette down in the ashtray and crossed the apartment, holding her head. Another one of her chronic migraines. She'd gotten a lot of them over the past few weeks. When she came into the bedroom, my dad stood to attention. The old lady was curled up in a ball on the floor. My brother didn't know whether to cry or breathe anymore. My mom put her hand on my dad's shoulder.

"Calm. Stay calm."

Her gestures, her voice. Mom knew what to do. The only one who could soothe the old man's crazy outbursts. I remember her skin was very pale. Nearly transparent. Her lips were almost gray. Her hands were shaking. Dad asked if she was okay.

"Call . . . call an am . . . ambulance."

She collapsed. I don't remember much after that. Firefighters. Dad crying. My brother crying. My grandma praying. In the hospital waiting room, the old man biting his nails until his fingers bled. My grandmother mumbling. My brother and me crying, sleeping, crying, sleeping. And then a man came. In a white coat. A young man. Tanned skin. My dad stood up. The man stammered a few words. Maybe it was his first time. Dad's eyes opened very wide, and he swallowed. And then he screamed, in a way I'd never heard him scream before and haven't since. On the bad nights, when my heart lurches in my chest and I feel like the world's splitting apart, I hear that scream, over and over in my head. Like a broken record the devil has bolted to a turntable. Then I sit there in the shadows, and I wait for my light.

6
YOUNGER BROTHER

M y head was already somewhere else. Every morning, like a robot or a zombie, I put on my scrubs and walked through the hallways, distributing big smiles to patients and doctors and nurses, but the truth was, I was like a ghost. Since my interview with Doctors Without Borders, I'd studied up on the situation in Syria. The war zones, the cities that had been bombed out, the weapons used. I was the perfect man for them: I was young, had a diploma, and spoke both French and Arabic. I'd be entering the old country with a bang. Soon I'd be done with France, and the mosque, and Imam Pharaon, and guys killing themselves with drugs. Goodbye to all that, and hello to my homeland and to helping these people, our brothers.

The daily grind was tough at the hospital, because we got our balls busted for the tiniest things. For example, if you wanted to pray, you had to do it in the break room. But there was a TV in there that was always on, turned to a twenty-four-hour news channel, that drove you crazy. People didn't want it turned off, and it kept us from having a peaceful place to go. So, to find somewhere calm, we had to use buildings that were disused because of asbestos—like bums. No respect for difference. They talked a blue streak about the separation of church and state and all that, but the truth is that they didn't want to admit that other people might actually believe. They were on a mission to turn us all into atheists.

And then God sent me a sign, bro. A guy from the NGO

called me. He beat around the bush for a good ten minutes before finally admitting that all the missions had been canceled. Fourteen French people had been taken hostage east of Aleppo. Shitty fucking luck. No more Syria. Back to the hospital, the salt mine, with the hopelessly sick patients and their aggressive families and the overworked interns. I endured each day as if in a half-coma, aware that, whether I was there or not, life was going on without me and lives were being used up. And I tried to convince myself, brother, that maybe the cancelation was a sign from up there, as if He were telling me, "Don't go with them," or something like that, but I couldn't do it. Every night I got out of those damn scrubs and hurried home so I could park myself in front of the computer. The world was making me insane. Everywhere, hatred was being poured on Muslims, like we were a plague that needed eradicating. Syria, Mali, Tunisia, Libya, Afghanistan, Iraq, Palestine—you had to suffer through some serious hardships from up above to earn His mercy.

Here, in France, Muslims were shit. Less than zeros in a society that teaches about equality and tolerance and respect. But the reality of daily life was dead children, raped women, bombs raining down on the earth. They were blowing everything up, and I was just a puppet in a hospital, playing assistant butcher for guys stupider than me, born in a different universe, who treated me like Uncle Tom on some Alabama plantation. It tore me apart. The French soldiers in Mali, nobody knew why or for who or how. And Syria—our homeland, brother, the place our father was always supposed to take us, was becoming a pit of filth and horror. People were being destroyed by bullets and bombs. They were dying of hunger and human evil and medieval diseases. And Palestine, bro—why wasn't anyone doing anything? They beat us over the head in school with liberty, equality and the rights of man, the UN, genocide, Rwanda, the Holocaust. Who could object?

Nobody. We have got hearts; we're humans before anything else. Of course we all agreed with that, but where has it gotten us? Our parents' generation was brought up on a steady diet of those values, and they've all spent their lives staring at their own shoes, not batting an eye. All of that stuff was just bullshit designed to keep us at the top of the food chain. Moralize to others and use it to keep them in their place.

One night I was staring out the window at the moon, thinking about the men who had actually set foot on it. Madmen who stretched the limits of life. So far as we knew. People who doubt the truth of it are the same ones who doubt there's a heaven, which—whatever, space comes from Heaven anyway. What was going to Cham compared to something like that? Three hours on a plane, a few hours in a car, a border. Everyone at the mosque was always talking about the old country, but—contrary to what people think and what the newspapers say—nobody wanted to go back and take a stand against Bashar. Like good French people, they were perfectly happy to just to criticize the injustice that was happening over there. What innocent people deserve to be killed by bombs? I wanted to help them. God had given me the good fortune to grow up in a peaceful country, to go to school and have a job, parents, a family. My real job was written in black-and-white in the Quran: *Whoever saves one life, it is as if he had saved mankind entirely.* That sura was what guided me. A beacon in my night, in the ocean of my life. I steered my ship by the Quran, my compass. My only hope was to leave, to go, so I could escape from the darkness and find the light. Launch my own jihad by saving people, repairing their lives and, along the way, my own.

Of course I knew it was a war, but did I have to kill in order to help make the world a better place? Over there, brothers were fighting against people with no hearts. I knew what I was looking for, whatever else I was going to find. I wanted to become someone in other people's eyes, not just a name, number, and job title on a badge. To build a new world, one of justice and peace.

I didn't quite know how to go about it now. I talked to Imam Pharaon about it at the mosque; I thought maybe he might have some humanitarian aid contacts in Syria. He just spouted a whole bunch of moralistic stuff at me, like, It's dangerous over there, you could die. I told him I wasn't going there to fight (but he didn't believe me), and that if I were sent to meet God, that was His will, not mine. He told me to settle down. "You're a good man. You don't have to sacrifice yourself over there. Let other people do that instead of you." This guy didn't believe in God. He put on a good show, but he was a phony—if he were a real imam, a real Salafi, he would have helped me. I wasn't afraid of death. I didn't give a damn. I wanted to save the world.

I started researching things, but I couldn't find anything much. To be honest, I didn't want to do anything stupid when it came to going to an unfamiliar country alone. I found a nursing conference in Strasbourg; it included a seminar organized by an NGO, Islam & Peace, which worked in Syria. The subject was medical care in war zones. I went with a Turkish buddy of mine, Ali, another nurse. The seminar was about first-aid techniques in war-torn areas. Conflict and catastrophe medicine, they call it. The seminar leader, a well-dressed guy in a suit and tie, pale-faced, with a subtly religious-looking little beard and doctorish glasses, spoke calmly and knowledgeably about the situation in Syria. My ears perked up. He was a Turk, a surgeon. He had come here from an area in northeast Aleppo, and he was going back after the seminar. His French wasn't totally smooth, but not nearly as bad as Pop's. He talked about daily life there, the bombs endlessly raining down, the mutilated people, the orphans, the lack of medical hygiene and materials. You had to make do with what was available: stitch wounds with fishing line; take out a bullet, and then, without X-rays, search around with your fingers inside the wound to make sure there was no metal left inside. Every day, serious injuries and death. To lighten the tone a little bit, he made a few jokes. For example, he described how he'd amputated a guy's leg and then, four months later, the same guy brought his son to be circumcised, saying, "He needs an amputation, too, but just the tip of his willy." After the seminar, I threaded my way through the crowd and found the man in front of a large pyramid of halal petits fours. At first I didn't know what to say to him, so I made some joke about the petits fours, how we were the only ones eating them and there were about three times too many of them, and it would have been better if they'd just given us a nice big plate of kibbe. He laughed, and we started talking. He told me his whole life story: his childhood in Turkey, coming to France at the age of seventeen, and then passing his exams at twenty-one and studying medicine. When the war started in the old country, in Cham, he'd left his position at the hospital in Strasbourg to do humanitarian work with this NGO, Islam & Peace. It was a large organization that raised a lot of money from French Muslims to help Muslims back home. We talked for a while about the organization's missions and his experiences over there. He gave me his card and suggested that we keep in touch. His name was Bedrettin.

Images kept running through my head. I daydreamed at the hospital and at night. In my nightmares, children called out to me for help. And I had it so easy: metro, hospital, mosque. In the evenings after work, I pored over the Islam & Peace website, reading every page several times and watching all their videos. Frankly, I was impressed. For once, people like us were doing a serious job. The NGO's books were public. The money came from donations. All their projects were described in detail, with eyewitness accounts and photos. The videos were really impressive, filmed with drones. The website was beautiful; it looked like some wealthy start-up in California had done it. No surprise, then, that in the upper right-hand corner, the donation counter kept going up and up and was already in the millions of euros.

I didn't waste any more time. I e-mailed the Turkish surgeon to ask what he was up to. He told me he was back in Syria, but the association was about to hold a charity gala in Paris. I went there, and it was jammed. Nothing but people like me. People of faith who weren't looking for problems in France but wanted justice. The directors of the association talked about all their activities. They were pros. I'd never seen anything like it. For once, guys like us were organizing; it was beautiful to see. Everything was impeccable: the PowerPoint presentations, the sound quality, the way the room was laid out; it was even better than the medical conferences organized by pharmaceutical companies. In Syria, the NGO ran four small hospitals north of Aleppo. They talked about orphaned kids, people who had been mutilated or were starving, the noise of bullets and bombs, providing medical care with no supplies, the lack of experienced personnel. They were looking for passionate, competent people. And I was the perfect link in that chain. I was Muslim, unmarried, spoke Syrian Arabic, and had several years of experience and no problems with my religion. When I got home, I sent an e-mail to Bedrettin and, jumping in with both feet, told him I wanted to join them.

He immediately video-called me. He'd lost the well put-together look he'd had at the conference. The connection kept cutting out, and the sound and picture were terrible, but we talked for almost two hours. Before hanging up, he told me he would talk to the NGO's directors and the local authorities. After that, I got out Mom's picture, kissed it, and prayed. I didn't fall asleep until three or four in the morning. The next

day, in the operating room at 7:45 A.M. (only a bypass), my
eyelids were sticky and I didn't give a damn anymore. All I
wanted was to get out of the operation to check my e-mail to
see if Bedrettin had been in touch. I couldn't think about anything else. When the morning was over, I looked at my phone.
Nothing. I refreshed my inbox every five minutes after that,
despairing. I didn't dare write to him, for fear of turning him
off. I couldn't sleep. Every morning when the alarm went off,
my eyes burned. This went on for three days. And on the
fourth day, during my lunch break, I saw the name of my
future boss appear in my inbox. "Bedrettin – Subject:
Welcome." They were going to take me on, although they
could only pay me five hundred dollars a month. But all my living expenses were covered, including food and lodging. A red
carpet. I still had one more procedure to do that day; I would
have sold everything I owned to skip it and leave right away.
After the operation, I took the stairs four at a time up to
Human Resources. I told them I was losing my mind there,
that I wanted to leave to do humanitarian work, and I asked
for a one-year leave of absence. A month earlier, a nurse had
killed herself. They signed the release then and there.

7
OLDER BROTHER

I went home, tormented, hit by a tidal wave of memories, drowning in anguish, my shirt soaked with sweat. Half an hour later, I snapped out of it. That was my brother at the bus station; I wasn't crazy. My last photo of him dated from when I got out of the army. I stared at it from every possible angle, all night, in different mental states, high on grass and then with a clear head, and the conclusion I came to, without any doubt, was that I hadn't been dreaming. Where was he? What did he want? Why hadn't he called? Asshole. He was a bastard and he always had been. Thought about himself first, before anyone else, before family, the old man, our grandma, me. The great nurse. The great Islamist humanitarian. Why did he want to save the world? To impress people. To be a big shot. To give everyone else lessons in morality.

I rolled another joint, hoping it would bring the sandman. It's weak and cowardly to smoke weed to get to sleep; it's for people who refuse to face their fears, who stuff them behind their pillows so they can get some peaceful shut-eye. But it's a sham. Pot doesn't bring you real sleep. It hits you hard, makes it so you can't keep your eyes open, but the pillow creases and dried drool on your cheek the next morning don't exactly suggest a good rest. Grass makes the nights as hazy as a hammam, all dark and humid, where you can't see more than a few feet in front of you and everything's slow.

Everything was slow. It was already morning. I was hungry. Empty stomach, empty head, empty heart, even. Because of last night, the joint, the kid brother. I was hot. Everything was too slow in my brain, as if I were still sleeping. A cold shower would do me good. Once my hair was clean, I combed my curls and trimmed my beard before putting on my suit. Black jacket, black pants, white shirt, black tie. The most fundamental thing about this job is being clean and polite, from your hairstyle to your car, and that includes your driving. Because the only thing that can guarantee you a nice fat wallet are the good reviews left by your customers. The algorithm distributes more fares to drivers with good ratings. I mean, I don't know that for sure, but that's what everyone says.

I never eat at home. There's no point, because then I'd have to do the dishes and shop for food, and I had other fish to fry. Coffee and bread and butter for two euros ninety, each and every morning on the boulevard de Belleville. Right across the street from my Muslim bros' mosque. Last night . . . my brother . . . ?

My brain finally snapped out of its trance when I read the ad placed by the soccer player Zlatan in *L'Équipe*. I don't know why the media assigns so much importance to freaks like him. For real, either this guy is crazy and the media just wants to generate buzz, or he's a self-promotional genius and he thinks journalists are idiots. Personally, I believe in mankind's basic intelligence and that, deep down, nobody's completely stupid. Yep, because God can't create anything imperfect. Everything he creates is perfect. It's humans who judge whether things are perfect or imperfect, by human criteria. God, He just *does*, and what he does, he does perfectly. Always. Period. If we really understood God, we would all love handicapped people, and blacks, and redheads, and Gypsies, and nuns, and pedophiles, and racists, and neo-Nazis, and even whores.

I've respected whores since reading this book in high school—I forget the name, but it's a book that will change your life. I understood people better after I read it. Even whores are respectable, because God created them. The guy who wrote that book was crazy, totally mental, but he was already a famous writer; he won some big prize, and then he published another book under a different name. It was about an orphan raised by a hooker. And the experts, the journalists and critics, all said that this new writer was better than him. And he said he was worn out, that he didn't have confidence anymore. And then he won the same prize again, even though you can only win it once; to be discreet, he'd put his cousin down as the author.

That guy was a real man, the kind who doesn't play the game anymore; he writes the rules of the game. He was an immigrant, like my dad. He'd come from Russia. I don't know what he did to become so successful. Big balls and a big brain, I guess. When I look around, I don't see very many immigrants who have it in them to break through like he did. Maybe because the doors are closed. No father, kind of like me, because mine's sort of a mother. All I mean by this is that I've got real respect for this writer guy, and for hookers. They exist because God decided they should, and they belong as much as anyone else. Humans are such bastards; they want to change the rules of the game that God dictated to them, to play pimp with human life. And then they charge you for morality. Get the fuck out of here.

Although, I really should learn to speak correctly, because if I said that at the mosque, with the crappy Arabic I learned from my Syrian father and my gypsy French, not only will they not understand me, they'll think I'm an infidel. But they can go screw themselves too, of course. They've turned Islam into a brand, which makes my head pound, because I can't manage to explain it. Life is terrible when you don't have the right words, when other people have to make you repeat everything so they can understand you. Life's more expensive that way, you know? Shrinks and lawyers will bill you double because you're bad at explaining yourself. They're pimps, too. They're there to help you and take care of you, but if you can't pay, they'll tell you elegantly and politely to fuck off.

It always takes me a little while to get going in the morning, for my central heating to kick in and my brain cells to start communicating with each other. It was my brother last night. I would have recognized him anywhere. His features, his height, the way he walked, his posture, the way he put his hand on the roof of the car and held his bag; he hasn't changed since we pretended we were famous soccer stars playing for FC Lilas. Even though he hates my dad, he uses the same ridiculous Mesopotamian gestures. I know them by heart.

I left the café and got into my car, pulling the summons from the police, headed FOR A MATTER CONCERNING YOU out of my jacket pocket. What did they want this time? I'd given them plenty to do when my brother left, and with my weed-related escapades before that. I dialed the number for Le Gwen, a cop I touched base with on the first Wednesday of every month. No big deal, just a routine exchange of pleasantries. Since *Charlie* and the thirteenth, we'd been having a whole new love affair with the police. Drugs, breaking and entering, car theft—none of that was a turn-on for the cops anymore. They're intelligence agents now, and despite being dead-tired, they're loving it. Gives them a new reason to live. And, to do the job properly and nab the big guns, they need eyes and ears on the street, people straight out of the *bendo*, the projects.

"Le Gwen here."

"It's Pilot."

"What's up, bro?"

Every single time, he greeted me like he'd been waiting for my call. Relaxed and calm, probably with his feet up on his desk, and no matter what I said, he just let it flow, handing out those *What's up, bro*s as easily as if he were some kind of ATM.

"I'll have a look at that summons. I don't think it's anything serious. I'll give you a call back as soon as I know anything and then you can stop by and see me, okay?"

We normally saw each other on the first Wednesday of every month, but Le Gwen liked it when I stopped by more often. In order to stay out of prison, I hadn't had much choice but to get buddy-buddy with the cops. It was the price I paid for my past, the years spent acting like Mr. Big of the *banlieues*.

I hung up and floored it toward the Gare de Bagnolet. The images from last night came back again. It was definitely my brother. At the ticket window, I bombarded the clerk with every *banlieusard* incantation in the book to get the list of passengers on last night's bus from Cologne. He started muttering things about how it wasn't allowed, he didn't have the authority, he could lose his job. He was an Arab, Moroccan, fortyish or so, and I told him to cut it out with the French, which calmed him down like I knew it would, because there's nothing worse than talking to a Maghrebi in French. It reminds them of colonialism and makes them feel like they're imitating their former oppressors. Anyway, after that he gritted his teeth and started listening to me. I didn't even have to say much; he could read all my doubts and anxieties in my face: Syria, ISIS, the Islamic State, terrorist. Words of fear. We didn't even need to say them anymore; they hovered like bees in the air; you couldn't see them but you could feel them, flying and stinging invisibly, landing on brains in flower to feed off the pistil, make honey, and take it back to the desert. The Arab clerk glanced around to make sure we were alone. His fingers tapped away on the keyboard with the enthusiasm of an informer. The printer spit out a sheet of paper, which he stuffed into an envelope and held out to me. I tried to take it, but he wouldn't let go. "Fifty euros," he said, remorselessly. A whole morning's earnings for a passenger list that hadn't cost him a cent. And they talk about racism. Scumbag.

8
YOUNGER BROTHER

Remember Lunatic's first album? Dad didn't want to buy it for us; he said it was trash music. So we stole it from the supermarket, hiding it in the shopping cart under the milk. Do you remember it, or not? The first song, "No Time for Regrets"? We listened to it in our bedroom, on the CD player Pop had given us for Christmas. We weren't allowed to tell the other neighborhood boys that we celebrated Christmas, because it was *hchouma*—shameful. Already, at ten and twelve years old, we were ashamed of our French origins. And do you remember the words? The chorus: *No time for regrets, our mistakes belong to us and no one else, born to make my contribution to progress*—those lyrics saved my life. Because, at the time, I wanted to die, to be with her again. Because it was my fault she died. I never told you, but that song brought me back from the brink, because it meant everything. I've wanted to save the world since that day, bro.

My NGO worked remotely with the Red Cross and Doctors Without Borders, but it managed its own operations independently. I left one month after they accepted me. Without saying anything to anyone. It was better that way. Like when you left for the army. No one would have understood, and no one would have wanted to believe me.

My plane landed in Athens. I dropped my suitcase at the hotel and made a beeline for the Acropolis. I had to be at the port the next day. I spent twenty-four hours walking every inch of that city. Everything was bad and good at the same time—bad because they were in the middle of an economic crisis, and good because the sun was still shining and the Greeks were still smiling. So I told myself that Cham couldn't be any worse.

The next day, we took a boat to the island of Kos, six kilometers from the Turkish coast. A backward version of the route taken by people fleeing the war. Our group was five people, dreamers like me, practicing Muslims, born to make their contribution to progress. The kind of guys you'll find in any religion. I was the only one born in France; the others had all just gone there to study. We shared the same crazy vision: to help, to build, to live, and to create a new world. Some of them were more pissed off than others, but Islam & Peace was no terrorist organization. Each person expressed his opinion and, without getting angry, we changed the subject. From Kos we went to Bodrum in Turkey, and then we boarded a bus. After two days of traveling through the mountains we stopped in Urfa, the birthplace of Ibrahim (Abraham), in southeastern Turkey. Everything had been going well until then. I saw familiar Arabic features all around me, guys that looked like they were from our neighborhood, hairy and with thick mustaches, and sometimes blue-eyed blonds—also like guys from home, with thick hair and heavy features. After spending three nights in an apartment in the northern part of the city, we got on the road to Cham, heading toward the border in a Jeep through groves of pistachio trees. A few kilometers from the border, we stopped in a village to change drivers. It was a hundred and twenty degrees outside—it felt like my skin was melting. People lived in houses like termite hills, built of hay and dried mud. It was like being back in the Stone Age. When you entered a house, the temperature dropped by a good twenty degrees. There was a sort of natural ventilation system, an ancient, ancestral thing—old-country A/C. The new driver was a guy from this village, about our age, with black skin, but not

African black—the black of poverty, real poverty, of spending his days in the fields. With his five remaining teeth and in terrible French, he told me they hadn't had running water for the past three years.

As we neared the border, I saw our country's flag. It made me want to cry. The dream of a lifetime. Since our *Jidda*—our grandmother—and her stories, and the ones our Uncle Hemmi told about our little village, Tadmor, and our Palmyran heritage. Our history. Our roots. The Turks had overdone it at the checkpoint; they were blocking everyone from crossing because of the Kurds. So we went west, along the border. On my left there were Turkish watchtowers, a fifty-meter-long minefield topped by barbed wire, and, behind a rocky desert, a few villages in the distance that we could make out thanks only to their minarets rising above the skyline. To my right, in Turkey, it was as green as paradise. The driver explained to me that the European Union had financed a dam project there and that, since then, they had planted olive and pistachio trees all over the area.

Our driver used a cane to press down on the gas pedal because polio had robbed him of the use of his right foot. At the next border station, we slowly approached the Turkish border guards. One of them looked into the car and asked me two or three questions in English. The Syrian flag, Dad's flag, our flag, red, white, and black, with its two green stars, fluttered just twenty meters away. In the distance, there were tents and hundreds of human silhouettes. The soldier knitted his brows and clenched his jaw, and then took a few steps back to let us pass.

The homeland was twenty meters away. So close I couldn't believe it. The first time one of my dreams had ever come true. We passed the flag. I don't know why—you'll laugh—but I suddenly wanted to sing "Hisseo Santiago," that song we learned in elementary school. Tears came into my eyes that not even the hundred-and-twenty-degree weather could dry. I turned my head so the others wouldn't see. And then I saw the people who were sheltering under those tents: sick children, displaced people, mutilated people, starving people. We got out of the car to give them water. Finally, home. I thought of you, and I wished you were there with me, and Dad and Mom, too.

9
OLDER BROTHER

From the Gare de Bagnolet, I headed for the mosque. It was Friday, and I always went there for the midday prayer. At twelve o'clock sharp, I stowed my shoes discreetly on the shelf in the entrance hall and tiptoed across the huge carpets. As usual, it stank of feet, mostly because of the old men who wore faux-leather shoes that made them sweat, and, whether or not they washed their feet or changed their socks, the smell would choke a horse. I'd been coming to the mosque since the kid brother went away. I found answers there. It did me good. In the end, if our father had done the job right, maybe my brother wouldn't have left. The old man had set religion aside; he never spoke about it. Grandma had a full monopoly on it, and even she taught us only the bare minimum, so as to avoid angering her son. You've got to have a strong spinal column to hold your head up high, and we were missing a few vertebrae. But we compensated, each in our own way. Me with cars and weed, drugs, grass, and the kid brother, at first, with a head full of daydreams and one hand on the Quran. I've never understood why or how he left. Anyone with half a brain would say he had it all—family, girlfriend, job, money, future—and that it made no sense at all.

No spinal column: not really French but not really Syrian either; not really natives but not really immigrants; not Christian but not Muslim. Aliens without knowing why. My dad has never told his side of the story, which means big pieces are missing, so we just imagine the rest. As for the other half of our story, the people who could tell it live far away, in Brittany. They're relatives without really being family. I don't know how to explain it, but it's impossible for us to understand each other. How can you find your way forward when you don't know where you've come from?

The preaching at the mosque was a little Westernized. Like reporters on TV news, the imam never talked about the world as it really was. He wanted to be a star with his picture on a poster more than he wanted to be a guide. And he attached a lot of importance to style, like, "pray pressed against one another," while Grandma had taught me to keep my distance, to pray in solitude. It was Friday, and the place was packed. Two or three of my friends were there—well, actually, I'm not sure if I should call them friends or just acquaintances. They drove me nuts. They acted like good Muslims but they came to the mosque in Real Madrid or Barcelona soccer jerseys. No respect. And they were totally clueless; the Real Madrid jersey has a cross on it. A Catholic cross. And they wore it to the *mosque*. And then they had the nerve to act high and mighty about what you should and shouldn't do.

The imam always started with the *khutbah*, a political sermon. He could hardly speak French to begin with; how could he understand politics here without being able to listen to the radio, read newspapers, or watch TV? I guess we'll just have to wait for the guys in our generation to become scholars and replace the old men.

After the service we went to K's house, as usual. He's a pretty together guy. Did political science at Sciences Po and knows what he's talking about. I made sure we got to know each other after my brother left; everyone knew they'd hung around together, and I'd thought maybe, eventually, that might help me to bring him back home, or at least to make contact with him. Every week, after prayer, we all went back to his place. He'd tell us the latest stuff we needed to know about the world, emphasizing certain important words as if he were slashing the air with a sword, like *West-ern-ers*, pronounced with the same obsessiveness as my dad when he said *Comm-u-nism* or *Ba-shar al-As-sad*. Sitting cross-legged on the floor with his hands on his knees, K would bend his head forward slightly while he talked, kind of like Sarko, or Denver, the Last Dinosaur. He'd arch his eyebrows and open his eyes wider and wider the more he laid out the world for us. There were eight of us, and all the regulars were there. It wasn't any kind of association or group; just a meeting of friends. K was strict about the rules. Never interrupt anyone else. Raise your hand to ask a question. Speak politely. No insults. Turn off your phone. Wash your hands, take off your shoes, and sit cross-legged in a circle. He was a fount of knowledge, a sage. He smiled discreetly whenever anyone asked a question. He always had an answer.

That day, he talked about the Jews and jealousy. His big credo was that we should never make trouble with Jews in France; we had to respect them and, if we were jealous, all we had to do was act like them, be organized, study or go into business, create a network. There was no point in being angry at them or attacking them. But, he warned us, respect doesn't mean friendship or sympathy. They were still the enemy; we just couldn't fight them in France. That wasn't the right place. The French are the arbitrators, and they will always protect the Jews; anything we do would come back on our heads. If you wanted to clash with the Jews in France, you had to do it with your mind. If you wanted to use weapons, you had to do it in their home country, in Israel or Palestine.

K always insisted that we couldn't allow ourselves to stand out; that we had to dress and speak like everyone else. No beards, no wearing *djellabahs* or *kamis* in the street, no Arabic words. He said God didn't care about any of that; what he looked at was the heart. I never stopped to think about why I kept coming to these gatherings, but I loved them. I learned all kinds of stuff I hadn't known before: geopolitics and history and religion. We even talked about films and music. One thing that fascinated me was the idea that "the enemies of our enemies are our friends." That day he told us, rubbing his palms together, what political realism was. That our mission was to serve God, and therefore Islam, and that for these reasons we had to study and understand how humans and societies function. It's a challenge the All Merciful has given us, to understand the system He has created. It's not very clear to me. I don't understand who Muslims' friends are or who their enemies are, because they're always at war against one another. For example, the Turks are Muslims, and they're allies with the Israelis, who are themselves the enemies of all Arabs, including Moroccan Muslims, who are friends with the French, who are both friends and enemies with everyone. *Ouloulou*, as our prophet, the French rapper Booba, would say. It's enough to make your head spin. But I didn't dare ask K, for fear of being thought an imbecile. It's because of the weed. Before all that, before my accident, my mind was a lot sharper. I was always one of the top students in my class in school. But that was before.

The other people at the meeting were also just regular guys like me; almost all deliverymen or drivers. Like most of the guys from our part of town, we'd all ended up in the transport business. No choice when your only degree is a vocational high school certificate and your only teacher is a car. Someone's phone went off; Ibrahim Maalouf's trumpet was the ringtone. It was mine. K stopped talking. It drove him insane when phones rang during these meetings. He took a breath. It rang again. I didn't know where I'd left my phone—my jacket, probably, which was hanging in the foyer. Then it rang again. He stopped talking again.

"Telephones off, okay?" he said to me, emphasizing the *okay* with his thick eyebrows.

"We're fighting the West so that we can live peacefully. To protect our brothers and sisters who are being subjected to the oppression of not being able to live according to the precepts of the Book. What is the harm in wearing a veil? Or a beard? In observing Ramadan? In praying, or eating halal? Are we harming anyone? I ask you. Those are the reasons for our fight. Islam has nothing against the West. But I have—you have—*we* have reasons to fight against the systems and the people preventing us from living the way we wish to. Where is the freedom the West is always bragging about so much? They talk about peace and friendship, and at the same time they're selling bombs, weapons, and ammunition. They talk about equality but support one rich, strong, and powerful country against another that is weak and without resources, which has been occupied for the past seventy years. Is it the Arabs who arrested Jews, who put them on trains and gassed them?"

Everyone shook their heads.

"My brothers, they are the lying ones. It was those for whom Islam is only war and death who did that. But Islam does not kill for no reason. Do we cut the sheep's throat for pleasure? No, it is so we can distribute meat among the poor, so we can eat it. And now, to make up to them, the West is letting the Jews punish the Arabs and the Muslims. The Jews aren't strong enough to hit out at their Western masters, so they attack our brothers instead. I repeat: the Jews do not control the world, or even the West. They're NATO's dogs, used by the United States and France to create a little holiday home for themselves in the Middle East. Just like in the Crusades. If they want to play, we will play, with our whole hearts and our passion and the sword of Allah the merciful. Amen."

"Amen," everyone repeated. Except for me. It wasn't a prayer, and I don't like it when people mix prayer and politics. As for the rest, I'd think about it. I'm not smart enough to decide whether I'm the fuckhead or he is.

At the end of the meeting I ducked out before he could talk to me. He would only have asked me to do something for him, like he always did, but I had no desire to engage with his darkness again. Since the war in Syria and the attacks, you couldn't tell who was who anymore. Good people might be killers, and vice versa. It was fucking terrifying, but you had to keep on living.

There were three missed calls on my phone from a number I didn't recognize. I called it back. A deep voice, touched with a Southern accent, answered.

"Hello."

"Hello; you called me?"

"Who is this?"

"You tried to call me three times less than an hour ago."

"Oh! That wasn't me. It was . . ."

"Who?"

"A young guy. I don't know him. He said he wanted to call a friend and he didn't have a phone."

"What did he look like?"

He hung up. I called back several times, but I never heard that Southern voice again.

10
Younger Brother

I don't know what I was thinking. I thought I would land like a dove in the middle of that death zone. We were driving toward the city of Al-Bab, forty kilometers from Aleppo. Nobody had said much since the border. We kept going, but as we kept coming across burned-out cars, the remains of artillery shells, houses riddled with bullet holes, our faces began to sag. The roads were dotted with civilians fleeing for Turkey, on foot, in cars, and on horseback. I was dead tired. We stopped. We started again. In a vegetative sleep-state, head against the window, arms folded, lulled by the sound of our gear rattling and the motor growling at each bridge ascent. With all the bumps and potholes in the road, my head kept jouncing off the window, and I woke up, eyes crusty, exhausted because we'd gotten up so early. The scenery outside changed from yellow to gray to green. Here, when water appeared, it transformed the dusty landscape into paradise.

A few kilometers outside Al-Bab, two guys got out of the truck. They lifted a large trunk out of the rear of the pickup and got into a car waiting at the side of the road. They followed us for a few kilometers before turning at the fork to Raqqa. The hospital was on the other side of Al-Bab, our driver explained. In the east. When we got there, Bedrettin and three other men were sitting on plastic chairs, drinking tea. They got up to greet us. Bedrettin embraced me in welcome. Next to him, a blond man in combat fatigues with a red beard, nerdy glasses, chubby cheeks, and a round belly nodded and smiled. A Kalashnikov leaned against his chair. The Turk told me he was the local emir, and the two other soldiers with him were *mujahideen* assigned to protect the hospital. He winked at me. You couldn't do here what we would do with Pop in France—speak Arabic so people wouldn't understand—and we couldn't speak French either, because in Syria, a lot of people speak it, or at least understand it. Behind him, what they called a hospital was a cinder-block building about the size of a large house, which had been given a coat of white paint to make it clean and visible in case of bombardments. The red Doctors Without Borders logo hadn't been erased; Bedrettin told me later that, following the French withdrawal, the NGO had turned this field hospital over to Islam & Peace. It was better that way. Our NGO got along well with the emir and the group that controlled this area. We didn't share the same convictions, but they were motivated by the same objective: fighting against Bashar and achieving peace.

I became the twelfth member of the medical team at Al-Bab. There were two of us nurses. In the main building, there was an operating room, a consulting room, a waiting room, three patient rooms with beds, and a staff room. Outside, a room dug into the ground was the pharmacy, and the morgue was in a tent.

I sat down with Bedrettin, the emir, and his two soldiers in front of the hospital, and we ate balls of kibbe. They planned for me to start working in a week; first I had to have some training and get used to the place. That afternoon we went into the city in a four by four that belonged to the blond man with the red beard, the emir, whom I ended up nicknaming Blondbeard, because Redbeard was a pirate, and you couldn't give a man of religion that nickname. Festive music echoed through the streets of the city and drifted through the car's open windows; there was a wedding happening. Bedrettin took us there so he could introduce me to some of the locals. We entered an immense hangar permeated with sound from car speakers. At the far end were men dancing in a circle, holding hands. Syrian-style. The groom was the only one in wedding clothes: shiny gray suit, white shirt, blue tie, Brylcreemed hair. "This is the most wonderful day of my life," he kept repeating. No women. They were celebrating the marriage somewhere else. From time to time, the groom called his new wife on the telephone so he could hear her voice before hanging up, smiling. Around him, several bearded men in combat fatigues took part in the festivities, while others slumped in plastic chairs, thumbs stroking the screens of their smartphones. Someone brought me another plate overflowing with kibbe, and I found myself sitting next to Blondbeard.

One by one, the men in combat fatigues came over to greet him. An embrace, a kiss on the cheek, a slap on the back. He introduced me to each of them as the new doctor. I didn't understand everything, because he spoke quickly, in the regional dialect, and I didn't dare ask him to clarify. He seemed really nice. The round face and genuine smile of a good man. Then he stood up and joined the men dancing the dabke, gesturing to me to follow him. My boss, Bedrettin, was talking to the only man who wasn't wearing fatigues. He looked like Blondbeard, only shorter and fatter. Same reddish beard, golden hair, snow-white skin, and a forest of chest hair spilling out of his shirt. He wore a flannel shirt, jeans, and dirt-caked work-boots. He could have been a young hipster from east Paris. All he needed was the single-speed bike.

I tried to follow the steps of the circle of men dancing the dabke hand in hand, shoulders swaying, but it was too complicated. Blondbeard told them to change the dance; this one was easier, just one step forward, one step back. Everything was different here; even the religious men were partiers.

Suddenly, there was an enormous, hideous noise, like jet engines. It was deafening. It even drowned out the wedding music. I thought maybe the guy guarding the entrance had fired his Kalashnikov in celebration, but the circle of dancers broke up immediately, and all the men made a beeline for their own guns. Then another sound became audible over the music: Blondbeard told me a combat helicopter was flying over the village. Those hadn't been celebratory shots, but a barrage of large-caliber machine-gun fire only a few streets away. The engine sound faded, and, one by one, the men put down their Kalashnikovs and rejoined the dancing. I'd get used to it, Bedrettin said. I slept at his place that first night. He was one of the rare men allowed to live alone in an apartment; local laws required unmarried men to live in barracks together. The next day I moved into an apartment of ten. The nine other men were soldiers. Three Syrians, two Pashtuns, three Iraqis, and a Turk.

Blondbeard came to visit. "You'll be fine here," he said. He took me on a tour of the city in his pickup truck. It was quiet; there was no sign of fighting, and some people were in the streets, mostly men, but a few women. We came to a river. It was crazy; you'd have thought you were at the public swimming pool in Bobigny. *Mujahideen* bathing, diving, swimming, playing in the water. Blondbeard pulled off his jacket, T-shirt, and pants, and joined them. They were all very young, between about sixteen and twenty-five. I perched on a big rock and watched them. Blondbeard motioned for me to join them, but I was too embarrassed. It was so weird; I'd anticipated arriving in a country at war, and in the first two days I'd been to a wedding and spent an afternoon at the old swimming hole. Aside from the helicopter, life seemed pretty pleasant. On the way back, Blondbeard asked me what I thought of Bashar al-Assad. I said he was a bloodthirsty madman. "He's an infidel," was the reply. "But a good enemy."

11
OLDER BROTHER

After I left K's place, an Uber accounts manager called me to tell me he wanted to meet with me for a review. Supposedly, my revenue was plummeting. For example, that day it was 3:15 in the afternoon and I'd only made sixty euros. I just didn't feel like it. But I really do love it when my tires crunch against the asphalt, when my hands, welded to the steering wheel, make the car dance around the curves; eyes on the road, I forget the red lights, pass on the right, merely slow down at the stop signs; the kilometers fly by, and my boat just cuts a clean path through the world. Once the door is closed and the cabin is pressurized, the atmosphere changes; I fly up into space and sail through the universe.

The past few days, though, I just hadn't been feeling it. It was the job taking it out of me: eight, ten, twelve hours a day. Suddenly, I wanted to enjoy life a little. I headed for the 120 in Saint-Denis, because there were always a lot of people there on Fridays, a lot of stories to hear. Oh well, I'd make some money in the evening. It's better to work evenings and weekends anyway; it may make you a loser, but it fills the coffers and the fridge. The 120 is a drivers' hangout, a restaurant, part traditional, part fast food. They've got everything: hamburgers, kebabs, pizza, noodles to go, steaks, skewers— all halal. After all these years, it's good for us to step into the twenty-first century too.

The place was jammed, as usual. All guys like me: black

dress pants, white shirts, hair cut short on the sides. I put my plate down at a table where some people I knew were sitting.

"Yo, Breton, what's up?"

They've called me Breton since the time some guys from our neighborhood who were at summer camp in Saint-Malo ran into us with our Breton grandmother at the beach. I was fourteen and my brother was twelve, and they never let us live it down; it spread all over the ninth arrondissement. Whatever. No big deal.

Hassen greeted me while soaking his disgusting, oily fries in Samurai sauce, a mixture of ketchup, mustard, and harissa. Even worse, he talked with his mouth open, with bits of salad stuck to his teeth. I must have been the only person in this place who actually knew how to eat correctly. Rule number one: you have to get the food to your mouth. But they did the opposite; they put their noses in it, like animals. Talk at the table was always about soccer, money, politics, girls. Especially politics. War, the government, the situation with taxi drivers. Hassen, apart from his passion for Samurai sauce, was also extremely active in a movement protecting the rights of private-hire drivers. He was no fool. He hadn't gone to college, but he wasn't stupid either, and he knew how to stand up for what was ours.

Everyone in this restaurant was more or less living the dream—if your dream was to eat a sandwich or a plate of meat in a dive smelling of grease and full of fat men with beards who harangued you with morality lessons if you so much as burped without saying *Alhamdulillah*. I don't know what it is about fat guys and religion. The fatter they are, the more they love to annoy everyone around them with religious talk. Same thing with fat women. That doesn't come from God, because He didn't tell them to eat like pigs. But it's not really the fat people's fault; it's the skinny people who snidely judge their round cheeks and big asses. That makes the fat people feel vulnerable, and they look for something they can defend. If no one judged them, I'm sure they wouldn't feel compelled to beat everyone over the head with religion. What if all our problems were just because of fat and love handles?

The restaurant was so loud that I couldn't hear much of the chatter at our table.

"That's unbelievable. You hear about those guys from Sevran? Joël, Karim, Bathily, that bunch?"

"The Rainbow gang?"

We called them that because they were one of the rare gangs where guys of different ethnicities hung out together.

"Yeah, them. Those idiots. They beat a guy up day before yesterday, at the RER station. Dude's in a coma. They're in jail."

"Why'd they go after him?"

"The guy was kissing his girlfriend, and they came over to mess him up a little, to tell him it's not cool to do that, because they're religious and it's offensive."

"In a *coma*? No way, man, are you serious?"

"They're crazy. So yeah, the guy defended himself, and they jumped him, right there in front of his girlfriend. Five against one."

Hassen always knew everything that was going on before anyone else, because all through the day, drivers would call him to talk about work stuff, and along the way they'd tell him the latest word from the street. Yann, a French convert to Islam who went by Younes, started to get worked up.

"See, things like that make me want to go ape-shit on everybody, man. Be religious on your own time, behind closed doors, brother. Why do you have to go around beating everyone over the head with it? Those guys, those homos, they should all be exterminated."

Like all converts, he went over the top with it. More royalist than the king.

"We must not be reading the same Quran, man. Where does it say 'Police each other'? I'd love for them to show me where it says that. If it had been a guy from the neighborhood, an Arab or black dude, they wouldn't have done anything. They would just have said hi, like, 'Salaam, my brother,' hand over heart. But because it was a little white guy, they beat the shit out of him. They're racists! I swear! They might as well go support Marine Le Pen, you know. They're cockroaches. They should be thrown out of the mosque, those little assholes."

When Younes talked, everyone listened and nodded. He was a former gang leader who'd found a way out with Islam. It was him I'd moved all the weed for. Younes had converted so successfully that it was like he was one of us, part of our tribe; not black or Arabic, but still a foreigner. Galley-slave job, anti-racist, anti–Marine Le Pen, just like us. Nikes on his feet, short-sided haircut, and even Islam. His brother was a lawyer, which was how he'd always managed to evade justice. I asked if I could talk to him, because he knew a little bit about law. I was worried about the summons. Le Gwen still hadn't called me back, and I was afraid something shady was up. Younes read the FOR A CASE CONCERNING YOU letter and smiled before answering:

"I wouldn't worry too much, bro. You can ask them why they're summoning you, and they have to tell you. If it were serious, they would have already picked you up at six o'clock some morning."

There were only a few French natives and not very many non-Muslims at the 120, but there were some: West Indians, Christian Africans, Portuguese. One of them was Mickaël. Last name: Da Sousa. He was the buddy I'd gotten busted with, but Le Gwen hadn't been as lenient with him. He had to wear an electronic ankle monitor because the prisons were full and the judge didn't think he was "a danger to society." And that was true; his only crime was moving weed. You can say that's bad, but the reality is that other people are out there transporting weapons, alcohol, tobacco, antidepressants, Coca-Cola, and those things are just as harmful to humanity. It had taken a while for us to start speaking again. Mickaël said it was my fault, and I thought it was his. But things were all right between us now. We had the same passion: cars and driving. And the same job, private-hire driver, though I worked for myself, and he couldn't yet because of the bracelet, so he slogged away for a boss.

"They're taking the ankle monitor off soon, and I'm going to Portugal. Think I'll stay there."

After two years trapped in the *bendo* because of the electronic ankle bracelet, he said, he wanted to see the country, and after talking with his uncle, he decided that living in Portugal, in the quiet and sunshine, was better than an iPhone and an Audi on the French concrete. I'd been to his village once. It was a tiny little hick place in the middle of nowhere on the Atlantic coast. Population of fifty, if that, wedged between the hills and the ocean. The village was beautiful but there was nothing to do; nothing but old people, and not even a café. Mickaël told me he'd help his uncle make wine and cater to French tourists on the farm to earn some cash.

"And if I learn to speak good Portuguese, maybe I'll go to Brazil. Come whenever you want."

I dreamed of Thailand, myself; the azure-blue sea, fine-sand beaches, champagne, coconut ice cream. But so as not to upset him, I said I'd think about it.

Little by little, the 120 emptied out. It was almost five in the evening and I found myself alone with Mehmet, the owner of the place, a Turk. We'd been friends forever. In my life there was my brother, and there was Mehmet. He has plenty of faults, but I've learned to live with them. Managing this kind of restaurant means knowing a thousand and one stories, because a lot of people come through here, especially drivers.

And being behind a steering wheel eleven hours a day means you get to know people, and you hear a lot of things. Mehmet was nicknamed Demytho, because he was a demi-mythomaniac—half a liar. Whatever he said, part of it was true and part of it wasn't. I mean, all of it was *based* on truth, but he always felt the need to make his stories more interesting. He should have been writing books rather than slinging hash twelve hours a day to buy a house on credit. I was reading the latest news from *Le Parisien* on my smartphone when his big hand landed on my shoulder.

"Hey, my brother! I heard somebody saw you at the mosque in Aubervilliers. Pharaon's mosque."

With Mehmet, you never know who the mysterious "somebody" is.

"Pharaon?"

"Yeah, the Egyptian, you know? The imam at the mosque in Aubervilliers."

I knew who he meant, but not what he was talking about. "So?"

"Brother, don't do anything crazy. You know that mosque is the boarding gate for Cham."

"What the hell are you talking about, man?"

"I'm only thinking of you, bro. Be careful, and stay away from that mosque. Pharaon is shady, and with things the way they are and all the spy stuff the government is up to, you'll end up in Syria as a best-case scenario, or, worst-case, in a new Guantanamo."

Pharaon was an Egyptian imam everyone respected. A fount of knowledge. Not some moron making Internet videos, reading interpretations of the Quran translated using Google.

Mehmet seemed serious about what he was saying. I didn't know how to answer. I didn't care what he'd heard about Aubervilliers; it had nothing to do with me. The Turk always had to gossip. All Turks are the same way; every Sunday, they have weddings and invite between five hundred and a thousand guests, just for the gossip. The network gets activated during the party afterward, from table to table, old lady to old lady; information moves faster than on the Internet. By the end of the night, everyone knows who's scamming who, and how, and for how much, and who slept with who, and a thousand other tidbits. I didn't want to say anything, but I was desperate to know if he'd heard anything about the guy I'd seen at the Gare de Bagnolet. His hand resting on my shoulder, he leaned down and whispered:

"I'll tell you something, but you can't tell anyone else. You have to promise me."

"Come on, man. You always say that, like you're Huggy Bear or something."

Composing my face into a serious expression and inclining my head slightly, I promised him I'd keep my mouth shut.

"Something's going down next week. I don't know what, or where, or when. But stay away from Pharaon and those guys, that whole scene. You're my brother, and I don't want you mixed up in any bad shit."

The problem with Mehmet is that you never know if he really heard something or if he's just making it up. It's like people who let out silent farts. No way of knowing who did it, but the smell tells you that someone did.

The events of the previous night kept running through my head. Mehmet went on talking, eventually coming to the subject of his last tax audit. The auditor had figured out that he was under-reporting his income. When adding up the number of kilos of flour he'd bought, Mehmet deducted the number of loaves produced, and therefore a theoretical number of sandwiches, which didn't fit with the income he declared. Anyway, he now owed a bunch of cash to the taxman, which made him angry enough to burst a blood vessel or two. His voice practically trembled with rage. The guy was always talking about money. It was infuriating; he didn't even realize how obsessed he was. He had a pretty successful life thanks to this restaurant. Twelve hours a day surrounded by the smells of French fries and meat so he could fill his pockets. The guy was money-crazed, wealth-crazed, work-crazed. Otherwise, why would he put up with all these asshole drivers and religious beardos, all the stale, fatty smells, and the long hours? You'd have to be truly passionate about money to do all that.

Up there in the universe of my head, somewhere between Mars and Saturn, I was at the bus station, watching my brother get off the bus and then disappear into that car.

"Hey, Mehmet, I think my brother's in Paris."

"What brother?"

"My *brother*, man. Band-Aid."

Band-Aid had been his nickname since he became a nurse.

"How do you know?"

"I don't know if I was dreaming or what, but I saw him last night at the Gare de Bagnolet."

"Why didn't you go up and talk to him?"

"Didn't have enough time, man. He got into a car, and I couldn't catch up with them."

"You? *You* couldn't catch up with them? No way."

"It was the cops, man. They pulled me over on the way down to Montreuil."

The Turk scratched his head. "You sure you aren't losing it again, like in the army?"

He knows almost everything about me, and vice versa. He's my oldest friend. He married a Kurdish woman and had two kids, which set his community buzzing. A good, nice girl, not some old slag who hangs out in cheap hotels hoping to give hand jobs to rappers or soccer players. The only thing is, she's not really Muslim. She's Alevi, which is a different, softer version of Islam. They're weird about God, but I really like them, never had a problem with them. To each his own; no problem.

But yeah, our people, the "real" Muslims, don't like updates, no doubt because they can screw up the system.

We sat silently. He slouched in his chair, his belly spilling over the top of his jeans, his double chin scratchy with stubble, dark circles under his eyes, and his face haggard, exhausted from the lunchtime service. I was lost in thought, with my elbows on the table and my hands clasped. Where could my brother be?

"So what did you mean? What's going down next week?"

"I'll tell you something, but you can't say anything to anyone."

Mehmet told his stories the way you drive a car in the *banlieue*: tires squealing, running red lights and stop signs. But the more the story stretched out, the more he started stammering. Couldn't control his own emotions. The more he stuttered, the more I figured the line between truth and lie had been completely crossed. He had to think about it in order to add the next lie to the previous one. Someone told him that they'd heard from a driver, Issam—no, wait, it was Pedro, a Portuguese convert—that some guys had come from Syria by way of Germany to blow up a car. And he knew that the Portuguese guy actually worked for the cops, and that he'd only pretended to convert to Islam so he could get inside info from Islamic circles. I wasn't sure about any of it, and I had no idea if I could really believe him, or what I could do with this information—and why would the Portos want to help the cops?

"Where did you see him, your brother?"

"Gare du Bagnolet, I told you."

"Eurolines?"

"Yeah."

"And what did he do? Why didn't you speak to him?"

"He got off a bus and left in a car."

"Where had the bus come from?"

"Cologne."

"Isn't that in Germany?"

I froze up then. Like in the army, in Chad, in front of the map. And the guys that started firing on our Jeep. And the way that soldier, Mendy, screamed. He died right in front of me, his eyes closed. There was nothing on the bus passenger list; no trace of my brother. I hadn't thought about it, but if he'd been in Cham, there'd be no reason for him to come back under his real identity. Since the *Charlie* shootings that was all over; no more doubts for the authorities. You don't come back from Syria without a reason.

12
OLDER BROTHER

Le Gwen called me back about the summons after I'd left the 120. Nothing major, but I needed to come by and see him. It was a way of pumping me for information. No signed contract between us; just my word and his. The first time I went to the station, I stood for five solid minutes on the sidewalk across the street, just admiring the building. It was beautiful. The architect had really outdone himself. The front was all stained-glass windows in blue, white, and red. At night, from a distance, the place looked like a church. Closer up, it looked futuristic. Who knew if it made the cops inside work differently; it didn't change anything for me. Since I was a teenager I'd been engaging in a sort of dance with the cops titled "I Love You; Me Neither." The police were public enemy number one for us.

I remember the winter day when the Drancy cops sprayed a guy we called Rainman with a fire extinguisher. He was a Tunisian from our neighborhood, a total mastermind. A few months before it happened, he'd already taken in four hundred thousand euros. The guy was a magician; a money magnet. Very few losses on his deals, and he hardly ever had to break anyone's teeth to get them to pay up. One payment in advance was the minimum, but he often billed for two or even three. He had guys ten years older than he was working for him. And despite everything, he stayed modest. He'd eat with us sometimes at the 120. Never talked about his takings or his art. Never said a single word more than he needed to. He was one of those guys who was better at making you talk about yourself than the gestapo, and without even asking any questions. Just a cool gaze and a slight, reassuring smile. Of course, the revenue office knew what he was up to, but without proof they couldn't arrest him and put him on trial, and no trial, no prison. That's the rule of law. France's richness made Rainman rich.

He disappeared, too, about four years ago. Just like my brother; one day here, next day gone. People say the guy had enough money to pad the pockets of everyone in the neighborhood for three generations. Four million euros, is the rumor. I think he'd just outgrown this place, so he took off with the swag. Maybe to crazy town, maybe to Brazil, or Thailand, or Dubai. Anyway, they were dying to catch him, but he always slipped through the nets. An artist. So they ambushed him. I was at a tram stop that day. The cop car slowed down, a dented gray Peugeot 307. Pulled up alongside him, and the front passenger-side window came down, and the cop took out a fire extinguisher and went to town on him with it. His whole head was covered in white powder and he was screaming, "My eyes, my eyes!" That same night, vengeance came in the form of Molotov cocktails thrown at a Renault Scenic patrol car and the local station. The message: "Let us live."

The first time—the real first time—my telephone rang after my kid brother disappeared, I was summoned for a matter concerning me. "Concerning *him*," I'd wanted to correct the person on the phone. I went down, sat in a chair, gave them my full name, date of birth, nationality. When they asked me if I had a criminal record I said no, and the person answered, "Really?" and then tapped away a bunch at his keyboard and then said, "Not yet." I listened, said "Yes, sir" and "No, sir," took a nice slap in the face, and went back to the city in my old man's taxi while he ranted about Soviet-style bureaucracy. What was my kid brother up to while I sucked it up and did the dirty work? I'd been visiting the cops for more than two years now. That's self-sacrifice, man. When I went down with Mickaël, Le Gwen got me off because I could be useful. He pulled some strings behind the scenes so that all my problems melted away. Not even a suspended sentence; nothing. I kept my mouth shut and no one knew. If they found out, in my hood, I'd be done for. Nothing worse than whoring yourself out to the cops. It ranks just below pedophilia in terms of morality. Made things a bit complicated with Mickaël, of course.

I parked my car in the parking lot of my building and headed for the police station on foot. It was seven in the evening. They directed me to the second floor, as usual. I went into a room, and Le Gwen was sitting there. Smarmy little French smile, Breton, seasoned veteran, self-confident, pointed chin, hair cut short on the sides, bushy eyebrows, open-necked blue shirt, expensive but ugly. A life spent locking people up—but they'd end up shutting him away too, in a wooden box in a hole in the ground, and they'd bury him with no one there to mourn; not colleagues, not informers. Nobody'd be bringing flowers, either. Whatever happens, you start life in a box; you live it in one, you finish it in one. First your mother's belly, and then a bassinet, then your bedroom, school, the dance club, your car, the office, your house, and in the end? A casket. Boxes. Always boxes.

"How's it going, Callahan?"

Harry Callahan, in case you don't know, is a crafty police inspector played by Clint Eastwood. Spits out words like machine-gun bullets. One of my dad's heroes.

"Fine. Your summons is shit. Just no more points on your license, bud. No more private-hire driving."

It took a minute to sink in. My entire new life was thanks to Le Gwen. The old cop had helped me to find a job. He'd given me the idea and referred me to a friend of his. For a year I'd driven for a boss, then gone on my own. Then he put pressure on the urban housing department to help me get an apartment. It might not seem like much, these little boosts, but it made it possible for me to join the adult world. It was what Pop had never managed to do.

"You get me? No more private-hire. You'll have to surrender your license and take the test again."

"What the hell is this bullshit? What am I going to do? I wasn't even notified that I didn't have any more points!"

"You were supposed to make sure, bud. You should have received a letter."

The truth was that there was a huge pile of leaflets, flyers, and letters in my front hallway. You'd have thought I had some kind of bureaucratic phobia. I just don't really like opening the mail. Too often, it's bad news. The last time I'd gotten a letter from the cops, my address was written on the envelope by hand, like a love letter. I was curious, so I opened it—and bam! A summons. Fuck me, man.

"Okay. I have a solution. So you're out of points, but as long as your license hasn't been withdrawn, you can still drive. So what I'll do is, I'll hold things back so you don't get summoned and you don't sign the papers, okay?"

I didn't know how to thank him. Over the years he'd become kind of a second father to me. I think my family situation—my mom, my grandma, my brother, and my old man—had softened him up.

"Now, we're going to do things right. You're going to find yourself a driving school and sign up for the test, and as soon as you've got a test date, I'll release your summons. Then you won't have a license anymore, but if you pass the test the first time, it should only be for a few days."

The cops always had their secret little ways. If you got a traffic citation, handing over a couple of soccer tickets usually made it go away. As long as you had something to offer, they always found a solution.

"Anything new with the beardos?"

He never really took his eyes off the prize, Le Gwen. He'd say a few words, fold his hands on his desk, drop his gaze, and then look up and ask the question, eyes glinting. You had to play hide-and-seek with truth and lies to avoid falling into his trap. Grandma used to say everything was a question of balance. "Your father was born on the very day my father died," she'd murmur. Since Mom died, I'd created my balance with my own two hands. My legs shook, but I resisted for a few seconds, the blood pounding in my head, my fists clenched, barely breathing, and I started to calm down again. If I had more control I could have held myself back, not letting out even a breath, and kept my mouth shut for years. But on that day, I didn't give a shit.

"My brother. I think he's back."

It just came out without thinking, like the time I kicked that guy in the head. Sometimes life hangs by only a few words.

"What?"

"A guy told me he saw him at Bagnolet."

"But you didn't see him?"

Balance. My fists flexed and my knees trembled. Head up, abdominal muscles clenched, breathing calm. I concentrated. Held on.

"No."

"Does your dad know?"

"No."

"He searched everywhere for him for two years. Why haven't you told him?"

"Heart. It's not a good time. Plus, he's in the middle of selling his taxi license."

"What does that have to do with it?"

"You wouldn't understand. He's got nothing. Just his own melon, that's it. Nothing else. A ruined retirement; just the minimum old-age pension. Seven hundred euros. That's only

enough to eat one meal a day, even at Lidl. So, for us, the
license is everything. Twenty-five years of work. Hours every
day with your ass planted in the driver's seat, looking for hands
in the air, ears peeled for a call from dispatch just to earn a few
bucks, to fill the fridge for your two street-rat kids, evenings
spent staring at the TV, falling asleep alone, no woman . . . So,
selling the permit means earning himself a well-deserved, comfortable last few years."

He doodled in his notebook. I thought I'd given him a
major scoop, a home run, but he didn't even give a shit; just let
it go by, without even blinking.

"What else?"

I figured I'd repeat what the Turk had told me. That kind
of half-information always went over well. "Everyone's saying
it's going to blow up soon."

"How?"

"Dunno. Nobody's saying why. I tried to find out more, but
I don't think anyone actually knows. They're talking about
Germany and Aubervilliers. You know who I'm talking about.
Pharaon and those guys."

"And that's all you know?"

"You know how it is. Lot of talk, but who knows what's
true?"

Le Gwen tried again to squeeze a little more information
out of me. He felt the balance of our relationship, too, of the
way we were going. We'd all been carrying on a kind of old-
fashioned letter-based romance with the cops in recent years.
The cops sent summons letters or wrote out tickets, and we
responded by tagging or throwing stones. They wouldn't have
jobs without us, because assholes like us take up most of the
hours in their day. The real bad guys, they don't catch them
very often. When it does happen, it's just dumb luck, or
because a cop is smarter than the criminal. And without them,
we wouldn't have anyone to judge ourselves by. We were close,

man. Buddies. They'd even become my confidants over the years. It was in my contract—otherwise I'd be off to the pen. No choice. Telling them the buzz on the street was the price of my freedom. Whatever had been said most recently by the nutjobs who talked more about Cham than about Islam. We had a deal. They shut their eyes to my past, and I opened my ears to save their future.

13

OLDER BROTHER

Barely twenty-five years old, and her tits are already down around her belly button. When she's naked, those big boobs of hers hang halfway down her stomach, but when she's dressed, she's got a nice rack, sculpted by those amazing modern bras that can turn nothing much into something premium. Women's clothes these days can turn anyone into a magician, man. Big ass? This brand of jeans can disguise it and make it look perfect. Flat ass? This other brand can turn it into a bubble like Beyoncé's. Big feet? Right this way, madam, I can make you look like you wear a size six. All of it causes some weird space-time distortions, man. Girls can use makeup to make themselves look like an extra-small in the face, but the ass is still size extra-large.

I'd just given her a good hard one, and the rules of life state that after sex, men go to sleep. But I can never fall asleep just after I've gotten some. A good, hard ride, sliding my dick home—it's like an electric shock to me, like a drug. And afterward, lying on my back, my eyes on the ceiling, and my cock sticking to the sheets, my head boils over with ideas. Just like with a joint.

I'd picked this girl up in a hookah bar on the night of a Champions League final match. She was talking with her friends, Arab chicks who used so much self-tanner they were bright orange. I was with my crew: Mehmet, Mickaël, Hassen, Younes, all the guys from the 120. I swung it so we moved to the table next to theirs. She was different from the other girls somehow; I'm not sure in exactly what way, but she didn't reek of cheap hotels. For me, picking up girls is a breeze; the gates open as soon as they find out I have an apartment, because hooking up in a hotel costs an arm and a leg, and, frankly, it's kind of boring. In the hood, everyone goes to hotels to fuck. You can't bring your piece back to the house in front of your parents, so it's either outside in some discreet alleyway, or in a car, or at a cheap hotel. So with an apartment, you become king of the skanks.

My girl was sleeping like a princess in heaven. I could feel her breath tickling my nose and I stroked her hair. I thought maybe I really was into her. You know, in love. I don't know. There's another girl too, and she definitely makes me feel like I'm getting tasered in the heart. But I can't end things with this chick; it'd break my heart. Maybe I'm just a coward.

Noiselessly, I slid one leg out of bed, then the other. I delicately lifted up the covers, kissed the girl on the temple, and stood up; no sudden moves, so I wouldn't wake her. Her expensive lace panties were under my left foot. Unable to stop myself, I lifted them with a big toe to make sure there wasn't anything on them. Best to know who you're fooling around with. You never know; life is full of surprises—who knows how thoroughly she wipes her ass.

I padded silently across the room. It was late. I selected *The Bridge on the River Kwai* from my DVD collection. One of my favorite films. I've lost count of the times when, on a Sunday afternoon, Pop and I sat on the couch together, his arm across my shoulders, watching this flick about a Japanese colonel commanding a prisoner-of-war camp in Thailand during World War Two. Saito, the Japanese colonel, has to build a bridge, and he joins up with an English prisoner, Lieutenant Shears. The best scene is when Saito is preparing to commit *seppuku*, suicide by disemboweling himself, to save his honor, because the bridge construction goes to hell. The Japanese believe that the stomach and the guts control one's emotions, so to make amends for their mistakes, put it right, or preserve their honor when they don't carry out an order from a master, they plunge a sword into their own abdomen. It's fascinating.

I've always hidden my weed and my rolling paper in the DVD case for that movie. And I commit *seppuku* with every joint; then I wake up and come out of the woods and go back to the city, and there's always a Lieutenant Shears to tell me I've done something stupid.

On the balcony, I fired up the joint so that I can forget. This is my crib, my bubble, my little corner, my world. It had rained; I was cold, and the bottoms of my feet were wet. I'd gone out without a shirt on, and the cool wind bounced off my skin. Moist and suspicious, the night smelled like a whore who'd taken early retirement. There was nobody out at this hour; nothing but asphalt under the streetlights. In the distance I could hear the sound of traffic; no one around but taxis, private hires, and people burned out by alcohol or drugs. When I smoke a joint, I love to hold the smoke in my lungs for a few seconds. It crackles in my nose, and then it's hot in my mouth and my throat and chest. I close my eyes, and it all goes foggy; everything evens out and I feel good, as if I set down my backpack, full of the weight of the world.

Your mind becomes sharper, stronger, freer. You forget all the rest; you're swimming in pure reality, no waterfalls of prejudice and fear sending spray up to make the world hazy. Deep down, what I want is to give it all up. Fly away, into the sky, save the world, win races and World Cups, make movies, even write books, and, hell, swim laps in a pool of money, too. It makes you crazy, driving around snobs and middle-class white dudes eleven hours a day in a city that won't ever be yours, and to see that city living its life from behind your windshield, only to end up giving computer whizzes and the tax man half of what you earn. It's fucked up, bro. The suit and tie are fucked up. It's all a bunch of shit, but you have to live with it, because without it, it's worse. People don't even respect you anymore.

Even the police used to talk down to me. It drove me out of my mind. The worst kind of slavery is when some pissant nobody talks down to you, but you have to talk back to them with respect. The unwritten laws are the hardest ones to abolish. So, driving people around brought me some cash, but nothing else. There's also the respect you hear in every sentence people say, that you read in their faces. Is that enough to live on? A little. Respect is the welfare of social relationships. The base, the bare minimum. To make the rest bearable, my method is to roll a joint, light it, and breathe in the smoke. Without weed, I'd be a robot. I wouldn't even be able think anymore.

All I know is that us guys from the projects, we do what everyone in society does: we reproduce our parents' lives. Here, aside from a few rappers and athletes, which are a hedge, a smoke screen hiding a forest of robots, nobody's life has turned out the way they wanted it to. Just like our parents, my bro. The world keeps turning, and its balance is constant. I wonder why we live. We dig our heels in about weed, and social conflicts, and religion, but we're here to enjoy life above all, otherwise why would God have bothered creating us?

The moon shines down on the concrete plain—*it* managed to separate itself from the earth four and a half billion years ago. I worked up a gob of spit to salute it. Breathed in the smoke, cleared my throat, prepared to spit on the world. My gums were still bleeding. I leaned over my balcony railing and got ready to let go. I'd been living my life rubbing shoulders with the asphalt for too long; now I wanted to tell it to go on without me. The spitball fell in slow motion; so slowly that I had enough time to see everything it did. Floor after floor, it sucked my neighbors' lives into it. They all wanted to spit right along with me, to say goodbye to the concrete and asphalt forever, because deep down, with the exception of a few varying family circumstances, we were all living the same factory assembly-line life. Mass-produced for struggle.

I was sleepy now, from the weed. Just before spitting out the loogie, I noticed a guy walking with a bag slung over his shoulder. It was dark and everything was kind of hazy, but he had the same walk as the guy at the Gare de Bagnolet. He walked toward my building and stopped at the entrance. He consulted the buzzer list, then looked up. The loogie was falling straight for his head, precise as a drone. Thank God, he took a step to the left to press on the buzzer, and it missed him, splattering on the sidewalk next to his shoe. The guy pressed the buzzer. It rang in my apartment. It was my buzzer? The guy down there? Who was this asshole buzzing me in the middle of the night? He's going to wake up my girl, the idiot. He buzzed again, twice, three times. The chick woke up, and I could hear her complaining in the bedroom. Dammit. I whispered a few soft words to calm her down and pushed the button on the intercom.

"Hello?"

"It's me."

I barely had time to pull on a pair of pants; I had to open the door without a shirt on. He was there, in front of me, with his boyish face and the same curls falling over his eyes. He'd always stood out in the neighborhood because of his look. A careful, perfect haircut, not like the rest of the deadbeats in the city: very short on the sides and long on top, sculpted with three different kinds of hair gel. That was why I'd never been able to understand how he'd gotten involved in other people's bullshit, because even physically, he had always kept himself slightly apart, remote. He even refused to have the same look as anyone else.

His proud face made me want to hit him. My teeth clenched; my head pounded. *Tum, tum, tum,* my heart thumped in my chest and the blood surged through my veins. I felt like ants were crawling all over my damp palms and my arms, and my stomach turned over so that I thought I might be sick at any moment. Tears lurked in my eyes like Viet Cong soldiers, threatening to burst out. I wanted to both cry and scream, to howl out my rage, to rip his face off to see if there was another one underneath. He didn't move. Didn't speak. His chin quivered. One good right hook and he'd go down, TKO.

The duffel bag over his shoulder, the low brows, the wet eyes, a gaze that came from somewhere far away and carried the whole world within it. That bag, and all the troubles he'd been through—he'd come back to put them down at my door. At the end of the day, my problems with the cops had been partly because of him. But there you go; in this shit family, honest people like me and my dad have always had to put up with the divas, my grandma and my brother. Did he think that life was a movie, maybe? That you could just come back like that, in the middle of the night, with no warning? Who did he think he was? Just standing there in the hallway, soaking wet, like a stray dog. But I never asked anything of him; I spent three years running after him, gone three years unable to sleep. And now His Majesty just shows up, just like that, out of the blue. He was the one who should apologize. Little shit. He hadn't changed, hadn't grown up. His hands were trembling. He slid them into his pockets to hide them from me. He was my brother, the man I hated most in the world.

He read all of that in my face. Everything I'd been wanting to say to him for ten years. An adult smile touched his face. The Viet Congs hiding behind his pupils leapt out and streamed down his nose and over his lips. So that I wouldn't see them, he pulled me into his arms, laid his head on my shoulder, and whispered in my ear, "Thank you. I'm sorry."

He's my brother. I love him more than anything. More than

heaven, God, my mother, my father, my grandmother, the girl in my room, the other chick, my car, my dark suit. He's my flesh and blood, my best friend, my partner in crime, my accomplice, my twin, my associate, my colleague, my double, my comrade, my "whatever you want," my everything, my reason for living.

He sat down on the sofa, perched on the very edge, like he might get up and bolt at any moment. He was still shaking, and I brought him a glass of water. He sat there without moving. Glass in his hand, staring into space.

Dad. Syria. My brother. Why did he leave? Bagnolet. The beardos from the bus. Germany. The Turk? Bombings! Why did he come back? I relit my joint and wrote off the rest of the night, because out there, on the horizon, I could feel the sun rising again, bringing warmth back to my world.

14
OLDER BROTHER

When I went to get water from the kitchen, I glanced at a photo stuck to my fridge door. The old man had taken it. At the time I'd gone missing too, before reappearing like magic. In the snapshot, my brother and I have our arms around each other, big smiles on our faces. He'd just gotten his nursing-school diploma. I was wearing combat fatigues; I'd joined the army. On an impulse, I'd fled the city, afraid it would suck me in and that I end up in prison. Three months before college entrance exams I'd waved good-bye to any chance of a degree; universities weren't for us, anyway. Half the guys who got in never finished. They took the scholarship money and spent it on vacations in Spain, and a year later they were in temp jobs. The few who did manage to hang in there and finish ended up in the hell of not being able to find a job. They still had the pride and glory of having a college degree, yeah, but I don't need any fucking glory. Glory never dried my tears, or filled my stomach.

The army was another world. A real profession. I'd met some soldiers at a job fair organized at my high school. Secretly, without telling anyone, I'd studied for the written test and prepared for the physical ones. To hell with everyone preaching to me about morals, and the naysayers shitting all over my ambitions. It was my life, not theirs.

I smashed the entry exams. A ten-kilometer orienteering course with a thirty-kilogram pack on my back? Nailed it. A week alone in a tent? No problem. The parachute jump? Yep.

Hello, army. Welcome to the parachute regiment. After a few months at training camp in the south of France, I took off for the southern hemisphere. The minute the airplane door opened, the hot desert wind grabbed me by the throat, like a hyena. After nine hours spent in the dimness of the military plane, the sunlight was blinding. I stepped down onto the tarmac with a hand shielding my eyes. My world had opened up, wide, immense. I was in Chad, bro. A magical, mystical name. Met my first enemy right there; it saluted me, big and round and yellow, beating down on my head, heavy as lead, enough to drive a lion insane. I took a few steps toward the dunes, which were peaceful as a little mountain range. They shifted with the wind. I squatted down and plunged my hand into the sand, to rub my forehead with it. The thousands of tiny grains slid between my fingers and fell back into the void.

It was there in Chad that I really became French. White, Portuguese, Arab, black, it didn't matter; the uniform erased any differences. We were all the same. Bros like me. Damaged by life. Before the army, it had sometimes been drugs, sometimes fights, sometimes poverty, and often family problems, a father or mother who had gone to be with the angels, a divorce. Sometimes it was just a little bit of bad luck, or just getting mixed up with the wrong people. The most dangerous ones were the guys who saw the army as a calling. Everyone in our little society arrived the same way, full of blather and certainty about life and themselves. But riddled with flaws, and full of doubt. The army stomped all over us to make us stronger. It plugged up the holes and beefed us up to disguise our flaws, but it never repaired a single one of them.

Six months after my arrival at the camp in Abeche, in the eastern part of the country, near the Sudanese border, I was summoned for a medical appointment. The doctor held me back for a minute; he wanted to talk to me. The day before, he'd received my blood and hair analysis results. He put down his cigarette and sighed resignedly before explaining that there was too much cannabis in my samples. "Cigarettes, okay. But grass, no way. Especially for you."

I'd had a few fuckups recently, a little bit of brain fog. But it wasn't my fault, I was sure of it. Nothing wrong with my mind. One evening we were driving toward the capital when the lieutenant ordered me to fire on an enemy vehicle in the distance. I took aim and fired. All the other guys in our vehicle started screaming at me, asking me what the fuck I was doing. I was sure I'd heard the lieutenant give me the order. The disciplinary committee blamed it on fatigue and gave me a few days off to rest. Two weeks later we were doing a night march along the Sudanese border when I took out a cigarette and lit it; no one said anything to me about it. The sergeant had forbidden us from smoking. You can see the light of a cigarette three kilometers away, twelve kilometers with night-vision goggles. I just wasn't thinking at that moment, and I disobeyed orders. Just as I took my third puff, in the middle of the dunes and under a full moon, there were detonation sounds, and sand exploded up in front of us. Sniper fire. We had to make an emergency withdrawal out of fear that Sudanese rebels would send a vehicle to trap us. The army took our psychological problems into account in the field; not enough, maybe, but they paid attention to us, because even warriors have a conscience.

The doctor picked his cigarette up out of the ashtray and jammed it in the corner of his mouth. He was the kind of guy who needed tobacco to get through life, like a crutch. "No more joints," he said. I denied it, the way I'd learned to do with the cops. He didn't even try to understand. "Hallucinations, anxiety attacks, the shakes. We know what causes that stuff. You think you're the only one? It's my job to make sure you don't screw up. I don't want any one to get killed because of something stupid." The deal was that I had to stop smoking weed and give him the rest of what I had, or be thrown out of the army. I didn't try to understand either and just signed. As a bonus, he wrote me a prescription for a week off to rest. I went back to spend it in France, and it was there, in the airport parking lot, that the photo on my fridge was taken.

A few months later, on a spring day, we were driving towards the capital city, N'Djamena, in a convoy of three Jeeps. Eight hours on the road, nothing but sand around us, the sun beating. The French flags painted on the sides of our vehicles were reflected in the local people's binoculars as we went by. When we went through villages, depending on the region, the people would come out and applaud, run and hide, or throw rocks at our Jeeps, baring their teeth with rage. Our only GPS had broken. The lieutenant asked me to guide him using the topographical map. I unfolded it. It was highly detailed: villages, mountains, hills, altitudes, and distances, with figures everywhere. I stroked the big sheet of paper, my eyes drowning in the rivers and regions and seas. In the very upper-left corner was a small map of Africa expanded to include the Mediterranean and the Middle East. You could see Syria. Pop's country. And ours too, a little bit. Someone was speaking to me. I raised my head. The sun whispered in my ear to turn to the left. I looked at that big yellow ball that had been hammering down on my head for almost two years, and told the lieutenant to make a left. The boss asked me if I was sure, because we were supposed to follow the river. Mouth dry, hands trembling, I took another look at the map in all directions and nodded my head yes.

After two hours, we stopped near a stream. I dunked my head into a small pond. It wasn't a dream; I was in Chad, in the military. The lieutenant told me we should have gotten there by now, and that I'd made our journey longer. I asked a fellow soldier where we were going; he thought I was joking, and we started off again.

Fifteen minutes later, in the rearview mirror, through a cloud of dust, I saw the second Jeep signaling to us with its headlights. The lieutenant kept driving, blindly. I didn't have time to say anything to him before the other Jeep overtook us and cut us off.

"We're in Sudan," the other driver said.

The blood rushed to my head. I wanted to throw up.

"What?" the lieutenant asked.

"Didn't you see the sign by that village? Everything's in Arabic; there's no more French. We're not in Chad anymore."

At that time, France was conducting military operations to maintain peace in Chad. In Sudan, just next door, the civil war was sending thousands and thousands of men to meet their maker. Officially, the army wasn't supposed to set foot across the border; it was forbidden by international conventions.

The lieutenant looked at me. His anger was calm and hard. The kind that demands an explanation before it strikes.

"I think I made a mistake. I don't feel too good."

"Fucking hell. There's a rebellion in this area. We're not supposed to be here."

After a few more choice insults, we turned back the way we'd come. Pierre Mendy, my best friend, took charge of the map while I climbed into the back seat. The base had been informed of our problems. As the sun sank lower in the sky and darkness fell, panic started to nibble away at our courage. Jostled by roads full of potholes, amid the noises of rattling chassis and rocks hitting the car, the soldiers told old stories about girls; others dozed, some cleaned their guns. Nothing went as planned; that was everyday life here, and it was the only thing you could be certain of.

It was totally dark now. Suddenly, our ears pricked up. A volley of gunfire had just ripped through the still, dry air. "Kalash?" whispered Mendy. The first Jeep slowed down and the lieutenant switched off the headlights. "Guns ready, eyes open." We scanned the dunes and boulders; no visible threat. Another salvo. Sand erupted in front of our Jeep. Then silence again. This time, the lieutenant cut the engine. He stuck his arm out the window, signaling the others to stop. "Get out your night-vision goggles." We didn't even have time to process the order before a hail of bullets came down. They were coming from the right, the left, from right in front us, from the top and bottom of the dunes. We leapt out of the car to hide behind the tires. These were heavy weapons being fired. Bullets hammered against metal. Our patrol was broken into three parts, each hiding behind its own Jeep. No way of identifying the enemy. They were everywhere, like ants. The lieutenant's orders echoed off the hillside, barely audible. For long minutes, each of us returned fire as much as we were able. The perimeter of my life shrank down to a few meters. Our only hope was the radio inside the car. Mendy stuck his arm inside. Too short. He told me to boost him up a little so he could rummage around. Above his head bullets were shattering the windows before thudding into the sand. A hero. This went on for almost forty-five minutes, until we heard the rotors of our two helicopters chopping the air, dispersing the enemy with machine-gun fire. Death toll among the French paratroopers: one. My buddy Mendy.

The doctor called me in again. This time, my problems were serious. He couldn't take any more risks. I had a sickness, and it had put twenty soldiers' lives in danger. He wrote a short note at the bottom of my file to justify my being sent back. One word was written in capital letters and underlined three times: SCHIZOPHRENIA. Goodbye, Chad. Goodbye, army. Hello again, France. Salaam, Bobigny.

15
YOUNGER BROTHER

The next week, I started my work at the hospital. It was a shithole. We had nothing, and everything was urgent. I didn't know which way to turn. When patients arrived, our first job was to decide which category they fell into: relative emergency, absolute emergency, or about to die. There were wounded people and sick people, but also starving people and crazy people. The place didn't have the resources to manage everything. Bedrettin planned an operation every day, in the morning, and in the afternoon he consulted. In emergencies, he wouldn't do the consultations. He told me pretty much right away that I was going to have to do more than nursing, and learn to make pre-diagnoses and do certain medical procedures. It was the old country, a land at war, a madhouse, but at the hospital everything was well organized. To avoid confusion, we kept a file for each patient recording any treatment history.

How many times did I see a father or mother run in with a dead child in their arms? All you could do was comfort their anguish by going to the burial. The hardest thing to take was the lack of medical capacity. People would come in with a heart problem; you could see it in their cold hands and pale lips, and in what I heard through the stethoscope—but there was no way to determine the cause without medical imaging. Often they were non-life-threatening illnesses, but without a firm diagnosis, we couldn't do anything. Bedrettin said it was fate; that we could just as easily have been born somewhere else, in another country, to another family, and not ended up here. It was God's will. My boss always operated on the lungs; the heart didn't speak to him; it was too complicated, took too long. Myself, if I thought someone had a heart ailment, I prescribed the minimum. If the heartbeat was a little bit fast, I told the patient to exercise every day. To do squats. That made them laugh. "This isn't France," they'd say.

I tried to leave the war out of it. It was there anyway, all the time, everywhere, and everyone was used to it. When I first got to the hospital in the mornings, before heading for the operating room I'd stop by the patients' rooms to see how they were doing. There were as many civilians as there were soldiers. Some serious cases. People rescued from underneath buildings or with gunshot wounds. There was one guy that looked just like you, like your doppelgänger or something. I'll never forget him, as long as I live. We were on the way back after a meeting with the Syrian White Helmets. I was driving the pickup and ended up going out with the ambulance-drivers to see something else. A few hours earlier, the area we were driving through had been bombed by Bashar; you could still smell the sulfur. I stopped to take a leak, and as I was emptying my bladder on the remains of a building, I suddenly thought I heard a voice. I jumped, pissing all over my shoes. "Help me," it said. My blood ran cold. I ran back to the car and told my two colleagues I thought I'd heard a voice in the rubble. They got out of the pickup and we went to have a look. The same voice called out for help: "For the love of God, I'll give you anything you want! I'm buried up to my neck, please get me out." One of the ambulance drivers said, "We're coming," and we climbed onto the debris of the building. "I'm behind here," the voice said. We lifted away some rubble that was blocking a sheet of metal. The guy's head was sticking out of a pile of rocks and dirt, his face and hair white with dust. He looked like a statue. "Help

me, dear God. I've been here for hours. My family is underneath. Hurry." We didn't have shovels or anything. We got
whatever gear out of the car we thought might help us dig,
and after an hour of work, we got him out. Spine, leg, hips,
shoulders, stomach—all crushed, broken. We put him on a
stretcher to take him to Al-Bab. He begged us not to leave,
to dig for his wife and children. I didn't know what to do, or
what to say to him. His condition was critical; he could die at
any minute from a hemorrhage. But I couldn't tell him that
his wife and children were undoubtedly dead, either. Finally,
we couldn't hold out any more; we loaded him into the back
of the truck and started for Al-Bab again. He screamed and
called out to God the whole time. Fuck, I feel sick to my
stomach every time I think about it.

Every once in a while we'd get news from the NGO on the
Internet; fundraisers, galas, supply donation drives. When a
pickup came from Turkey with supplies, the driver would also
bring meat and butter. We didn't eat much because of
rationing. Blondbeard always took a little to distribute it to the
fighters. People were dying of hunger, and I couldn't stand it.
Luckily, the nine guys I lived with gave me part of their
rations, which I then gave to the kids at the hospital.
Sometimes I met other people from France; all guys from our
hood, total street rats. Some of them came alone, just like
that, to join the war, and since I was the only Frenchman and
none of them could speak proper Arabic, I found myself kind
of shepherding them around and helping them get situated.
They all talked about Raqqa, Al-Baghdadi, Bashar, about dying
as martyrs and turning into green birds fluttering around the
throne of Allah. Blondbeard always told me to send them to
Deir ez-Zor, because they needed fighters there. It wasn't my
war, though, so I let them go to Raqqa. Bedrettin had told me
to be careful, because the line between our NGO and the local
group was getting finer and finer. Blondbeard was putting

pressure on us to give medical care to soldiers first. We didn't have much of a choice.

On the day of the *Charlie Hebdo* shootings, everyone celebrated. The *mujahideen* drove around the city in their pickup trucks, firing their Kalashnikovs in the air. They danced in the town square like they were at a wedding. Blondbeard ordered sheep to be sacrificed and meat distributed to everyone. It was insanity. It was so strange to think that central Paris had become just like this place. I couldn't wrap my mind around any of it. The two terrorists claimed to be part of the Al-Qaeda group in Yemen, but here, our guys talked about it as if some of our people were responsible. It wasn't my idea of jihad. In war you had to be honorable, and that's what people did here. But I kept my mouth shut. No choice, really. The *mujahideen* I was living with didn't understand anything; they hadn't gone to school. They came from Iraq and Afghanistan. To avoid them, I found ways to go home late, and after dinner I'd go back to visit the patients. I worked so much that after seven months I felt like I'd completed an MD. Bedrettin let me operate. He was still the one who made the diagnoses; often he forced me to practice. It was mostly always the same thing: bullet wounds, cuts, gouges. Clean and close the wound, check it again, and then stitch the skin. One day a woman in a burqa arrived, obviously in a lot of pain. Said her shoulder hurt. She was Blondbeard's sister-in-law. She didn't want to take off her robe, but she had to, so we could examine her. I told her that, telling her it wasn't forbidden if it was to receive medical care. She didn't want to listen and demanded that a woman examine her. We had to call Blondbeard, who came right away and commanded her to take off the burqa, so she did it, keeping her face hidden. Holy shit, she was beautiful. God damn, I wanted to fuck her, bro. I immediately got hard as a rock. I couldn't take it anymore; I was jerking off two or three times a day—secretly, because it was haram. She had

skin like silk, white and soft, and perfect tits, big as melons—
normal, because she was pregnant. But I swear to you, at that
moment, pregnant or not, I'd have taken her back to the supply closet in a heartbeat.

She'd dislocated her shoulder firing a Kalashnikov.
Blondbeard explained to me that she was the commander of a
unit of female soldiers. At seven months pregnant! Sure, no
big deal. Bedrettin told me to watch and listen. He took her
hand and wrist in his hand and asked her what time the next
prayer was, and gently lifted her arm and turned it inward. A
few seconds later she thanked us; her shoulder was back in
the socket. She stopped crying, and her first question was
how long it would be before she could fire a gun again. Crazy.
I had to stop myself from laughing. Bedrettin told her to rest
until after she gave birth. "She's nuts," he said later. "There's
a risk to the baby." And sure enough, a month later she was
back. She went into labor during a training exercise with her
group of combatants. We were short on space, so we put her
in the staff room. I brought in the ultrasound scanner. The
baby hadn't turned, and the umbilical cord was wrapped
around its neck. There was a very high chance it would suffo-
cate. So we told the woman we were going to do a C-section.
For Bedrettin, you learned by doing. And in Syria, with the
number of cases we had to treat, learning happened in real
time. He showed me the skin fold underneath the woman's
round belly. "About three centimeters above the pubis, make
a fifteen-centimeter incision. About as long as your hand.
Otherwise it's too hard to get the baby out. Sketch a line with
a pen first so you'll be sure to make a clean cut."

I drew the scalpel across the woman's white skin. Blood
poured out. I started shaking. Bedrettin grasped my wrist.
"Breathe. This is normal."

He pressed a compress against the incision. I had my fingers
inside the opening and I could feel the baby under them. "Cut

into the fat now and lift some of it out, if you can; that will make the job easier." Next to me, Blondbeard and his brother, palms raised skyward, chanted prayers. "Okay, now part the muscles with your fingers. Let me show you now." He cut into the uterus and widened it with his fingers, then pierced the water sac. The baby was there. All purple. The umbilical cord around its neck. "When it's like that, I cut inside the belly. Best for the baby. And clean afterward. It's not procedure, but without supplies, we've got to work the best we can." He placed a metal instrument over the incision, a kind of retractor, and then shoved it behind the baby's head like a shoehorn, to lever it out. He pushed hard. I was shaking. I thought he was going to tear open the girl's belly, or rip the baby's head off. A few seconds later he gave the baby a few raps on the back and then blew first into its nose, then its mouth with a straw. The baby started crying. It was breathing. Bedrettin told me to get a towel. We had no midwives. It was my first delivery, and my first cesarean.

"Give the baby to the father, and give the mother some water." Since we had no anesthetic, we'd given the girl codeine and, to muffle her screams, put a towel in her mouth. "We're not done. Now we have to sew everything back up." Way too stressful for me. Bedrettin had said it wasn't a very complicated operation technically, but with the woman, the husband, the family members, and no assistance, doing a successful cesarean was a hell of a feat.

That night, Blondbeard invited me to dinner at his house. He congratulated me on the cesarean and then, like Guendou, demanded to know why I wasn't a doctor. I explained that in France, medical school wasn't for people like us. He didn't understand. So I told him that, where we'd grown up, at school, the teachers didn't give us a good enough education to get into medical school. He said it didn't surprise him, that nonbelievers had no reason to help us raise ourselves. Blondbeard reminded me that, to become as skilled as

Bedrettin, you had to have unshakeable faith in the Almighty. For him there was no difference between nursing and medicine; the goal was to care for people. I liked that, his way of seeing things. He always said that you were learning to live at every moment of every day, that you were learning until your last breath. So I took him at his word and listened to every piece of advice my mentor gave me, observed every medical move he made. Now, Blondbeard considered me one of their own. Almost like a son. It was crazy, man—a new profession, a new family. I was finally somebody, brother.

16
OLDER BROTHER

T*hump. Thump. Thump.* My heart pounded in my chest, reacting as much to the grass I'd smoked as to my brother's return. The ghost at the bus station had been him, after all. His expression, his hairstyle, his clothes—everything had changed. He was my brother from before, the way he should have been before he went down the wrong path to find Allah. I didn't know what to say to him. He was sitting right there in front of me, with a vague look in his eyes, murmuring a few words: "Well, I'm here. I'm glad to see you, really glad." I was torn between delirious joy and wanting to hit him. As if he'd fallen from the sky. He'd come from so far away, practically the great beyond. To tell the truth, I'd given up hope that he was still alive. He was a man from the past who had suddenly appeared in the present.

We stayed like that, talking about everything and nothing, my apartment, Dad, our memories. Neither one of us had the courage to get into the hard stuff yet. No one had prepared me for this, for a scene straight out of a movie. It wasn't my thing. You learn in the streets that you're the one who causes the unpredictable to happen, not the one it happens to. But his silences, his eyes, his smile—they all said he had a lot to tell me, and that it was going to take some time. The kid brother had grown up.

"You want to sleep?"

He said he was okay, but I knew we'd both be better off after some rest. I showed him to the spare room, the one I'd never used for anything, as if it had been waiting for the kid brother all this time. He set down his duffel bag and stretched out on the sofa bed.

My girl was still in bed in my room. She'd fallen asleep without turning the light off, and I could hear her soft breathing. I lay down beside her on my back, hands folded across my middle, staring at the ceiling. Thoughts were bashing around in my head like bumper cars. Finally my eyelids got heavy, and I drifted into sleep. A series of images floated through my mind. I was sitting with my brother. Back in the beloved country of his childhood, he was talking to me, a saber in his hand, his face menacing. Then, suddenly, we were in a bowling alley. Above each of the lanes were the flags of the different countries involved in the war in Syria. The bowlers, who were the leaders of the countries, came up and introduced themselves to my brother. He greeted each one by slicing his head off with one stroke. The bloody heads fell, one after another. And before they could hit the ground, he grabbed them by the hair. Then, with a demonic smile, he rolled each one down the lane toward the pins. A strike, every time.

The bowling alley became like an ice rink filled with blood. He screamed at me to watch him, to take his photo and put it on the Internet. My lips were glued together. I couldn't cry out. I found the strength to stand up and strangle him. The bastard almost suffocated; then, by some divine force, he peeled away my fingers one by one and made me sit down again. I stood up to try again, but I failed. Finally, I accepted that he was the stronger one of us, and stayed sitting down, drinking my Coke. My brother suddenly spun in a circle and transformed completely from head to toe. Now he looked like any guy on the street. He started talking to my girl. My beauty. Not the girl sleeping next to me, but the love of my life. She was sitting next to my mother. He asked her to dance. She smiled, handed her purse to my mother, and, like a careless queen, stepped into his arms. He welcomed her like a brother-in-law, but suddenly the killer's face came back. His hand turned into a saber. She didn't move. And then I saw her head fall.

I screamed so loud that the whole neighborhood must have thought someone shot my mother. The girl woke up and put her arms around me. The bed was drenched with sweat. She stroked my hair to calm me down. I got up to piss. The door of his room was half-open, and I peeked in. My brother wasn't there. *Thump. Thump. Thump.* My heart lurched. I pushed the door open and put one foot into the room, and then the other . . . stepped further inside, flipped the light-switch, and pulled back the duvet.

Curled in on himself like a beaten child, he was snoring softly, the way he had from earliest childhood. My hand trembled and I clenched it into a fist. The urge to hit him for what he'd done to my girl washed over me again. But I knew I'd been going a little bit crazy for a while now. I went into the bathroom and took a leak, then got back into bed. When I lifted the duvet, my girl's smell wafted into my nostrils and straight to my brain. It made me hard, and I slipped an arm around her to caress her tits, then slid my hand down between her legs. She groaned at me to let her sleep. I tried again to get her going, but I think my nightmare-fueled yelling had dried her up for the night. I moved back over to my side of the bed.

I woke up in the morning, when she kissed me quickly before rushing off to work. Little brother was still sleeping. It was ten o'clock already. It had been a few days now since I'd worked a decent shift or earned any decent money—but my flesh and blood was back home, so screw it. I got up. He was still there, in the bedroom, in the same position, like a newborn baby.

I went down to the corner store to buy a few things for breakfast. When I got back, I started a pot of coffee and switched on the radio. That woke up my brother. I still couldn't believe it.

"Good morning. Sleep okay?"

He was groggy, his eyes bulging, his hair sticking straight up like a circus freak's. Where to begin? What to talk about? What was he going to tell me? He came back into the kitchen. Better wait a bit before talking about the hard stuff. I started with factual things.

"How did you get my address?"

"On the Internet. I found a company in your name, with this address. I came to have a look yesterday during the day and your name was on the buzzer, but I figured you were at work, so I came back at night."

He buttered his third slice of bread. "Fuck, I missed this. A traditional baguette with butter and jam."

His way of manhandling the butter has always driven me crazy. He cuts out big chunks, impossible to spread. And it makes the whole stick of butter all deformed, like some kind of bizarre modern-art sculpture, like the one at my lawyer's office—he's the brother of Younes, the guy who converted. Normal people start with the top of the stick, gently scraping it. But anyway.

"When did you get back?"

"Yesterday evening."

I swallowed. I tried not to flush. I stared at him for a few seconds. I didn't know what to say. He was lying to me. I'd seen him at the bus station two days ago. I bought myself a few minutes away from him by getting up to piss. As I emptied my bladder, I reminded myself that I was no coward.

"Why are you lying to me? Huh? Why are you lying? I saw you at the Gare de Bagnolet the day before yesterday, getting off a bus."

Now he was the one who didn't know what to say.

"What do you mean, you saw me?"

"I saw you. You, your fucking face, there. You got into a Citroën and drove off toward Montreuil. What fucking game do you think you're playing? Don't start out by telling lies when you've only just gotten back."

He took a deep breath and started to talk. He wouldn't look me in the eye, kept fiddling with his spoon. He hadn't come back alone, but with some smugglers. It was thanks to them that he'd been able to come back into France. And before coming to see me, he'd had a few items of business to sort out.

"But I like to keep well away from that kind of stuff," he said.

"What kind of stuff?"

"Nothing special. Papers, all that. I went to see the guys from my NGO."

"*What* NGO? Are you fucking crazy? You've been gone three years, and I have no idea who you were with or where you went."

It was bizarre; none of what he was saying made sense. It was like he was drugged, or in shock.

"Islam & Peace. That's my NGO."

He started over, at the beginning. He'd landed in Nouak-chott, Mauritania, on the edge of both the desert and the sea. Then he'd gone to Timbuktu, in Mali, with his NGO and a Turkish doctor. A surgeon. There, in a field hospital, he had served as the doctor's assistant and learned in concrete terms how to treat patients.

"I'm almost a doctor now."

"Damn, on top of everything else, you want me to believe that you were in Mali!"

I knew he was lying. I'd been told he was in Syria. Even though it was a long way away, people found out everything. Everyone knew someone who knew a guy who'd gone to Syria. There were barely two thousand Frenchmen over there, so of course none of them was a secret. One guy had even shown me a picture of him with a bunch of soldiers. I slammed my fist down on the table.

"Stop fucking lying, you son of a bitch!"

My coffee cup fell to the floor.

"Stop lying or I'm going to kick your ass, I'll throw you out the damn window and then run you the fuck over with my car, you get me?"

Fuck. The guy had been missing for three years, and now he just showed up like it was no big deal. A flower in the barrel of his Kalashnikov to tell us that everything was fine, that he'd been treating cases of the flu in Africa. Now he got angry, too.

"Calm down, okay? Don't talk like that. Especially about Mom."

He looked down and stopped talking. I felt like my brain was boiling. Emotions, you know? For ten minutes we sat in total silence. You could cut the tension with a knife. So much for the reunion. And then I thought about the old man. He had the life experience you needed to handle stuff like this. All I could think to do was to call him. And we'd have to go see him right away anyway; he'd been worrying about his son for three whole years.

"We'll go and see Pop. Right now. I'll call him. Don't argue."

He looked up as if I'd mentioned a demon. "No way. Especially not him. Wait before you call him. Wait. Wait, okay?"

"What, are you afraid?"

"I just don't want to, that's all. I'd rather go and see Mom first."

I've never really been able to put myself in someone else's shoes. Easy to say; hard to do. It's an art. If I were my brother, I'd have told the old man to go fuck himself, too. You never know; maybe Pop would have had him thrown in prison to teach him a lesson. He'd spent some time inside himself. He didn't give a shit. Maybe he would have had me sent down, too. He'd never forgive him, that's for sure. No way. When I went back through my memories, I could see my dad working like a dog to give us a good life in France. I realized it on the day Le Gwen saved my ass, and I'd gotten back in line. But my brother?

The very first time the kid brother brought up humanitarian work was on a Friday. I remember because that was the only day of the week Dad insisted that we all have dinner at home as a family.

"Why you want to go off and do humanitarian work? There's Pompidou Hospital for that. Civil service. Good salary. Retirement. A wife, have kids, calm life."

"Life makes no sense. All those people dying because of the war, the famine. I can help them, Pop. I want to help."

"So what you call what you do at the hospital now, then? You helping people, no?"

"It's not the same thing, okay?"

Little brother was pulling out all the stops, doing everything he could think of to give Pop the finger. To give everyone the finger. Under his beige *kamis* he was wearing an old Nike

Paris Saint-Germain track suit. Birkenstock sandals on his feet. It was more comfortable, he said. And then there was his little folding bike. He'd bought it at the flea market in Montreuil. When it wasn't raining, he went everywhere on that bike. He said cars were blasphemous. All of it drove Pop out of his mind, but he never said a word. I was old enough to understand that he was terrified that my brother was spiraling out of control. He thought it was just a phase, though, that one of these days he'd get over this period of youthful stupidity and fall back in line like the rest of us. Besides, he'd gone through a sort of rocker-hippie-communist phase himself, in Syria, in the '70s and '80s. And now he drove a taxi and had two sons.

My old man put up with some unbelievable shit. Family was more important to him than anything else. Above all, we had to be *together*. At Friday night dinner, he accepted that everything had to be halal, even though he ate pork and was no more Muslim than a pair of Nikes. Bizarrely, my brother never said anything to him, though he always was the first person in line to preach to anyone else.

As usual, on Friday, my dad had ended his work day early. I didn't have a job at the time. I was zoned out in front of some TV reality show, my eyelids drooping, courtesy of Mary Jane, when the old man got home. He muttered a disdainful greeting in Arabic and carefully hung his leather jacket over the back of a chair. Then he wrenched his shoes off his stinking feet before pulling off his shirt and tie and unbuttoning his pants so he could breathe. And then, also as usual, he sat down to read the news on the laptop I'd bought him with money from running drugs. Not that he knew about that, of course.

Every evening he started by reading *Le Monde*, then *L'Orient-Le Jour*, a Lebanese newspaper, then he'd finish with the Syrian papers. After that he went on Facebook, to follow the progress of the conflict that way. Aleppo had been spared for the moment. My grandmother still lived there. The war had screwed up the old man's plans. He'd figured on moving back to the old country when he retired—to Latakia, on the sea, just across the water from Cyprus, dipping his toes in the ocean, drinking beer, and gossiping with his old buddies from home. "Al-Assad family is too strong. If they ask me, I tell them, not possible to win war against al-Assad."

The longer the war went on, the longer my kid brother's beard grew. He was constantly out with the organization he belonged to that distributed meals to the homeless. Pop wouldn't stop harping on the fact that it was Muslim. "Why don't you join a 'normal' organization? Why does it have to be Muslim? Does it matter? Human is what matters!" The word "normal" started an argument in our house pretty much every week. For the old man, "normal" meant "secular." Because my brother was smarter than Dad, he never got into any kind of philosophical debate. He just talked about choice, communities, beliefs. Dad would just end up grumbling into his mustache and then start clearing the table, letting the subject drop.

My grandma came to be with us when the conflict hit Aleppo. She showed up in a state of complete shock. Pop quickly put her in a nursing home. Each of us had his place; one in a taxi, another out pounding the pavement, the third always either at a mosque or a hospital, and the old lady stuck in a bed waiting for someone to love her. My brother was constantly badgering Pop to take Grandma out of that place. That almost got a laugh out of the old man; he knew nobody was going to take care of her.

Some members of the family in Syria disappeared. We didn't know if they were in Turkey or somewhere else. My grandmother retreated into silence. She never said a word; only her eyes and her hands talked. Little brother asked questions about Syria, the family, her mother, her father, religion, the village, the war. She squeezed our hands and answered with a soft expression or by raising her eyebrows slightly.

Every time he went to visit, he wore his religious head-covering. That put Grandma in a bad mood. She'd sigh and close her eyes for long moments before opening them again and listening to him. She stroked the kid brother's hand more and more. As if to hold him back, keep him there. And he just sounded like a broken record. I don't think Grandma understood everything he was saying, and I didn't either. It was a weird kind of Arabic, full of religious words I didn't know.

And then, one day, he moved out of the house. To go live with a friend. There were suddenly only two of us at the table on Friday nights. One time, and only once, he came back for dinner. His expression was closed and he didn't eat anything. The atmosphere was icy. Three days later, his telephone number was disconnected. After a few weeks with no word, we got an e-mail from him. He'd left for a year-long humanitarian-aid mission in Mali. It all happened really fast. He left in a hurry.

W e were in the kitchen cleaning up from breakfast when my dad called.

"How are you, *ibni*?" he asked.

I covered the phone's mouthpiece with my hand and whispered to my brother:

"It's the old man. You want to talk to him?"

He shook his head. Pop was calling me to catch up, just because.

"Everything okay at you place? When you coming to eat with your Baba?"

"Friday, Dad, like always."

As I spoke with our dad, my brother gestured frantically for me not to say anything. The old man's harsh voice vibrated so strongly through the phone that my brother could hear everything he was saying. I saw tears shining in his eyes. He turned his head away so I wouldn't see, and wiped them away with the corner of his sleeve. I told Dad I'd call him back and hung up.

"It was weird to hear Pop's voice. I'd forgotten his voice."

"You should have talked to him."

"No, not right away, not like this. After. We'll surprise him. What did he want?"

"Just saying hi, checking in. He's changed, you know."

He didn't understand what "change" meant. My brother had never known how to act like a son. Without realizing it, he had always defied the old man, challenged him, as if it were a competition. I don't know why. Because of Mom. But whatever. I could never explain it to him.

We decided to go to the cemetery to visit our mother. I took a quick shower and plonked a baseball cap on my brother's head. He needed to stay secret, for now, at least until I could go see a lawyer.

He smiled like he used to do, back in the day, when he saw my car. Like he was happy for me. He must have been even more shocked to see me with an apartment, a girl, and a nice car, than I was to see him back home.

It wasn't far from the bottom of the twentieth arrondissement to the Cimetière de Pantin. Reflexively, I took an alternative route to avoid running to anyone we might know. My brother pointed at the green sticker in the upper right corner of my windshield.

"What's this thing?"

"My private-hire license. I work for myself; I've got my own company, but there are other guys who work for a boss and don't use their own car. They just drive and earn a fixed amount per hour, plus a commission on each fare. They have a purple sticker. They're pretty much slaves."

"My brother the boss, ha ha ha!"

"Yeah, man, it's all right."

Business was good in the beginning. Uber had just launched its services in France, and they needed to recruit drivers and win over customers. They paid forty-five euros an hour, just for driving around the city. The platform's goal was to show customers that there were a bunch of drivers, so someone could pick them up really fast. When the customers logged into the app, they could see little cars moving all over their phone screen, like ants on a map of the city. Forty-five an hour just to be available, driving around aimlessly. For years they paid me for not doing much at all. I was raking it in. A third of that forty-five euros went to taxes, which left me with thirty euros an hour in my wallet. Nice wad of cash, right, bro? Some days I made two hundred and fifty, three hundred euros, and there were some months when I brought in four thousand. Driving changed my life, bro. A suit, an apartment, a smile, a girl. Living the dream, just about. But that was in the beginning.

You can drive your car right into the cemetery where my mom is buried. It's so weird. You're free to annoy the dead with your exhaust fumes. Anyway, we drove down the little lanes. It took me back to the day of the funeral. Dad in his sunglasses and black cap. My grandma also in sunglasses, like Vito Corleone's mother, and us on either side of her, walking with halting steps. For hours, everything felt like some sort of hallucination; the old people crying, our other grandmother and the family that came from Saint-Brieuc. When they lowered the coffin into the grave, it hit me that it was really all over. Until then, I'd still been expecting her to pop up with a big smile and gather us into her arms. My brother closed his eyes. The men in black threw a few shovelfuls of dirt onto the coffin. Then the city worker came with a backhoe and filled in the grave. Underground. She was never coming back. We've gone to visit her several times a year since then. Pop never remarried, and I've never dared to ask him why.

We parked the car under some trees in the cemetery and got out like zombies, drunk on sorrow, but with each step toward the grave, the sadness lifted. We felt more like ourselves again. It's stupid to say, but cemeteries are comforting; you realize you're not the only one mourning somebody. Each grave is a memory, a soul, a history, buried underground. Only the living remain, to remember and to grieve.

At Mom's grave, I passed my hands over my face and murmured my prayers. Little brother watched me out of the corner of his eye. It must have surprised him to see me praying. And I was surprised that he wasn't. He used to harangue me about religion all the time. He stood off to the side for a few minutes, not saying anything. I couldn't concentrate on two things at once—my prayer, and what my brother was doing. Then he stepped forward and sat down next to the grave, and kissed the tombstone, stirring the dirt a little bit with his finger and murmuring things I couldn't hear. When I was finished, he smiled at me. His lips were trembling. He turned his head away so he could cry. My grief, I'd let it go when I came back from the army. It isn't so much her death that makes me sad as it is the absence of her arms, her voice, her lips, her hair. Thinking about her comforts me. And, every time I take a pull on a joint, she's with me. I'm in her lap and she's smiling at me.

My brother had let his hair grow; it looked like it used to in high school. Pretty brown curls that fell into his eyes. He'd also shaved his beard. Sitting there beside the grave, with my jean jacket over his shoulders and his pale skin, he looked like a European rocker or a hipster. I bit back a laugh, and, wordlessly, we stood to leave. His shoulders back, hands in his pockets, lips pressed together, he took deep breaths. His chest quivered and his eyelids held back eighteen years of tears. He got into the car and, like a pasha, gestured for me to start driving. No, he hadn't changed. After a few minutes, he came back to the land of the living.

"Do you live with that girl I saw last night?"

"Nah, she's just my girl."

"Is there anything to it?"

"Eh, it just is what it is. It happened fast. Nothing serious. We each have our own life."

He stared out like the window, like he wanted to tell me I was almost thirty and it was time to settle down.

We went back to my place, and I waited until we were at the table before saying anything else to him. I hadn't thought about it, but nothing in my fridge was halal. Too much of a pain. I asked him about it before I started fixing lunch, and it didn't seem to freak him out too much. He sat down, and so he couldn't avoid my eyes, I put my plate down across from him.

My life was pretty uneventful. Organized. Everything in order. After living with chaos for a long time, I'd realized what a pleasure it was to be organized. Pleasure has always been my end goal in everything, but I used to jump into things without thinking—and I suffered the consequences. I had to make amends, after that. For fucking things up in the army, too. And school. The desire to have some order in my life, so I could enjoy it better, came through my talks with Le Gwen. The cop. He was a fuckup once, too. Worse than me. And then he became a cop. His story made me dream of better things. I found a goal for myself, and a reason to believe in it. To make something great out of my life. Wake up in the morning without needing to work, read the paper, listen to the radio, take walks, think, shoot the shit with my friends, have a girl on my arm in the evening, and kids I'd teach to read. I needed cash for all that, and to get the cash, I had to pay my dues. Work. And that meant I needed to have an organized home. A place for everything and everything in its place, you know. Get my life in order. And one day, all of a sudden, without even realizing it, you're at the top of the mountain you've been gazing at. And then you just keep going up, toward the next summit. It's simple. You just have to breathe a little bit, sometimes, to catch your breath.

I smoked a cigarette before eating. My brother was sitting across from me. The unstable element. The grain of sand in my well-organized life. A sudden reappearance. Not a mirage. Not a hallucination. Not a ghost. A flesh-and-blood man with his own weaknesses and contradictions and lies, and his own reason for living. It was a mess, all right, and we were both in it up to our knees. We'd need all four hands to get out of it.

Whatever happened, he—and the old man and my grandma—
was the only family I had. I could already tell there were
rumors going around the city about my brother's return. There
are people who'd tell me to report him, to protect myself.
Others from whom I needed to hide him at all costs.

He asked me for a cigarette. He told me he wanted to stop,
and that he hadn't been able to smoke much while he was
away, because cigarettes were expensive and hard to find.
Then it started to come out. The truth. It just flowed naturally.
He told me about his time in Syria, in a voice like a radio host
on a nighttime show. Soft, slow, serious. Cigarette after cigarette, he talked about geopolitics and war and medicine, about
kids suffering from malnutrition, but never about himself. Like
a kind of robot, telling me only what it was programmed to tell.

"Wait, I don't understand. So you were in Syria! I knew it.
But what were you really doing for three years? Why did you
lie?"

"You think the truth is easy?"

He dropped his gaze and flushed.

"I was a doctor."

"What kind of a doctor, you motherfucker? What do you
mean you were a doctor?"

"I learned on the job, in the field. There was no choice. I
was the most qualified person there a lot of the time."

A tear glimmered in the corner of one of his eyes. He got up
from the table and asked me for another cigarette. Leaning
against the window, he took deep drags.

"All of that's over for me now. I want to get back on my
feet, start doing things right again. I have a profession, a
diploma."

"What are you talking about? What's 'all of that'?"

"Islam and everything."

I itched to shove him out the window. He was doing his
goddamned Serge Gainsbourg rebel thing again.

"What kind of idiot are you? You're fucked, man. It has nothing to do with Islam. You went to Syria. You're done. You know about *Charlie* and the Bataclan, right? The cops are everywhere; they'll find you, and quick. You don't know how they gave Pop the third degree when you left. You are toast, man. You think life works like that? Like Aladdin's genie, like you snap your fingers for something magical to happen? You should have thought of that before."

Now he started acting like Omar Raddad.

"Let them come, then. I have nothing to hide. There's nothing to say. I'll tell them, Mali, Turkey, Iran, Iraq, Yemen, Somalia. That's where I was. But I didn't do anything. I swear on Mom's life. I was a nurse, okay? Band-Aid, remember?"

"Say whatever you want. But, my brother, if I saw your picture on the Internet with all those soldiers, don't you think the cops know about it too? Of course they know. They're monitoring us and Dad, too. Believe me, they already know you're here. I'm going to see a lawyer for you tomorrow."

"Do you think that'll help anything?"

"He's the brother of Younes, the guy who converted. He works in the court in Bobigny. Don't worry; he's dealt with this kind of thing before."

"Who is Younes?"

"Yann, the French guy, you remember? Used to wear the FC Staines jersey, number five."

"No way! That asshole converted? Swear to God? You're fucking kidding me!"

"Yep. I swear."

"So is he circumcised now? They make him cut off the tip of his dick, or what?"

We both burst out laughing.

The next morning I booked it to the lawyer's office. There was a painting of a blindfolded woman on the waiting-room wall, holding a scale in her right hand and a sword in her left. At first I thought it was Marianne, the symbol of France, but I wasn't sure, so I asked my smartphone: "Woman, sword, scale, meaning." It answered back: "Goddess Themis." The Greek goddess of justice. The scale she holds is to weigh arguments against one another, the blindfold is so she will judge without prejudice, and the sword is for handing down the sentence.

The lawyer's office was in the new part of town by the Bibliothèque nationale de France. Modern, with glass buildings and wide sidewalks, full of light and space. It was nothing like the ragtag Paris I loved. Haussmann and all that hoo-ha, like in Walt Disney's *Ratatouille*, you know? And the office was on the rue René-Goscinny. No lie. Images of Astérix and his buddies were all over the place. Ridiculous, man. So at number thirteen on this street, behind the white facade of a brand-new building, through a heavy glass door, was a lobby with a fifteen-foot ceiling. Slate tiles on the floor, mirrors all along the left-hand wall, and, on the right, a metal sculpture a meter wide and almost as high as the ceiling, all to remind you that you had come to a Very Important Place. Again, crazy. A bizarre thing, that sculpture; it looked kind of like warships fighting with the ocean. A plaque next to it said F. Guimez, who I guessed was the guy who cobbled the thing together. I don't understand life sometimes. *We* get up in the morning, get in the car, get people where they need to go, so we can put food on the table for our families. And then there are *them*, the ones who get to just stand still, clear-headed, and bash a chunk of iron around and then sell it to someone else who's got so much money he'll happily fork it over to buy a piece of someone else's dream. It's a drug like any other. Everyone's got his own madness; everyone, his own shit, his own life.

The secretary behind the reception desk told me to have a seat. The coffee table had the usual pile of magazines, and their latest covers. Islam here, there, everywhere. Crazy; they're all crazy. As if Islam itself decided to carry out these attacks, just decided it one morning with a snap of its fingers, just for fun. It might sound bizarre to say it that way, but they didn't really understand what Islam was. Allah forgive me, but Muslims shop for shoes the same way as the rest of us, bro. They find a pair they like, in the size that fits, to walk toward whatever they're looking for. What relationship does a mosque have to some idiot who blows himself up? What does a woman who wears a veil have to do with a madman who cuts people's heads off?

Across from me, the lawyer, Younes's brother, spoke calmly. It was weird to see a guy from the street talking like the ones who hold the reins. A boss. As he talked, he fiddled with a beautiful pen, the kind jewelers sell. He seemed to know his job well. I'm not saying that because he had a suit, styled hair, and perfect skin. But the whole thing—the office, the look, the style—felt professional. When he spoke, I felt in my heart that he was still one of us. I described the situation with my brother to him as best I could, without letting on that he'd come back, but saying I was in touch with him by telephone. That made him smile. It was a casual smile, but I couldn't tell if it was because of my words or the mess we were in. His chest puffed up and he set down his luxury pen.

It was complicated for my brother. In the old days, the cops would have had to catch him first. And to hold him, first the cops would have to have suspicions that he'd gone to Syria, and then be sure of it. After that, for him to go to prison, the law would have to prove that he participated in a jihadist or terrorist movement. That was under normal conditions. But now, all they needed to throw him in jail was proof of travel to and from Syria—because, other than journalists and some humanitarian-aid workers, no one went to Cham by chance anymore.

As he talked, I was already picturing myself in the court-house in Bobigny, watching my brother be transported from a police van to the witness stand, cameras flashing, a T-shirt thrown over his head, wrists cuffed together, and a guard on either side of him. Like a boxer dazed after taking an uppercut to the jaw, I pulled myself together, away from the hazy images and the courtroom, and spoke about humanitarian-aid work again. The lawyer stopped, surprised, and, trying to hide a mocking smile, coughed out a few words that threw me right back against the ropes again:

"*Your* brother? Humanitarian-aid work?"

Even I didn't believe what I was saying. But I had to tell the lawyer. No lies about my brother. Ever. At least, I hoped not. And then we needed to talk about us—my dad and myself, that is, as we might be accused as accomplices.

"For you, it'll depend on how excited the cops and the judges get."

My telephone vibrated. Too much information. I started over, froze, tried to think and ask questions at the same time.

"If I understand you correctly, if my brother comes back, there's a good chance he'll go down."

"The fact of having gone to Syria, for any reason, is already evidence. Other than journalists and the Red Cross, who goes to Syria? You think people just visit Palmyra randomly, for no reason? Palmyra is finished. They've blown it to smithereens.

They're cutting people's heads off over there, you know. You're not innocent if you go to Syria now."

"What's the connection? Why are you talking about Palmyra? That's our village, our hometown. But that has nothing to do with it."

"It's just an example."

"But he went to do humanitarian-aid work!"

"With what group? What NGO? Give me some more info and we can always start a file. But remember how long Free Moussa took? The humanitarian who got arrested in Bangladesh?"

"Free Moussa has nothing to do with anything. He was in Asia."

He laughed.

"Listen, I like you. But let me do my job. Believe me, it's got plenty to do with it. The authorities are cracking down on Muslim groups, Muslim NGOs. I guarantee you they won't go into it in very much detail, NGO or not. If you go to Syria these days, you're considered suspicious, and your brother knows it, otherwise he would have come here himself."

I couldn't figure out what he meant. Did he know my brother was in France?

"And what's the risk to me?"

"You?"

"Yeah. Me."

"Have you done anything wrong?"

"No."

"The only thing is if he comes home, and you help him."

"So?"

"You'd be designated as an accomplice."

"In what?"

"Aiding and abetting terrorism."

"But I'm telling you, my brother hasn't done anything. He's a humanitarian-aid worker."

He sighed.

"You know what *taqqiya* means?"

I'd heard about *taqqiya* on the "Food for Thought" radio show. It was when Islamists came back to France pretending they'd abandoned jihad. Dressed like your average Joe. Alcohol, drugs, sometimes girls. And then two weeks later, they'd end up mysteriously blown to bits in a metro station or concert hall. A new, freaky kind of spy.

"Yeah, I know about *taqqiya*. What does that have to do with anything?"

"Well, it's the number of guys coming back and claiming to be all pure and innocent, saying everything's fine, and then one day they blow themselves up."

"You're nuts, man. Who told you he was back? He called me, I think from Turkey, and said he wanted to come home. He's doing humanitarian work, okay?"

"Look, I'm telling you this for your own good. I'm not going to go over it all again. It's not about what he has or hasn't done. Did he go to Syria? Yes. So he'll be considered a terrorist. If he comes back and you help him, doesn't matter how, you're complicit. In this country, they even arrest people who let undocumented immigrants stay with them. So, for terrorists . . ."

His suit and his perfect hair didn't budge an inch no matter what case he dealt with or how serious it was; he was a machine. We talked for ten more minutes or so, and then he excused himself, claiming he had an appointment. On the landing, he shook my hand, looking like a Frenchman. A real Frenchman. Not a white guy; a Frenchman. Someone who had made it. Who'd crossed the line, moved up, left the hood behind.

"Next time, I can help you. It won't be free, but I'll give you a good deal."

It wasn't enough to talk like us; that didn't make him family. Nobody back in the hood would ever have the balls to give off that kind of vibe. Of course I would have slipped him a twenty.

20
YOUNGER BROTHER

I n the spring, Blondbeard, our emir, found a pretty house for me and Leïla, my wife. I'd spent the previous winter in the shack with the other local guys. We only had a wood-burning stove for heat, and despite what you might think, winters over there are really harsh. It gets down below freezing. Snow everywhere, white-out blizzards, icy wind slapping you in the face, making your eyes water, cutting straight to the bone. They don't have the equipment or the clothes to deal with it. During the winter months, the fighting calms down. Then, as soon as March hits and things warm up, the bullets start flying again.

At the beginning of April, the emir's cousin took me to a *madafa* near the border, a building occupied by unmarried women and those whose husbands were away fighting. It was a sort of boarded-up house, no windows, dirty and rat-infested, run by an old madam who made the women's lives miserable. Everything possible was done to break their spirits and make them want to marry. Soldiers would come and talk with the old lady, who acted as a middlewoman. She'd show you photos of the girls on her smartphone, and the *mujahideen* would make their choice.

I just wanted a house and a steak. A nice filet, preferably, but what I wanted more than anything was to get out of my current place. Because unmarried men weren't allowed to live alone. So I met a few girls at the *madafa*. There was a room where you could sit and talk. They were all waiting for their

Prince Charming, you could tell. Naive. Innocent. Veiled from head to foot. But in secret, the madam of the *madafa* would show you photos of the best-looking girls. To pique your interest. In the beginning, I wanted a total hottie, but when I thought it through, the most important thing was for her not to want kids. God sent me a widowed mother of two. An old sweetie of thirty-eight. Leïla. We started arranging the wedding immediately, the women on their side, and the men on theirs. I hoped for a discreet celebration, but people went all out to celebrate the marriage of their doctor: me. Four hundred people and twenty sheep. More than for the emir's son's wedding.

Since Bedrettin had left for Mayadin, in the southeastern part of the country, I'd been running the hospital. It was bizarre. I thought back to our first meeting in Strasbourg and to everything we'd experienced since then. There were only six of us left on the team; the others had been killed during a bombardment of Aleppo. Without Bedrettin's experience or knowledge, I did what I could, the best I could. In one year, he had taught me to administer routine medical treatments, as well as some surgical procedures. The first thing was to treat the ones that were in immediate danger of death, and then the ones that could be easily helped. All I could do with the seriously wounded was to patch them up before they were transferred to the hospital in Raqqa by pickup truck. They were short-staffed there, too. They were being forced to sneakily import surgeons from Damascus, whom they had to pay a fortune to operate. The price of risk.

Since Bedrettin's departure, I hadn't had any more contact with Islam & Peace. The emir had become the intermediary, and, every month, he gave me an envelope of cash. Everything was expensive and inflation was out of control because of the foreigners arriving with their dollars and euros. The Syrians couldn't afford to buy anything anymore. Every morning I went from my house to the hospital to deal with my army of mutilated and wounded. It was my thing. I was the one who ran it. We treated people and they went away happy. Happy to be alive, even if they were something less than what they had been before. Because, whatever happens, martyr or not, one thing all mortals have in common is the fear of death. No one is certain about what happens after you die. Personally, life scares me more.

The front was thirty kilometers away. Occasionally I went there with Blondbeard to get a sense of what was happening. It was a mess. Sometimes ground was gained; sometimes it was lost. It became a game. Through our binoculars we could see the plumes of smoke created by artillery shells. Our people never fired on cities or villages. Not like they did.

One day Blondbeard's brother-in-law came into the hospital with blood streaming from a cut above his eye—a cut from the ring belonging to Blondbeard, who had hit him. The brother-in-law was responsible for the construction of a tunnel they hoped would enable them to attack the enemy from the rear. A team of prisoners of war was under his command. On the day of the fight, there'd been a collapse at the building site. Five prisoners were hurt, one seriously. The brother-in-law refused to bring them to us for medical treatment because they were infidels. When the emir arrived at the work site, he had a fit. All he wanted was for the tunnel to be finished quickly. And to build it, they needed manpower. If the prisoners didn't get medical care, the *mujahideen* would have to dig the tunnel—and while they were doing that, they wouldn't be able to fight.

After the fistfight, the prisoners arrived at the hospital. Broken hands, arms, legs, cracked ribs. Their feet were frostbitten because they'd been forced to work barefoot. We cleaned and bandaged them up. I don't know why, but I had a feeling something bad was about to happen. The first prisoner who arrived, the leader of the group, had stared at me with his blue eyes. As if he were trying to antagonize me. Once we finished patching everyone up, Blondbeard had them locked up to convalesce in a house that was being used as a prison in the northern part of Al-Bab. A week later, one of them pretended to be sick. When the guard came in, they attacked him, took his Kalashnikov, and fled on foot toward the border. Unfortunately for them, the brother-in-law caught them. And hanged them right across from my house, near the main square of Al-Bab, so that everyone would see them. The next morning, the guy's face was seared into my brain. His face was blue, his tongue hanging out. It scared the hell out of me—and everyone else in town.

Blondbeard wanted to capture a village on the front line, near Akhtarin. Snipers hiding in a tower blocked the advance of the *mujahideen*. Bashar's Shiites had already killed almost twenty of our men in the past few months. The tunnel, the one Blondbeard's brother-in-law was in charge of building, was supposed to help us avoid a no-man's-land badly exposed to sharpshooters. It was impossible to get in there and eliminate them without risk of being shot. First the snipers would aim at the legs, as a warning. But when Blondbeard pig-headedly sent in some Iraqi fighters to capture the tower, they started aiming straight for the chest. Our men dropped like flies. They brought guys in to the hospital who'd been hit by twelve-mm shells, with holes in them three inches across. Often, by the time they got to the hospital, they were unconscious, or on their way to heaven. Or hell.

Al-Bab was one of the crossing-points for French guys coming to Syria. They all wanted to head to Raqqa, but for a lot of them, the adventure ended in Deir ez-Zor. The Stalingrad of Syria. A slaughterhouse. Our guys had been fighting for two years against the Damascus forces to take the city. New recruits normally went through a *muaskar*, a kind of three-week boot camp, where they got in shape, learned to shoot, to have military reflexes, to respect the chain of command. But the local emir of Deir ez-Zor was crazy. He was a Libyan who hated the French. He said they were subhuman, called them apes, and sent them into the thick of it after two days of training. It was a French guy who told me this. Yassin, an Arab from Lyon. He'd come from Deir ez-Zor and wanted to go back to France, so he headed for the Turkish border on foot. I don't know what happened to him. And I kept my mouth shut because if they arrested him, it was prison at best—but death by Kalashnikov firing squad, more likely. He was a guy from home, a kid from the streets. A good guy. Cham wasn't for him, that's all. What he told me about Deir ez-Zor was freaky as hell.

Everywhere in the city, snipers and soldiers fought amid the rubble of buildings demolished by bombardments, rocket attacks, and machine guns fired from helicopters. Yassin told me about another French guy. A converted white guy. A lunatic, sort of like Rambo, the kind who'd run fifty meters and slide while firing off a volley with his Kalashnikov. He'd been out in the desert for four days, and Yassin was assigned to flank him. A lot of the guys didn't speak good Arabic, or if they did, it was Maghrebi Arabic. So they talked in English. But the French and their English . . . Well, it was a shitty mess. So, anyway, the French worked together and figured out the commanders' orders using a few words of English and sign language. In the hell of Deir ez-Zor, this squad including of Yassin and the headcase had been assigned to capture a water tower. There were a dozen of the enemy, hidden behind a butte. The French convert had just arrived but didn't hear anything. So while everyone was hiding, this other dude would wait for a pause between bursts of enemy gunfire and then jump out to fire back a few bullets of his own, even though he didn't really know how to shoot yet. Insane. So, to capture the building, the sergeant told the young French guy to run toward the entrance at his signal. The others would cover him. At the signal, the *mujahideen* leaped out and opened fire on the enemy. The guy bounded forward like a rabbit. There were thirty meters to cover. After the first bomb exploded, he dodged the crater left by an artillery shell, and just as he was about to make it inside the water tower, there was another explosion. Just one. Immediately, he started screaming. A sniper's bullet had hit him in the lower back, ripping open his stomach and bladder. Shit squirted everywhere and sprayed all over the inside of his gut. His intestines were hanging out. The guy managed to keep going until he reached a car and took cover. Yassin and the others hid a few meters away, behind a dirt mound. The guy was waiting, hiding behind the car, for them to come and get him. But the sergeant ordered them to let him die because he didn't want to lose two more men to save some asshole who didn't know how to fight and was going to sit at God's side as a martyr anyway. The guy lived for three days, in agony, amid the bombs and bullets and the noise of helicopters, just a few steps away from his comrades. The smartass boys in France talk a good game, but that's what the reality of Cham is. You march or you die. The men there will rip your throat out. You don't count in anyone's eyes but God's.

The night before the November 13th attacks in Paris, Bedrettin called me. Everything was going well for him in Al-Mayadin. He was running a bigger hospital, with a staff of forty. He was the only doctor and was still training on the job, with his books. Later, I found out that he didn't give a fuck about Islam and the jihadists; he'd gone to Al-Mayadin for the money. They'd offered him twenty thousand dollars a month. He couldn't say anything because the *mujahideen* only earned a hundred dollars a month. To be honest, I think now that the guy might have been a kind of Turkish agent who'd infiltrated

Syria. He was too good to be true. Too bizarre. And he never talked about himself. There was something about him that was off, but I could never say just what.

The day after November 13th, Blondbeard came to find me. "So?" he asked. I didn't know what to say. I'd spent the whole night watching the news on satellite TV. I wasn't afraid, because I knew neither you nor Pop were likely to go to the Bataclan, or into the French parts of town. But yeah, deep down, there was still a risk that something had happened to you. Then I suddenly remembered that we'd gone for a Christmas celebration at the Bataclan one year, with that group Mom belonged to. We each got a remote-control car. It seemed to strange to me.

I prayed for our dead. I'd come here to fight that kind of injustice, and now assholes from here were doing the same shit to innocent people in France that Bashar was doing here. I figured I'd better pretend to be happy. I hated myself for it. I thought about Paris for days. On the Internet, I saw everyone writing *Je suis Paris*. But then I opened my eyes, and the real truth was right there in front of me. All the time I was treating innocent people at the hospital and dealing with the consequences of the American bombardments and Bashar's artillery shells and the Russian attacks, I hadn't been seeing clearly. *I am Syria* is what people *should* have been writing. But no one gave a shit because we were Muslims. So I decided that Paris was just another statistic, and I couldn't let it keep me from living my life.

21
OLDER BROTHER

People never change. Ever. Even back in the day, years ago, I was already at the controls of a race car. Number 10 on my soccer team. I was the driver, the one calling the shots, the go-to guy. The one who saw the holes in the opposing team's defense and passed the ball where it was least expected. Behind a steering wheel and on the field, the important thing is to see farther than five meters ahead of you. To have a comprehensive view of your environment and anticipate the next ten seconds. We never change in life. Ever. Soccer, driving, life, they're not like a chess game. You don't have much time. You look at the options, and in a split-second you make a choice. The broader your view, the better the choice you make. We don't change, and I was already fated to be an attacker. I wanted to be out there alone, me against the world. We never change, and back then my brother was number 6 on the same team. On the field, just behind me. A different role. Figure out the opposing team's game plan; fix the mistakes the attackers made; restart the machine; set the rhythm. He was on drums, and I was the soloist. You never change. We were always right there together, next to each other. Different; never in agreement; but never fighting. Thank you, Mom. Thank you, Dad. Thank you, *Jidda*.

Back then I didn't have weed or hash in my lungs, but my mind was already getting hazy. Easily distracted. My brother had been moved up to our team, so he was the youngest member. One Sunday morning, after a match the old man hadn't come to, we were waiting for the tram. The kid brother had passed me the winning goal. On a clearing shot from the opposing team's goalkeeper, he had jumped higher than the other team's attacker and headed the ball to me. I let the ball go between my legs to evade the first defender, then turned to wrongfoot the second. I was about thirty-five meters from the goal. Our two attackers were in the woods as usual, neither marked nor positioned to receive the ball; they hadn't anticipated my dribble. Thinking I was going to strike, another of the opposing team's defenders recentered to block me.

In the corner of my field of vision, right on the edge of my sightline, I saw a blue dot running. It was my brother. Instinctively, I sent a flick in his direction. The ball soared through the air and the kid brother received it perfectly. At that point, the goal was almost a done deal, because we'd practiced this combination on the Lilas gravel until we bled. While one struck against the defense by the wings, the other struck through the center, waiting for a backward pass. The ball came at me a little too forcefully, but I stretched out my leg and leaned forward so my strike wouldn't go wild. It flew like a missile straight into the left-hand side of the net. Goal! We'd secured first place, and we'd advance to the premier regional division the following season.

In the locker room, the ten Maghrebis on the team sang "We Are the Champions" and then "Ya Rayah" by Rachid Taha. Those guys were as much our friends as they were people to be a little scared of. They didn't want to see that we weren't Arabs like them. We had no problem with white guys. There was one on the team, and we were the only ones who ever talked to him. But they—I don't know why—they'd made up their minds not to like white people. Or black ones, either.

Whatever. Because we were strong, we were respected. In their heads, we weren't white. Which was another ridiculous thing. They said "French," but my brother and I couldn't call

white people "French," because we were half white—
Breton—and if we said French people were "French," what
did that make us? Mulattoes. And that, since we'd seen the
film *Roots*, was out of the question. Slavery was over. And the
old man had spent too much time drumming into our heads
how shitty Syria was for us to not want to be French.

Anyway, the world is complicated for no reason—but at the
same time, without all this bullshit, we'd die of boredom. After
the match, at the tram stop, sitting on a bench there in the middle of our concrete Disneyland, among the Scrooge McDucks
and the Donalds, we shared a pair of earphones connected to
our single Sony Walkman which we got by swapping with a
gypsy from Montreuil for a mountain bike pinched from a
black guy who'd stopped in front of the Noisy-le-Sec swimming pool for a piss. My brother's Nike Air Maxes were
pressed against my Nike Sharks. Sergio Tacchini tracksuit for
him, Lacoste for me, and Ärsenik rapping "Quelques gouttes
suffisent" in our ears. I bopped along with the music as we
waited for the tram.

Suddenly, two enormous guys appeared out of nowhere,
like Aladdin's genie. Both of them were easily six foot two.
Gigantic hands, huge bellies, big beards. One had on a white
djellaba; the other one wore a beige *kamis* and had a book
tucked under one arm. At first, they just asked us how we were
and what our names were. Guys like this—weird guys—had
been moving into our neighborhood for a while now. They
were way too obsessed with the mosque, like it was full of gold
or something. My brother started shooting the shit with them
about God and religion, prayers, the flock. They suggested we
go to the mosque with them to see for ourselves, and we said
we didn't have time. So one of the guys said that, if God had
said the same thing, I wouldn't exist, and the least we could do
was take a few minutes for Him, and not be ungrateful. He had
a point, and I shut up.

So, just like that, we followed them to the mosque in Aubervilliers. Pharaon's place, the Egyptian imam. For two hours they talked to us about our origins, about God and the Quran and Abraham, Moses and Jesus and Mohammed. I was fucking starving, but my brother had forgotten both fatigue and hunger. Just like at school, he was curious about everything, piling question on top of question. Once he even contradicted Kamel, the guy in the beige *kamis*. My grandmother had taught him a little bit about religion, and it's true that neither of these two guys seemed like the sharpest tools in the box. I kept looking at Kamel; I was sure he was white. It wasn't just his nose and his reddish beard that made me think so— Kabyles and Berbers can be redheads—but the way he spoke, justifying everything so excessively. Maybe he was Breton, or from somewhere in the north. Anyway, he was the more annoying of the two. He talked like a crackpot, acting like he was furious, without stopping for breath. In our neighborhood, we call those dudes "whites with a complex." All their friends are Arabs or black Muslims, and whether out of admiration or interest, or just because they want to belong to something, they always end up converting. You can become a Muslim, yeah, but you can't become black or Arab. You can't change your genes. And then after converting they always act like teacher's pets and preach to everyone about what religion should or shouldn't be. It doesn't get a lot of attention in the media, but they're a minority that's responsible for the majority of the problems. Whatever.

Finally, the two guys took us to a kebab joint we'd never heard of. "It's one hundred percent halal here," said the redhead. I wanted to say, "Because it's ninety-seven percent everywhere else?" But I kept the dig to myself. It wasn't the time to spoil the ambience; I was too hungry and the risk of not getting a sandwich was too high, given the guy's prickliness. He even harangued us about the sauce. Ketchup, mayonnaise, and all the other ones, he said, were haram—forbidden. Only harissa was permitted. Fuck, man. I mean, I like harissa, but it gives me the shits, and then it's Palestine in the toilet bowl for two days. We destroyed the sandwiches, and then my brother and I said we had to get home, claiming that our father would be worried about us. They insisted that we come back, that they would wait for us at Friday prayer, and that they would be serving mutton at noon. My brother wouldn't listen to me; he went back the next week. But it wasn't because I hadn't warned him that mutton was dangerous. He had an attack of food poisoning that lasted two days. He spent the whole forty-eight hours vomiting and shitting. He barfed like a dragon spitting fire, and his asshole was a geyser. But that didn't keep him from going back again.

It was like he'd discovered the origin of the Big Bang that day at the Aubervilliers mosque. His eyes looked like he was drugged, and he couldn't get the words out fast enough. Pop, my grandmother, Syria, the Quran, the universe, infinity.

"Do you believe we just appeared randomly out of nowhere? You see how perfect we are. And look at the round-about, that statue in the middle of it. How do you think that happened?"

He gestured to a rusted metal statue representing a slave breaking free of his chains.

"That? That thing? Come on, get the fuck out of here. It's the color of shit. Yeah, sure, so-called God, he made that. Whatever. 'Oh, it's disrespectful to God to say stuff like that' . . . Bullshit . . . You shouldn't listen to those old guys . . ."

Soccer went well for us the next year; a whole string of good matches, cups, medals. We dreamed of Paris Saint-Germain, of careers as soccer pros, like the De Boer or Baggio brothers. One Sunday morning, the PSG recruiter responsible for the 9-3—Seine-Saint-Denis—signaled to us from the bleachers. Samuel, a West Indian. We were both invited to take a test. In the car on the way there, our old man kept saying that playing soccer didn't make you a man. He wanted us to pursue noble professions. Medicine, law, engineering. The kid brother wanted to punch him. I just looked out the window, saying, "Okay, Dad."

The previous evening, I'd made the greatest discovery of my life. My first joint. Stressed, I'd gone down to see Moha, an older neighborhood kid who was squatting on the first floor of my building. He exhaled a lungful of smoke and held the joint out to me, saying Mary Jane would mellow me out. My feet took me back home without the help of my brain. In my hazy, half-asleep state, the room seemed to spin like a merry-go-round. Pop called me and I pretended to be asleep. The kid brother was furious when he realized I was stoned. We shared the master bedroom back then, the one Pop has since moved back into. We wanted to be together. We got up together. We slept together. We played together. We lived together.

On the PSG training grounds in Saint-Germain-en-Laye, the test started out well. There were a lot of people there. My brother and I told each other to keep it simple, not try any fancy tricks, because we needed to stand out. Other than us, everyone there was black. Without meaning to be, the recruiters were a little bit racist, convinced that black people were stronger physically. Everyone said that. But we had experience both on the playing field and in the street, and we knew that wasn't true. They were just like the rest of us: the proof was that when there was a fight, the black kids' punches weren't any stronger or weaker than anyone else's.

On the field, I was moving well. Control, precision of passes, return of the ball. My brother had also found a good rhythm, being where he needed to be, when he needed to be there. No fancy moves, but no misfires, either. At one point, alone in front of the goal, after a brilliant pass from my brother, I readied my leg for the kick. I could already see the ball going

into the top left corner. I could already see myself as a pro. At
that exact moment, my life changed. Life hangs on the word *if*.
If the assassin hadn't slammed into me with my foot in the air,
hadn't smashed into my knee, I might not be spending my days
driving a car. It was a killer's tackle, a disgraceful thing. His
cleats tore into my skin. After that? My brother came running
and delivered a solid right hook to the guy, who fell like a ton
of bricks. Final score? Two disqualified, one injured. In the car
on the way home from the hospital, Pop was happy. Goodbye,
childish dreams. The old man had seen it all coming. Read
books. Learn. "We start your political training, your brother a
little young still."

As usual, Dad started out well. Syria, religion, politics,
democracy, equality. All of that was new for me. This was after
the September 11th attacks, and the old man explained to me
that we'd never know who was behind the plot or why. The
United States, he said, would use it as an excuse to start a war.
Which happened. But then, as soon as I started doing better,
he got tired of the whole thing and gradually abandoned it. So,
like a stupid asshole, I let it drop too. I spent all my time playing video games. My knee was messed up; I could hardly walk.
Four months in a cast, and then two more on crutches. At
night, my brother could hear me crying. So he'd talk to me, tell
me I had to keep the faith. During the school vacation, to pass
the time, I hung out with my buddy Moha at the Barres-
rouges, one of the neighborhood parks. Weed helped me to
forget the hours, the minutes, the pain. I left it all on the
bench, and dribbled between my thoughts. The kid bro kept
on playing soccer by himself, but it wasn't going as well anymore. The other guys were harder on him, which was normal,
because I wasn't there to protect him. He kept going to
Pharaon's mosque, too. He never talked to me about it,
because I was depressed and he knew I didn't give a shit about
these stories of prophets and angels and stars.

By the next summer, I'd passed the tenth grade, so, to get my spirits back up and to get us out of the neighborhood for a while, Pop took us on vacation to Argelès-sur-Mer, near Perpignan. The three of us spent a week in a studio apartment. There was hot sunshine, fine sand, cool water, and girls everywhere, throwing themselves at us. All day my eyes were like windshield-wipers, going back and forth from one tight little ass to another. If you wore sunglasses you could stare all you want and nobody would know. I asked one seventeen-year-old blond to put sunscreen on my back. That girl was a knockout. My brother didn't want anything to do with it. He'd been a zombie since vacation started, his nose glued to a book. A big book, with a pretty cover. So despite all the hot chicks covering the beach, he was absorbed, spellbound. I asked him what he was reading. He didn't answer, just straightened up and showed me the book. The Holy Quran. "Look," he said, pointing it out with his finger, "the left-hand page is in French and the other one's in Arabic. So it's helping me learn the old man's language, too, and there's a ton of interesting stuff. Philosophical stuff."

Was this really the place to be reading the Quran? My brother had always been good at doing anything, anywhere, anytime, any way. Whatever.

L ife is bizarre. Everything was nice and calm and tidy
and then, all of a sudden, the past caught up with me. I
would have liked to be like nature; you know, going
along on my way no matter what happened. Nature doesn't
care if we try to resist it; it always finds its way; it doesn't worry
about the past or fear the future. With a river, you can build a
dam, but the water will build up and overflow it. A tree's roots
will grow until they crack concrete. Waves? They'll carry away
sand castles, wear away the coastline, leap over seawalls with
the force of a tsunami. The wind will rip off roof tiles and whip
itself into tornadoes that ravage whole regions. But I was only
a man, a son of nature, and I had to get used to the idea that
my brother had come back, and that I needed to manage my
life with him in it now. But, in his own mind, was he really
back?

His story was bizarre. I'm no specialist, but Aleppo and that
whole area, they talked about it on the radio like everyone
there had gone completely crazy. I didn't know, man. But he's
family, and I didn't have a choice. I was going to be part of
whatever came next—or rat him out to the cops. But that was
impossible. It would have killed the old man. I didn't know
what to do; I was just a driver. Tell me where to go, and I'll
drive the car. Tomorrow, the future, was the important thing.
Who cared what was in the rearview mirror? The past never
brought anything but tears.

The apartment smelled like roast chicken. A new brother

was in the kitchen. Wrapped in an apron, he was running his knife through some onions—*mincing* them, as a chef would say. You would have thought he was our dad: old-fashioned and strange and changeable, jumping from pillar to post, from one mood to another, without leaving you time to understand what's going on. But at the same time that was what made him unique. Slippery as a fish, exasperating as a cat. A member of my crew, my clan, my blood. I put my cigarette down in the ashtray. The lawyer's words were going around and around in my head. What if the cops knew? Maybe they already had my telephone bugged. They could be here in ten or fifteen minutes.

Little brother was the cook this apartment had been lacking. I had the kitchen redone when I moved in. Knives, cutting boards, casserole dishes, frying pans, a colander . . . Out the window, I watched the headlights of cars weaving between the raindrops. A revolving light flashed in the distance. A police car. It came closer. Stopped a few meters from the building. Two police officers got out and walked toward my building. My hand trembled. My blood ran cold. Fear. It started in my belly and surged up through my chest and into my ears. They were going to bust us. We were finished. Fucked, so stupid. I watched them enter the stairwell of the building next door. Fuck. They'd made a mistake. We had to get out of here, fast. Now. We'd drive to the end of the world, go underground, hide out; we wouldn't even breathe until they'd forgotten about us.

He was still at it with his vegetables. I was wrestling with fate, while he was wrestling with knives and a baking dish. Bastard. He'd come back and scratched at the door, *meow*, *meow*, as if asking for a dish of milk. He was destroying my life. Maybe he hadn't done anything; maybe that was actually the truth. But what other people thought of him was what counted here. When he left he might as well have been Osama bin Laden Junior, no matter what he said at the end of the day, the idiot. Maybe he had regrets; maybe they were what drove him back to Paris. He could cry all the tears in the Tigris and Euphrates by way of apology, but who would believe him; where was the proof? No paradise for us; we'd all go to prison, with him at the head of the line, our story splashed all over the news and in the papers. A nightmare. He hadn't seen the protests after *Charlie*, the prime minister's statements, the deprivations of citizenship and all that stuff. Mr. High-and-Mighty did what he wanted. Son of a bitch. The cops got back in their car and drove away. My heart stopped pounding, but my cheeks were still hot and flushed from the adrenaline.

My brother had set the table even more nicely than the old man did.

"It's like we're at Pop's on a Friday night. How long have you known how to cook?"

"I learned. I had the time . . ."

He'd answered me with the smile of a little boy whose elementary school teacher has just praised him. The guy had always had an insane knack for anything having to do with aesthetics and precision—like his father. The aromas from the kitchen were filling the apartment, making my stomach growl. I stood at the window, dragging on my cigarette, as he carefully carved the roast chicken. Beautiful movements: slow, precise, self-assured. Beautiful work. I'd tried carving once, and the truth is that it's not a skill that comes naturally. It's almost like surgery. He dished it onto the plates without speaking, like a perfect soldier. He sat down. I stubbed out my cigarette. Like two men neither dead or alive, not zombies, but half-dead, half-alive, facing each other, eyes unfocused, shoulders parallel, around my little square table, each waiting for the other one to whip his tongue out of its holster.

"What did the attorney say today?"

He'd fired first. I had my answer. I took a long drag on my cigarette.

"It's a long story."

"What did you tell him?"

"What I said I would. My brother's abroad, he'd like to come back to France, what are the risks?"

"But you told him about Syria, and all that?"

"Yeah."

"What did you say?"

"Humanitarian-aid work, okay? You think I was going to tell him you were off in jihad?"

His good mood evaporated in a split second. The magic word transformed his smile into anxiety. The old brother was back.

"You shouldn't have told him anything at all. What if he tells the police?"

"You're nuts, man, that's Yann's brother. You're a moron. If anything happens to us, they'll kick his ass. I just said that when you left, the cops questioned us, Dad and me, because they thought you'd gone to Syria. So now, we don't want any trouble when you come back."

"But you really said it was for humanitarian-aid work?"

"Yes, okay? But he told me we'd need proof. And he also said that, in any case, just going to Syria, these days, is grounds for being arrested for terrorism and put in jail."

The attorney's words seemed to depress him. But what had he expected?

"Think, okay? You can't stay in France."

"Where do you want me to go?"

I wanted to hit him.

"God, bro, you always act first and think later! How should I know? Figure out a plan!"

"What plan? I can't talk to anyone! You have to help me think of something."

"You're crazy, man. You come back, just like that. You've put me in deep shit, don't you realize that? Deep shit! If they catch you, I'm going down too. And I don't know how long they'll keep us inside."

He didn't reply. We stayed like that, without speaking. The roast chicken grew cold on our plates. I wasn't hungry anymore.

"You annoy the hell out of me. You always have. Why don't you ever listen? Why haven't you ever listened? You fucking . . . Who the hell told you to go fuck your whole life up in Syria?"

"Shut up, man! Stop harassing me about Syria!"

"Who told you to go to Syria? Was it me? And now you're here begging me to save you. I had a hard enough time saving my own life, bro. You know what my life is? Busting my ass ten hours a day in a Japanese sedan, driving happy, successful people around the city."

"Stop throwing Syria in my face! Everyone makes mistakes!"

"Mistakes? Are you nuts? My God, you're completely insane. What mistake? You were in the war, bro. You were against Bashar, among people who hate France. You have nothing but enemies!"

"I got scammed. They fucked me over. Get it? You need me to use smaller words?"

I went out on the balcony to smoke a cigarette and calm down. He started cleaning up the kitchen. I was dying to scream at him, without knowing why. I was furious. Furious that he'd put our whole family in the shit. From the balcony, I whispered at him so the neighbors wouldn't hear:

"Why won't you go and see Pop?"

He didn't answer, just continued clearing the table and tidying up the kitchen.

"Hey! I'm talking to you!"

"Look, just leave me alone. You're an ingrate, a fucking ingrate. Who got you out of the shit when you fucked up? Who brought you home from the club when you got smashed and were vomiting everywhere? Who made sure the old man was asleep when you took his car for your 'business'? Huh? Tell me that! So don't come at me with bullshit like I ruined your life."

"Shut up, you son of a bitch! Just shut the fuck up!"

The glass door to the balcony was still open. I went inside and closed it quickly so the neighbors wouldn't hear.

"Fine, you know what? Drop it. I'm out. I'm leaving."

"Where are you going?"

"Don't know. I'm out."

"Where will you go? You're going to get yourself arrested."

"I'll manage. Don't you worry about me."

"Fine, piss off, then! With your bullshit and your fuckups and your Syria!"

The doorbell rang several times. I went to answer it. It was the old lady who lived in the apartment below mine.

"Are you the one screaming like that? What's the matter with you? It's ten o'clock at night."

I wanted to smash her head against the door. How dare the old bag come up here with her fucking panties in a twist?

"I'm sorry, ma'am. I fell asleep on the sofa, and I must have rolled over on the TV remote."

I don't know if she believed me. She turned and went back downstairs without wishing me a good night.

My brother had gone into his room. I went in after him. He was lying down and had opened a book. It was like seeing a mirage. The last time I'd seen him with a book in his hand had been when he was in nursing school, reading a textbook.

"I'll leave tomorrow morning, okay? I'll leave you in peace."

"Okay. Good night."

I had nothing else to say to that son of a bitch anyway. I didn't press it, just went to my room. Maybe I shouldn't have said anything to the lawyer, but we don't always do what we want in life; we often just do what we can, and I'd do whatever I could to make my brother's life better. I went back into the living room to get my *Bridge on the River Kwai* DVD case. Roll a filter tip, crumble the grass between my thumb and index finger, lick a cigarette, unstick the paper, empty the tobacco into my palm, mix it with the weed with my index finger, get out a cigarette paper, put the rolled filter tip on it, roll the paper with strong, practiced fingers, moisten the paper with the tip of my tongue, stick it, roll again, this time the end of the paper; light it, take a deep drag, let it rise, hot in my chest, my mind slowing down, exhale the smoke, and fly away. Turning on the TV, I stumbled across a documentary about Palmyra. A marvel, an ancient city in the middle of Syria. Our home, there, beautiful. Still standing after two thousand years. The lunatics destroyed it. I didn't understand anything in life. Maybe we'd go there one day with the old man. All three of us. In the desert. My brain got lighter, head whirling, mouth sticking, eyes drooping. I don't know why but it was like I'd already seen these images. Palmyra. Someone showed me, but I couldn't remember. Maybe the old man. The image changed. Now this one, I mean it, I was sure I'd already seen this building. Upright columns. But where? Mixing it up with somewhere else, probably. A mixture of Chad and Rome, I guess?

The angel Gabriel came down and stroked my hair. And I fell asleep, hand under the pillow, dreaming of Mom. Because she was there, my sweet mother, the one who appeared when I went up to the Garden of Eden to smoke grass. Not dead, still there, in my head, in my heart.

23
Older Brother

H ello?"
"Yeah, I'm listening. It's the driver. I can't find you. Where should I come to get you? Is it Nanterre, or Courbevoie?"

"Uh, I'm not sure. Wait, I'll look out my window . . ."

I'd just been commissioned for a fare in the business district of La Défense.

"Can you see the big thumb? Next to the Grande Arche?"

"I'm almost there."

In La Défense there is a kind of underground maze of parking lots, delivery bays, taxi stands, and even a supermarket and a restaurant. You have to be careful not to get lost; one wrong turn and you can end up on the highway. The next exit is more than thirty kilometers away. The thumb the customer was talking about was a giant sculpture, more than ten meters tall.

"Hello? It's the driver. I'm here."

"Oh! Already! Sorry. I'm running five minutes late. Can you wait for me?"

I typed "Thumb La Défense" into my smartphone. "Work of art by the sculptor César," it replied. Twelve meters tall, weighing eighteen tons. It had been erected in 1994 on the forecourt amid the towers. It was 12:30 P.M., and uptight assholes in business suits were scurrying along the sidewalks, anxious to feed their paunches. Everyone went crazy over that big thumb. I got out of my car to take a closer look. Skin texture, wrinkles, the nail, the curve of it, the thumbprint. Great art, man. The smartphone told me a bunch of anecdotes over the next three minutes. This wasn't the only thumb; César produced a lot of them, in all different sizes, to stick them right up the a . . . of the people who could afford it, including the public authorities, who'd sucked more than enough tax money out of us to pay for a bronze thumb. I mean, I don't know how much that thing cost, but a thumb like that, like a Roman emperor's, like Caesar's, sculpted by a guy called César, was a hell of a trip.

There were works of art all over La Défense. I'd walked all around here one night, stoned, with my friend Moha. We'd stolen a guidebook to the area from a Fnac and we looked at all the sculptures, just talking about nothing. Some of them cost millions of euros. They were our brothers, those artists. As messed up in the head as we were. We laughed our asses off. The decision-makers had put works of art everywhere among the towers, convinced it was good for people. But no one gave a shit about them, and no one understood them. You'd have thought they were just decorations. To understand, you have to take the time and have the interest. Otherwise, no one gives a damn about any of it. Art should smack you right in the face at first glance. Then, when you analyze it, you discover all the details. And then you decide it's a masterpiece.

"Hello? This is the driver. Where are you?"

"I'm going to need another five minutes. I have to finish a report."

A report! To hell with this guy, man. I had other things to do. I was losing fares waiting around. A guy sat down next to the thumb, holding a package in his hands. Curly hair, navy suit, white shirt, blond beard. He looked like a Syrian, with his bushy eyebrows, but a well-dressed one. There were a bunch of military types walking around, too, probably freaking these assholes out with their assault rifles. What if one of them went berserk and started lining everybody up? Fucking hell, I thought. I'm still a little stoned from last night. I should write all this down; it would make some good stories. What if the guy with the blond beard suddenly blew himself up? He could have a belt of explosives on under his suit. The thumb would take off and end up stuck in the sky's asshole. He looks like a well-put-together dude, but he could be a terrorist. *Taqqiya*, like the lawyer said. You never know.

Another dude joined the guy. Younger. Yellower. He quickly greeted the man with the blond beard and they sat down together on a bench nearby. Started talking. Holy crap, the younger one looked like he was at death's door. Even from a distance I could see the dark bags under his eyes. What could they be talking about?

"Good. You've absorbed what I taught you."

The younger one tried to hide his smile.

"The best way to be discreet is to surround yourself with people. At this time of day, people are walking around, eating, talking. And we're talking, too, just like them. The art of dissimulation is not to hide; it's to be invisible. And to be invisible, you have to blend in with your environment. Like a chameleon. Have you eaten pork yet?"

"No."

"Well, you're going to taste it now. Here, take a sandwich, and don't argue."

The younger guy looked surprised. Just before he took a bite, he looked up at the sky. Maybe lightning was going to strike him down. He bit into the sandwich, the bastard. Son of a bitch. He just ate pork. He seemed to love it. Sin is always far away and close at hand at the same time. Just a mouthful away from hell.

"Not bad, eh?"

The younger guy chewed, pretending to be disgusted.

"The party's in five days. Next Wednesday. Make a note of it in your head and nowhere else, and tell your team to do the same."

The man with the blond beard continued talking.

"The munitions specialist better keep a low profile, or it's all over. And what are you using to buy the stuff? Careful with credit cards, and not too much cash, either."

"Actually, we don't need it. There's another solution."

The man with the curly hair crumpled up his sandwich bag. He stayed silent and closed his eyes for an instant before murmuring something incomprehensible in Arabic.

"Be careful."

Two women in suits and stiletto heels walked by, asses swaying. The man with the blond beard smiled and winked at them.

"In five days. Wednesday. Make a note in your head and nowhere else."

My customer arrived then, and the two guys vanished from my thoughts.

"Are you the driver? Hello, I'm Mr. Granet. Sorry to be late."

Fuck, man, I was crazy. I let my mind spiral out of control over two guys sitting on a bench. Too far. This was no good. I should really stop smoking weed one of these days.

Another siren. What time was it? It was daylight outside. I felt like I'd slept for three years. Those Dutch labs were producing stronger and stronger shit. One day my brain would end up totally fucked. I was beat. Exhausted. Over it. My head felt heavy, my eyes stung. I pushed open the door of my brother's bedroom. Little asshole was still asleep. On the floor next to his bed was the book he'd been reading the other night, *1984*, by George Orwell.

After a few minutes' hesitation, I forced myself to put on my suit. I had to bring in some money; I hadn't worked since the kid brother turned up, and the fridge was emptying fast, with a capital F. I was shaving when I heard him pissing.

"So you haven't left?"

He waited a couple of seconds before answering. The couple of seconds it took to decide whether to scream at me or go along with the joke. He went with the joke.

"Nah, I called the cops to report you."

I didn't know what he did with his days and nights. He'd been here four days already. He asked to use my laptop in the evenings and I always found it on the coffee table in the mornings. I'd been like him when I came back from the army: stuck, locked up, unable to make myself move. It makes you nuts. After the accident in Chad, the doctor prescribed pills, supposedly to help me heal. All day I watched the darkness and the blood flowing around me. Like a zombie, I went from the TV to the computer, from a movie to a TV series. The only breaks I took were to go to the bathroom and eat. Taking a shit, or eating a steak, broke up the routine. At first, the old man left me alone. Months went by and nothing changed. Out the window I could see the locals, family from way back, going about their business, living their lives—and I, sitting there in the dim half-light, was letting mine slip away. One day I went downstairs. Big Moha was still there, with his joint, his gypsy face, his snaggleteeth, and his fucked-up brain. I stopped taking my pills and started smoking weed again, and, bit by bit, I found my footing in the hood: soccer field, shopping center, hookah bar, kebab joint. Conclusion: Mary Jane breathed life back into me.

In the shower, as the cold water streamed down my face, I realized that it was up to me to find a solution for my brother. Despite his courage and his studies, he couldn't do it himself. He seemed smart, and maybe he was, for scribbling in answer-books and giving people medical treatment. But for practical things, it still, as always, came down to me. Like the lawyer said, he couldn't stay here. I'd have to come up with a way for him to disappear, fast. But where? Who could I ask? And how would we do it? I had to find a plan, find a place, put him there, get my affairs settled here, and then join him. With the old man—and Grandma, if possible.

At 9:15 A.M. I put my hands on the steering wheel. To get back into the swing of things, I headed for Belleville and the café where I often had breakfast, not far from the Salafist mosque. At the counter, the waiter served me my usual: Americano, croissant, glass of orange juice, and the paper. I scanned the headlines: the final polls before the elections; the war in Syria; attacks in Turkey; a health-care scandal. Then I turned to the local news section, which is 1) practical, 2) more important, and 3) relaxing. On the page devoted to Paris Rive Gauche, the top headline in the right-hand column read "Burglary at Hôpital Pompidou."

Someone had swiped a bunch of chemicals from the hospital's medical supplies. The police and the hospital's security staff hadn't noticed of any breach. Despite heightened security measures, someone had managed to get in and out without being seen. The article didn't give any information about what kind of stuff had been stolen, but it must have been important, because the hospital director requested an around-the-clock military presence.

I was distracted from the paper by a voice on the TV announcing a debate on private-hire vehicles. A platform was closing down . . . due to competition. "They can go fuck themselves!" spat an old man sitting at the counter. Must be a taxi driver. And, from the mouth on him, I'd have bet a hundred euros that he was Kabyle. This was the eleventh arrondissement, an area in which members of the bohemian bourgeois— bobos, we called them—and the Arabs and Chinese uncomfortably shared space. A zone of territorial competition between fancy candy shops, egg-roll and spring-roll vendors, clothing wholesalers, organic food shops, tearooms occupied by white-bearded old Chinese men and cafés by dark-skinned Arabs, Montessori schools, bicycle repair shops, couscous restaurants, vegetable-sellers, Kabyle-run bar-cafés, Muslim bookstores, sellers of cheap knockoff handbags, boutiques where you could buy authentic, very, very expensive handbags by completely unknown designers, and grocers who sold everything from crème fraiche to single cigarettes. And, of course, mosques.

In reality, there's no competition; everyone cohabitates and mixes together. Kind of. Some posh bobo places an order with a Chinese caterer, who buys his vegetables from an Algerian greengrocer, who frequents the same Kabyle café as the bobos, run by the "good" kind of immigrants. At two o'clock in the afternoon you can sip your coffee at the counter with Miloud or Heikel, who come from the high plateaus of Kabylia, and that same evening raise a glass of red wine with Morad from

Oran or Moha from Tlemcen—and this changes your life. Some Chinese people come to the café, too, the more open-minded ones, or the alcoholics to buy scratch cards or lottery tickets, or bet on the horses, or play gin rummy. In the candy shops, the Maghrebis and Chinese magically manage to understand one another by speaking a sort of Creole specific to the eleventh arrondissement. This same language is a source of conflict when the napkins expected by Arabs are rectangular instead of square.

The sidewalks are filled with Asian women pacing back and forth. The walking ladies, we called them. They spend the whole day just shooting the shit with one another. At first glance they'll smile at you, and you know immediately what their job is. Since passive soliciting was made illegal, these watchwomen of lower Belleville have been constantly on the move, so the cops don't take out their ticket books. They wait instead for a client to hail them. The rest happens in an apartment, a stairwell, or maybe the back room of a massage parlor. People say they're the cheapest in Paris, and that a blow job plus vaginal sex is only thirty euros. For twenty euros more, you can even fuck them in the ass. Never confirmed the rumor personally, myself. Too dirty.

Amid all these people are mosques and men, some young and some not so young, with their beards down to their belly buttons and their *kamis* worn over tracksuits and their plain old shoes or Nike Airs on their feet. The kind of shoes weed dealers used to wear in the late '90s. These guys are often on bikes, not out of some kind of bullshit bobo desire to be eco-friendly but because they claim cars are haram. Why not, I guess? Those green assholes say stuff like, "Nature is a gift, and we only have one planet, so let's protect it," and the Belleville beardos say, "Nature is a gift from God; man is made to live in nature and not in sin. Protect all of that, and travel by bike." The bicycle fad around here must annoy the hell out of the police, and I'm sure the statistics on facial-feature checks would bear that out. How do you tell a bearded Muslim on a bike from a hipster on a fixie? It's a serious problem. The other day at the café, there was a bobo kid who told me some hipsters filed a complaint about all the facial-feature checks the cops are doing, and the prefecture actually listened to them. Immigrants, with all their religions blended together and mixed up, have been complaining about that shit for fifty years, and no one listens. Some republic.

So the cops had to suspend their checks, and the statistics went down. One of the squad officers from the nineteenth arrondissement found a solution: he noted all the brands of bicycle and used that as a criterion to judge a person's situation. Hipsters buy new, expensive, fixed-gear bikes from bike shops. Huge frauds. The beardos buy old, worn-out bikes, often Peugeot folding ones, from private individuals on the Internet. Since that discovery, the checks have started up again, this time successfully. So now, instead of being criminals for looking wrong, people are criminals for having shitty bikes. And soon enough, the protests came along with it. Imagine a funeral procession headed by a bearded Muslim in a djellaba holding a sign that reads "No to the stigmatization of Peugeot folding bikes," like a good French citizen who loves to complain. Who'll say he isn't integrated then?

I left the café, and the app assigned me to take a guy to Sentier, the historic quarter where the Maghrebi Jews lived, the Sephardim. The old man has always told me they were as much Maghrebi as they were Jewish. Anyway. The rider was going up the rue d'Aboukir. In the rearview mirror, I could tell from his face that he was employed by one of the Silicon Sentier companies. In the past few years, this area has become the mecca of French start-ups. Not too expensive, and right in the middle of the city. This dude had a look on his face like he'd just lost the World Cup. Dark circles under his eyes, empty expression, knitted brow. He looked like Raymond Domenech when Zidane headbutted Materazzi. Anyway. He got in the car with a big cardboard box full of papers, pens, and folders. Surely, he'd just gotten fired. Poor guy, as of this morning. He asked me to turn on the radio. "Whatever station you want, just so the radio's on." The kind of customer who doesn't do well with silence. I do the same thing, when I don't want to think. I'll listen to anything, Radio Caribbean, Radio Mozart, it doesn't matter, as long as it lets me turn off my brain and focus on the road.

On France Info, after the newsflash, they started talking again about the private-hire platform that was closing. I turned up the volume. A little bit more information had come out since this morning; the boss had held a press conference, and they played some clips from it:

"Right now, as they say in the Internet economy, 'the winner takes all.' There's not enough room for two platforms. Our main competitor is taking sixty percent of the fares, and the market is saturated. Too many drivers, too many platforms, and the client base has stopped growing, and is even shrinking, as some people are going back to taking taxis. Our only means of survival in the past have been advertising and communication, but we no longer have the resources to invest in them."

People talked about new start-ups like they were the future of economics and, via the domino effect, the future of humanity. So this bankruptcy was a big thing. The elites of our country, the head minister of the economy, had voted massively for these new companies, and made all the little peons like me get on board.

The guy in the back seat asked me to turn off the radio.

"I worked for that company . . . Don't really want to hear people talking about it, I'm sure you get it."

He could fuck right off, this dude with his face like a beaten dog's. He'd signed on to work for a company that hired lost souls to drive ten hours a day, guys who didn't know what else to do with their lives. They plunked them down behind the wheel of a nice shiny car and sent them out to rake in the cash. A third for the platform, a third for the bosses, and the last third for the drivers. And of the drivers' one-third, the government helped itself to twenty percent. At the end of the day, the drivers only take home twenty-five percent of what they earn. The guy in the back seat of my car, with his glum face, like a whore's at the end of a long night, helped all of that happen. He never thought, never said to himself, "Hey, wait a minute, we're exploiting people." No, he even thought it was all great, because it was so modern. To hell with their modernity, if you ask me. I'm sure people lived better lives during the time of the prophets. Yeah, there was sickness, and, yeah, there were wars and servitude, but at worst, all you had to do was find some forgotten little corner and cultivate a little patch of land, to not be dependent on the assholes gobbling up your living space.

"Have you been doing this for long?"

I swallowed down my venom. "Almost three years. You?"

"Same. You should stop. In the end, we're all going to be . . ."

"To be what?"

"Fucked."

Without the car and the suit I'd be back on the street, moving weed to get by. At least this guy would be getting unemployment to tide him over for a few months. He could take a trip somewhere nice and exotic with his woman and come back rested and refreshed, tanned and with no more dark circles under his eyes, send out two or three resumés, alert his network, and be back behind a computer screen in the blink of an eye, fucking over a new bunch of miserable bastards. The more time that goes by, the more like the old man I become. A motherfucking "Comm-u-nist." Because I used to believe in the American dream. Earn your T-bone fair and square. But that didn't last long. The only truth is that, once

I've paid the rent, I barely have enough cash to take my girl out on a date.

He got out of my car near Marx-Dormoy. Like a real-estate agent, he'd tried to sell me on his neighborhood for a good ten minutes. White people love moving into druggie neighborhoods and telling you how much they love the diversity. I'd have liked to click my tongue disdainfully at him the way our Malian neighbors did to my old man, but the truth is that he'd already gotten the full picture from seeing my face reflected in the rearview mirror. If I were rich, I'd live in a beautiful area, with beautiful buildings and beautiful girls and beautiful cars. But these dudes run away from all that; they dream of living like ghetto rats, with ghetto faces and ghetto breath and ghetto neighborhoods and ghetto parties. It's bizarre. Luxury doesn't exist anymore except in dreams, nobody knows who's who anymore, or who is what. In the French we speak in our part of town, we'd say these times are *à la haess*. Gone to shit.

25
YOUNGER BROTHER

I n the morning, before the raid on the tower, they came
to get me at the clinic. I hardly had time to finish the
cesarean I was doing before they bundled me into a
pickup. The tunnel was finished. Three hundred meters long,
six meters underground. Twenty fighters had gathered at the
tunnel entrance. Blondbeard's brother-in-law had finally managed to finish the construction, with what was left of the prisoners. Because of all the time he'd spent in the sun, the scar
on his temple stood out, a souvenir of Blondbeard's ring. The
brother-in-law gave the signal, and we started off, one by one.
I brought up the rear. As I descended the ladder, I looked up
to see the sky one last time. The shaft was barely shoulder-
width. The other guys were armed to the teeth. Besides their
rifles, some of the men were carrying rocket launchers or
heavy machine guns. There wasn't enough air, and the cave
smelled like farts. It was suffocating. That line, "You see, in
this world there's two kinds of people, my friend—those with
loaded guns, and those who dig. You dig," from *The Good, the
Bad, and the Ugly* kept running through my head, bro.

The prisoners had dug like dogs, barefoot and with their
bare hands, so other people could make war. You could see the
marks their bloody hands had left on the walls. Every one of
the guys I was with wanted to make war. Maybe they'd never
known peace. The man in front of me wore a black padded
vest packed with explosives. He moved forward with diffi-
culty, holding on to the damp walls of the tunnel. I'd heard

explosives were really heavy. His first name was Abou Johnny. Weird, yeah, I know. But there's a logic to it. It wasn't because he was a convert, but because he was very blond, with smooth hair, which made him look American. Blond hair here is usually curly or even kinky, but his was silky. His eyes were very blue, and his skin was white as snow, and he had a face like an angel's, in one of the stained-glass windows in a church back home. If he had on jeans and a baseball cap, he could have been a Google employee. You'd never know he was Syrian, let alone a jihadist. It just goes to show . . . Syria taught me "Son, all men are equal," and this was the proof. It was just the laws of men that made us unequal. Crazy or not, this dude would never have had to deal with any racism in France, not with that face. But our Pop, bro, with his mustache and his skin the color of Nesquik, was forced to trade his doctorate for a taxi license and a hunk-of-junk car. And you, my brother . . . and you . . .

Anyway. This guy was a real headcase. I'd delivered his baby in the clinic two weeks earlier. His wife was as crazy as he was. I barely had time to cut the umbilical cord and clean up the baby before she asked me to take a picture of her with the kid in her arms and a Kalashnikov next to them. The sister posted the photo on Facebook to "show the Islamic community Allah's generosity to his believers," as she put it. God save us from that kind of insanity.

The end portal of the tunnel was behind a butte, which would protect us from any snipers in the tower. Blondbeard, our emir, had been yakking about his plan for six months. The butte was an indispensable key to his success. Behind the butte, about a hundred meters downhill, was the village. And on the other side of the village was the tower, with a view of the entire surroundings. The houses had been abandoned by their inhabitants. The place was nothing but a military anchor point and an observation post for Bashar's men.

To protect us from snipers, they'd erected big sheet-metal shields the night before, which would allow the *mujahideen* to move around easily during the attack. For a year, our fighters had gone up against elite sharpshooters' bullets and ended up with us, in the hospital. It had become a routine occurrence. In the beginning they'd aimed for the legs, because it's more complicated to care for a wounded person than a dead one. It makes one less bed available, and makes it necessary to treat the victim. But the last four had come in with bullets in the thorax, whistling respiration and with blank eyes. In each case, we'd been unable to do anything much, and it was driving Blondbeard crazy. He was determined to take the tower today, and then to advance as far as the river to secure the village. He was even ready to sacrifice some of his men, so long as the mission succeeded.

Abou Johnny had a long discussion with Blondbeard's brother-in-law, the overseer of the tunnel. They developed a plan. From a distance, there didn't seem to be any movement in the tower. From across the scrubland, it looked to me like the television tower at Fort de Romainville. I don't know what the fuck I was doing, or how I had come to be there. More than two years I was stuck out here in the desert. No training, pretending to be a doctor. I'd come over with an NGO only to end up as a medic under the command of Blondbeard in a military operation. My first one. After an hour, Abou Johnny and the brother-in-law seemed to have reached an agreement; they shook hands, then embraced. Kind of like the couples on train station platforms on a Sunday night. It was peaceful. Abou Johnny knelt to pray. We waited nearby. The men were calm. No helicopters tonight, no bullets, no artillery shells, no mortars. It felt good, but it wouldn't last.

The young man finished his prayers, stood, and took a small mirror out of his pocket to fix his hair. Then he rejoined his men and embraced them, one by one. For two years he had been guiding them among the hills north of Aleppo. The soldiers' loyalty to the young man was surely greater than their faithfulness to Blondbeard. They talked about him like he was Rambo. He was afraid of being killed only because of the consequences it might have for his men, which was what allowed him to act in ways that were excessively risky for himself. He never once visited the hospital. Not a single injury. Not even a sprained ankle, which was the most common reason for the *mujahideen* to come to the clinic. Omar, one of the youngest fighters, started to cry. Abou Johnny took him in his arms and thumped him on the back, saying, "See you soon." Kalashnikovs strapped across their bodies, palms turned skyward, all of them murmured a final prayer.

Then, like in a theater revue, each one took his place. The first group started off across the scrubland to plant a sniper with a machine gun. Soon afterward, they started firing on the tower, with ten-second intervals between volleys. No response. I'd heard that when the enemy doesn't fire back, it's a bad sign. Now, a second group of four or five men headed out to hide in a house and install a second sniper with a machine gun. Then they started firing in their turn. Still no response. When the last group of guys hidden behind the shield began firing on the tower, Abou Johnny winked at me, shook my hand, kissed me on the forehead, and said, "Thank you, my brother. You gave me a son. You've earned your place with Allah." He walked away hunched over and, when he'd left the shelter of the sheet-metal, flattened himself to the ground. With a Kalashnikov strapped tightly to his body, he let himself slide down the slope until he reached the first house in the village. This was my first time being present during a military operation, and it was nothing like the movies. My heart. I'd been given a rifle for safety, but I didn't know how to use it. Blondbeard had been nagging me to go through training camp since I arrived, but I always avoided it by coming up with something I had to do at the hospital, and there truly was so much work that I didn't really have time for anything else. To cover Abou Johnny, the hidden snipers fired a hail of bullets, accompanied by repeated shouts of "*Allahu Akbar!*" Finally, the tower began firing back. Every four or five seconds, a bullet landed near us, often in the sheet-metal shield. Fortunately, it had been folded three times over and reinforced with wood. Impossible for bullets to penetrate.

During this time, Abou Johnny had made his way down the slope and into the village. From my vantage point I could see him moving from wall to wall, crouching, carrying his Kalashnikov and wearing his vest packed with explosives. Then he was outside my field of vision, and I couldn't move my head to watch him without risking a bullet in the skull. Like a metronome, the regular bursts of gunfire reminded us not to come out. This lasted ten or fifteen minutes. Nobody knew what Abou Johnny was doing, and the operation's success depended on him. The *mujahideen* tried to stay calm, but some of them panicked when bullets whizzed past their ears.

"*Allahu Akbar! Allahu Akbar! Allahu Akbar!*" they cried out to aid him, and the truth is that they must really have believed in victory to fight with such courage. Suddenly, we heard a scream. One of guys out in the scrubland yelled that young Omar had been hit in the neck and needed medical assistance right away. I crawled to get my gear and then went back for a blanket. "Too late!" the guy cried. "He has gone to be with Allah." Bashar's men hadn't been using Dragunov sniper rifles for a while now; the Iranians had given them copies of an Austrian gun, the Steyr. I could see it in the wounds. There's nothing much you can do anymore.

Suddenly, several Kalashnikov volleys coming from the village shattered the silence. Then no noise for a couple of minutes. Everyone was quivering. I was lying flat on my belly, and I crawled to the edge of the protective shield to try to see what was happening. It was too far, almost two hundred meters. If one of Bashar's guys had spotted me, he could have taken me out with a single bullet, but at that particular moment I was so full of adrenaline I felt like nothing could happen to me. The others felt the same. I felt like I was living, truly alive, like when I did a cesarean. After six months of preparation, we were at the end of the operation. Everything could still easily go downhill. I pictured the other man in the tower, surrounded by Bashar's insane Shiite militiamen, red bandeaus around their heads, screaming *"Allahu Akbar!"* too, but for different reasons. A louder, stronger *"Allahu Akbar!"* rang out from our side. And then we heard a deafening explosion. A cloud of dust rose up from the tower.

"Allahu Akbar! Allahu Akbar! Allahu Akbar!" They rushed toward the village, rifles in hand. I didn't know what to do. Men were running everywhere, *mujahideen* bounding down the slope in the direction of the village. I stood up, picked up the gear and the Kalashnikov, and went after them, letting myself roll like a bike wheel, full tilt, down the hill. Curled up in a ball, my face bloody, I waited for the gunfire to stop. We had won.

When we got back that night, Blondbeard had ten sheep slaughtered for the *mujahideen*. He was smiling ear to ear. Looked like a happy kid. He gave a long speech. His son, a boy of thirteen, came up on the platform to recite verses from the Quran and urge us to continue fighting. I wanted to go home. After half an hour, I said I had to go to the clinic and check on the patients, which I should have done, but I was too tired. At home, Leïla cleaned and bandaged the cuts on my hands and face. Then I tried to sleep, but I could still hear the bullets whizzing around me. My first real experience with war. I thought about the people at the concert in Paris.

The next morning at the clinic, the cesarean patient from the previous day had taken a turn for the worse. She had a fever of 105.8 Farenheit degrees. Her husband came to yell at me. He was a wounded fighter. He threatened to cut my throat if his wife died. I didn't understand what was wrong with her. She complained of intense pain at the incision site, but I'd done the same procedure as always. Before leaving for Al-Mayadin, Bedrettin had told me this would happen, because we weren't specialists and didn't have enough supplies. We couldn't be experts at everything. I made the hurried decision to open her up again. We'd left a compress inside her. When I took it out, blood flooded into her abdominal cavity. I started shaking. The nurse shook me, but he could see that I'd frozen up. He put in new compresses, without success. I must have torn away something that had clotted around the compress. When I removed it, the bleeding started again. And, it had become infected. Compared to Bedrettin, I worked like a butcher. The girl lost consciousness. Blondbeard sent us a pickup and a driver, and we rushed her to Raqqa. There, they had the facilities to operate on her. In the back of the truck, I checked her pulse every ten minutes. Raqqa was two hours away. Ten kilometers outside our village, I lost her pulse. The nurse wanted to do a cardiac massage, but it didn't do any good, she'd lost too much blood. The pickup turned back around, with its cargo of a dead woman. I didn't know how to break the news. I was already exhausted from the previous evening and the burial of Abou Johnny. The husband showed up at the clinic with a knife. Blondbeard's driver threatened him with a Kalashnikov; then, when he wouldn't calm down, they took him to the Al-Bab prison. It was an ancient, Roman-era water tank about twenty meters deep. They blocked it with a wheel-shaped stone, like a giant manhole cover. It was all almost two thousand years old, and it was fiendishly effective.

In the days that followed, Blondbeard could see that I wasn't okay. He was an intelligent man. Like a true manager, he knew how to handle the troops. He offered me more resources for the hospital, and a few days off to rest. But the truth was that I just couldn't take it anymore. Then, one day in late winter, as we were walking in a grove of pistachio trees, I put my hand on his shoulder.

"I'm going to France."

26
OLDER BROTHER

Where could we go with my brother? I'm no Tom Cruise, and this wasn't *Mission: Impossible*. We had to get away, and fast. Before things got out of control. I wasn't far from the 120, Mehmet's restaurant. After the news broke about the platform's bankruptcy, I floored the gas pedal in the direction of my second family. It didn't matter what time it was with Mehmet; he was always open, because drivers work 24/7 and they could be famished at any hour. So Mehmet the Turk had a joint of meat on the fire all day and all night. Between six and seven hundred sandwiches a day. He was raking it in. And the cherry on top was that it was one hundred percent legal.

It was barely noon on a Friday and the 120 was packed. After the announcement of the platform's closure, a flood of calls and texts had sent an entire armada of black cars toward the 120, the headquarters of the revolt. In the middle of the restaurant, surrounded by drivers, was Hassen, the head of the private-hire drivers' union. The guy has always been political: neighborhood association, anti-racism association, protests, political meetings, a card-carrying member of the Socialist Party, and even elected to the Drancy city council. One day it hit him that politics doesn't pay squat, so he put on a black suit of his own and got behind the wheel. For a year or so he was content, working hard, making money. But then his weakness caught up with him, and he created the union.

At first, no one gave a fuck about it. Normal: money was

good, bellies full, tears fewer. But then the financial wind shifted, and our bank accounts started to feel the pinch. In this life, everything's a question of survival. If you want to keep food on the table you have to have an advantage over the people around you. Be the most discreet, maybe, or have a diploma, or a particular skill. In my case, there was nothing protecting my job. All you had to do in the early days was buy a suit and a phone, get a quick certification, and take the wheel. If you didn't have the cash for that, you would find yourself a boss and drive for him. If you did have the money, you would get yourself a car registered in your name, take classes for a month to get your permit, and, bam, you're off and running. Well on your way to having your hair turn gray for the sake of a little *dinero*. So, of course, every down-on-his-luck asshole around made tracks for the job. The ultimate example were the dudes fresh out of jail. Wearing an electronic ankle bracelet doesn't keep you from stepping on the gas pedal. It's even the only job possible, really; no need for a CV. The platform doesn't give a shit about your past.

Little by little, with more and more drivers but only so many customers, there were fewer fares, so there was less money to go around. Especially with the clients ordering and paying through the platform, which made you dependent on a mobile app and an algorithm. Some drivers do better business than others, so the machine assigns them more fares. Why? *No sé.* Some weird thingamajig between the average rating given by clients, the rapidity of the trips, and the number of hours spent behind the wheel. As life's gotten harder, Hassen has become our Che Guevara. He's the one who negotiates with the platforms, because we don't know the right words to use. We would have gone in there with our emotions, but he was a politician. A chess player.

So, right there in the middle of all the anger, Hassen was explaining to the drivers that they had to wait, and the other platform should quickly pick up the clients.

"But what if people are fed up and go back to taxis?"

"Two things, my brother. One, we have a technological advantage. It's more practical for the client. One click, and no need for cash. Other than that, it's just business as usual, bro. We have to provide the best service if we want to stay in the game—that's how we beat them in the first place.

"And the LOTI drivers? Bro, it's because of them that the customers have taken their business elsewhere. They work like monkeys. Nothing but lowlifes. Just worker bees who collect their paychecks at the end of the month, while we're trying to build a real collective thing here, a united front. They drive any way they want, don't even know how to speak French. They're giving the brand and the profession a bad name. I swear on the Quran of Mecca, if there are any LOTI drivers here and you dare to open your trap, I'll knock you out. I've got a family to feed, house payments, car payments."

Some of the guys smiled discreetly; others nodded. LOTI drivers are drivers who work for a boss who provides everything: car, gas, phone. All they do is drive. But it's just more bullshit. LOTI drivers are the lowest dudes on the totem pole, the ones who really can't do anything else. The electronic ankle bracelet kind of dudes.

Another guy piped up.

"Right on, man. You've said it pretty well, and we work our asses off, that's as it should be. Yeah, there are LOTI drivers who fuck things up, but they're a minority, and we don't want to go down because of them. Instead of criticizing the French all the time, stop and think for a minute. Our problem isn't the whites, it's the sons of bitches who manage the platforms. We've got to get rid of the platforms, brothers. If the government ran the platform, I'm sure the commission would be lower. Sure of it."

"What are you talking about? You think we'd be driving if the whites left us room to do anything else?"

Driver after driver spoke up. Everyone had his own opinion on the platform's closure. I didn't know what to say. Regardless of anything else, in the short term, they were all going to turn to the competition, and the customers would do the same. Some of them were already driving for both platforms, but that meant a permanent juggling act with your phone, because you could be assigned two fares at the same time, and if you turned down a fare, your rating dropped.

There'd be even less money to go around in the months to come. You used to be able to make 300 or even 350 euros in one day, bro. Even with two days off a week, you could earn 7,000 or 8,000 a month. After you took out the platform's commission of 1,600 euros, 700 euros for VAT, 500 euros for the car payment, 600 for gas, and 200 for insurance, you were still left with 3,000 to 4,000 a month.

The stab in the back was when they lowered the rates to keep the customers happy. We suffered from that one directly. The platform could have chosen to reduce its commission. But no; it was always about making as much money as possible on the backs of the poor working stiffs. It's our own fault; we're like an army of starving losers jumping at the tiniest scraps until they're gone. Those sons of bitches. They've got it nice and easy behind their computer screens. They created the software, and we, being stupid as dogs, drive all over the city just to put food in the fridge. Now that the riders pay less, the people who want to keep earning a good living just pile on the hours. The idea of thirthy-five-hour work week has become a joke among drivers. A 200-euro day and you feel like you've won the fucking lottery. In the end, some poor saps work fifty to seventy hours a week for 1,500 to 2,000 euros a month, with a bunch of debt hanging over them.

Like many others, I've cheated the tax man. No choice. The idea is not to declare everything you bill for, so you pay less in taxes. You do what you have to do. Nobody's gone down for it yet. Fortunately, I bought my car with the cash left over from my previous life. Bam. Thinking about that made me feel a little bit better. Problems are like cockroaches; they always come all at once. Impossible to eradicate them completely. The only solution is to move somewhere else.

I was just about to leave the 120 when Le Gwen called me. It always sends a chill down my spine when his name shows up on my phone and there are people around me. Especially guys I've known for a long time. I picked up to tell him I'd call him back in five minutes. I said goodbye to everyone, got in my car, and headed for Bauer Stadium in Saint-Ouen, to get myself a safe distance away. You never knew if somebody might be listening. I called him back.

"Are you coming to see me about your permit? It's important, come soon."

The whole business with the points and the license had totally slipped my mind. If I didn't watch it, I wouldn't be able to drive anymore—although, really, I probably would, because they never actually check those things. All these regulations are ridiculous. We're all going to end up like the government minister who didn't pay his taxes. "Administrative phobia," there you go! Fucking hell, I've got other things to do besides passing my test again. Why does everything always happen to me, Goddammit?

"When do I need to come?"

"As soon as possible! Tomorrow?"

"Okay, I'll call you back to confirm."

I spent the rest of the day driving, customer-hunting, and it went fine. I handed out "hellos" like the ticket machine at the prefecture. Since it was Friday, I headed for the Gare du Nord. English tourists would be coming in for a weekend in Paris. Lot of good fares to be had. The algorithm assigns them to cars nearby. Best to stay near the station, but without being too close, or the taxi drivers would hassle you. It was all about private-hire driving on the radio today. On one hand, there was the closure of the platform, and on the other, there was the conflict with taxis. The minister of the economy gave a radio interview on the subject. Even though he was a former banker, he seemed like a good guy who understood what young people wanted. The journalist tried to trap him by talking about the condition of taxis since Uber came on the scene, but the minister was too clever for him; he changed the subject to the situation of young people in the *banlieues*, with philosophical arguments: equality of access to work, integration through jobs, social diversity, and all that stuff people who think they're doing good by talking say. He'd made the journalist look like an idiot, so the guy started sputtering, becoming aggressive, but the minister dominated the situation with his calmness. Respect! Because usually it's the opposite. He'd chosen to be on the side of truth and to say aloud what everyone was silently thinking: in the face of competition from private hires, the taxi drivers had started acting like mafiosos. Aggression, threats. It all must have been making Pop's blood boil as he listened to it. Debate, discussion, moderation—they were alien to his nature. The old man never doubts himself, ever. According to him, he's always right. And in this case he was convinced that private-hire driving should be outlawed.

In the meantime, we, the angry, screwed-up young people, had taken over the suits and the steering wheels; we weren't hanging out in the lobbies anymore. The minister proposed solutions for us, and he was the first one to do it in a long time, man. Because the others—the assholes, whether they were taxi drivers, bosses, politicians, or, generally speaking, everyone who gets up in the morning to go to work, has two kids, and votes for the same old crap every five years—they spent their time smacking us on the head the minute we moved a muscle to try to break the cycle of bullshit and get out. When you break through in sports or music, they clap for you like circus monkeys. But then there were the people from our part of town, who tried to move into their world. Forced to close their mouths to survive and forget where they came from. The world of assholes sucks. I'm no intellectual, but I have noticed one thing. The roots of a tree spread to where there's space. If the tree has water and sun, it will have the energy it needs to grow, and sprout leaves and flowers, and its roots will spread where they can. Potted plants? They never grow, they resist nothing, and you have to do a lot more to take care of them. There's a reason rap was born in the *banlieue*: the ground's conducive to it. Laws exist, but we disregard some of the rules to broaden the range of possibilities. We don't consider anything forbidden, and we explore the world. And that inevitably makes things happen—good things, and less good things, but it makes things happen. In thirty years, rappers have become the biggest-selling musicians in this country. At a time when they say young people don't read anymore, rappers are the only ones writing.

An English couple got in my car at the Gare du Nord. The man had a Rolex on his wrist. They had a reservation at a hotel in a really shitty *banlieue*, Clichy. Incomprehensible. As I drove back up toward the beltway, I offered up a few words in English to start the conversation rolling. Unlike with people who hail taxis, our clients are usually nicer to us. The conversations are better, and occasionally you can scam them just a little tiny bit; it doesn't hurt anyone, and it fills up the coffers. My rate that day added a few extra beltway exits. I only ever slip in a tiny pinch, and only with tourists. If you do it with Parisians, man, it makes them vote for the National Front. Gotta be on your best behavior with them.

The English guy, his watch, and his fat wife got out of the car. I turned up the volume on the radio. A spokesman from the taxi drivers' union was talking. His voice held the cumulative rage of all the drivers losing a little bit more income every day. The minister calmly let the missiles fly past him. The spokesman announced that there was going to be a big rally next Wednesday, to block off the Place de la Nation and the Porte de Vincennes. The last time that happened, at the Place de la République, it had turned everything into a huge mess. My dad would be there on Wednesday for sure. I knew him like the back of my hand: since my brother left, it was his only reason for living.

I picked up a couple of students in Levallois-Perret. They were going to the airport. They'd barely gotten in the car when the guy said they were in a hurry and already running late for their flight, which meant: "Can you drive any faster, buddy?" I said, "I'll do everything I can to get you there on time," the magical phrase that always makes the customer feel better. In reality, I wanted to tell him it wasn't my problem and they should have ordered a car earlier, because I didn't want to risk getting pulled over for speeding. But, thinking of the rating they'd give me after the ride, I held my tongue.

In the rearview mirror, I could see the guy's hand resting on the girl's thigh. It slipped down to stroke the inner part, before moving slowly toward her zipper. The girl pushed it away, discreetly, whispering a few words in his ear. The guy was too horny, and that didn't calm him down. This time he pressed his lips next to her ear, and his hand made another move toward her zipper. Then it slid up under her shirt, toward her chest. I could see the chick's irritated smile in the rearview mirror, but she didn't do anything else to make him stop. To keep things tantalizingly ambiguous? To make me jealous? Maybe she liked the look of me . . . ?

The girl might have been twisted, but the guy was even more so. Deep down, these two assholes had no shame. Getting it on in the back seat of the car of the poor working stiff driving them around. Well, it takes all kinds to make a world. We're not ayatollahs. But, shit, you can't go too far, either. It's not a question of morals, but girls and sex are a rare commodity. Putting yourself on display in front of everyone like that is ostentatious. It creates desire, frustration. And then reaction and violence.

My phone rang. It was Pop. I answered it with my hands-free headset, so as not to take my hands off the wheel. The old man was complaining because I hadn't showed up to dinner that night. It's true that this was a ritual I almost never missed. I told him I was overwhelmed by life. "But I can help you," he said. I wanted to say, "Come and save us, Dad," but my brother had made the decision to leave him out of it for the moment, and I couldn't afford to add another layer to the problem.

Hearing me talking to my old man on the phone, the guy in the back seat stopped his chest-groping cold. His knitted brow in the rearview mirror told me exactly what he was thinking: *Fucking thug.* It was all well and good for him to feel up his girl in front of me, because he was the customer. I was the service provider, slave to his money for the duration of the ride, so I had to respect the rules. No choice. I hung up. No point in rocking the boat over something so trivial. That's what sucks about a world where cash is king; you have to give in, otherwise you can wave goodbye to the money along with the people who have it. The asshole in the back seat muttered something in a low voice to his girlfriend, before crossing his arms and staring angrily out the window.

The two fuckwits got out of the car at Roissy. The guy walked away without a word, but the girl's goodbye was accompanied by an apologetic look. She was definitely into me.

When I was a little kid, I used to ride along with my dad to the airport a lot, to pick up customers and get the good fares. Taxi drivers like to call it Guantanamo. Pop had to wait in line for three hours for one client. Just killing time in his car. A prison. Since our apartment was in Bobigny, halfway between central Paris and the airport, every morning the old man would get behind the wheel and ask himself the question: Down into the mines—Paris—or up to Guantanamo?

I parked the car in the parking lot and went into the airport to see what was what, settling down at a café in the departure hall. The place was teeming as usual: rolling suitcases, hurrying flight attendants, loudspeaker announcements, baggage carts squeaking, military types making the rounds. There were all kinds of travelers: men, women, old, young, poor, rich, all religions, ethnicities, and nationalities; it was like the Tower of Babel, or Noah's Ark. Across from me, the destinations of departing flights flashed on a huge lighted board: Tokyo, Istanbul, New York, Rome, Los Angeles, Singapore, Islamabad, Moscow, New Delhi, Dakar, Rio, Montreal, Mexico, Bangkok, Kinshasa, Boston, Buenos Aires, Saint Petersburg. My brother and I could have gone anywhere in the world. He had nothing to lose, and I didn't have much. The car? I could sell it, or total it for the insurance. The apartment was just a rental. My job and my girl? I'd find others. Little brother was wanted, and we'd have to find a way to get out of the country without going through French border control. We had to make a plan to turn things around.

On the board, Porto and Lisbon caught my eye. I looked from one to the other, and the wheels started turning in my head. The ideas came faster and faster—like the shadow of a solution was hovering, and I was circling around and around it without quite being able to put my finger on it. Then, suddenly, like when Tintin shouts "Eureka!" all the pieces fell into place, and it came to me. I remembered last summer at Mickaël's family's place. It was magnificent, man. We spent a month with his family and his cousins. Everyone loved me. I was French, and a little bit Syrian, but no one gave a shit over there. Portugal was the good life. We could go there while we were on the run, figure out a plan to go somewhere else after.

Maybe Brazil! In the land of the samba, nobody would be looking for my brother, and he could go out in public without fear. There. That was the plan. Simple, quick. No complications expected. A brilliant plan. Better get started as soon as possible.

There was still the question of the old man and Grandma. The old lady, God preserve her, would be going to heaven soon, which was better for her and us. And Pop, when he learned what kind of mess my brother had gotten us into, would only have to bury his mother, sell his license, and follow us. Over there, we'd give him some grandchildren. That would keep him busy.

27
Younger Brother

I n Syria, in the evenings, I watched TV news to follow the
fighting. The only channel that worked was the Kurdish
one. The picture was bad and flickered a lot. I stuck a
fork behind the TV set as an antenna. Every night at eight
o'clock, before the Kurdish-language news, the day's martyrs
were listed. Not just Kurds, but also Arabs, Christians,
Chaldeans, Assyrians, Turks. The whole melting pot of Syria.
The offscreen voice reading the list punctuated the names
with "*Shehid Namirin,*" which, thanks to the Arabic subtitles, I
knew means "Martyrs do not die." One night I saw a picture of
a man I'd met. Danyal, an unassuming shepherd, who had
come to the clinic hoping we would treat his horse. I refused;
he insisted. He had paid a driver and brought the horse here
in the back of a van. He used the animal to fetch water from
the well. He had three kids. I felt sorry for him and took a look
at the horse's injured foot. It was a nail that had gotten stuck
in the hoof. I'd removed it with surgical pliers, disinfected it,
and bandaged the foot.

Danyal was Assyrian, part of a Mesopotamian people that
had been in the region for three thousand years, perched on
the borders between Turkey, Iraq, Syria, and Iran. Christians
who spoke a language descended from Aramaic. I read on the
Internet that the Turks had massacred them a century ago,
like the Armenians. He told me about the village in Turkey
where he was born. When the last Ottomans waged war on
them, the men had gathered in the church. It dated from the

Roman Empire. Seventeen hundred years. The siege lasted forty days. The church did not fall. There were still Ottoman bullets lodged between the stones of the walls. Like everything those people built, it was solid. They'd only built with stone. Well-cut blocks. Rectangular. Perfectly geometric. A race of builders.

I don't know how that humble shepherd got mixed up in the war. He was the kind of guy you saw in Kobanî. They would never give up anything. Not a centimeter of land. They resisted all invaders for almost three thousand years: the Babylonians, the Hittites, the Romans, the Seljuqs, the Ottomans, the Mamluks, the English. The Kurds were in the process of establishing a small state in Syria, and they left Arabs and Assyrians as administrative governors. The day I saw his picture on TV, I tried to imagine Danyal's whole life, from birth to death. What he believed in. Why had this peasant joined the Kurdish fighters?

At home, Leïla's son had been sick for a month. Nothing major, just a case of spring bronchitis, but medicine was lacking. The boy cried all the time. We lived in an Assyrian house, with thick walls, but you could still hear him. The other son never spoke to me. When I came home from work in the evening, Leïla always told him to give his father a kiss. He'd stand there sulking, arms folded, like a spoiled kid from back home. One day she forced him, pulling him by the ear. She practically tore the thing off. The boy rebelled, grabbing a shoe and hurling at my head, screaming, "He isn't my father!" She beat him with her fists for that. I went up to the roof so I wouldn't have to hear it. He wasn't my kid. And I didn't want to fight with her. I lit a cigarette. Even though it was forbidden. Here, you have no right to smoke. No right to do this. No right to do that. No movies. No music. The men were afraid of everything. Other men, women, friends, enemies, the sun, God. So they prayed. Prayer and death and no laughter.

The cigarettes were contraband from Turkey, and criminally expensive. If a guard saw me smoking, he was allowed to shoot. I had to stay alive. I smoked one cigarette a day, at night, on my roof. We were in the Holy Land, the land of the Bible; since the beginning of time, people here had been ripping each other to shreds in God's name. I looked toward the north. Behind me, the plains stretched out all the way to Cairo. 1,500 kilometers. In front of me, thirty kilometers away, was Turkey. Freedom. So close, but so far. It was as if Mom were calling me. But you didn't leave Cham without a reason. Some had tried and ended up blowing themselves to bits by stepping on a mine. Others had fallen under a hail of bullets from a Kalashnikov. There were also the poor guys who were caught up with by Jeeps. Decapitated or hung in the market square, to set an example. And then there were the rare ones who made it out . . . and then came back. The Turks often sent them back. Well, they'd drop them off at a checkpoint, and they'd be recovered there and taken straight to the marketplace for a date with the sword or the rope. You didn't leave Cham; you stayed until the end of time, and prayed and fought and made babies. It wasn't a war, it was a revolution; you marched or you died. The border was so close, and so far. Freedom, too.

P ortugal? What do you mean, Portugal?"
"POR-TU-GAL. You hot for Portugal?"
"What am I supposed to do in Portugal?"
"You're a nurse, idiot. You can find a job anywhere!"

"No, I mean, I know that. But where would I go in Portugal? Where would I stay?"

"Well, I've got a plan. You'll go stay with my buddy Mickaël."

"Who?"

"You know, Mickaël, the Portuguese guy."

"The one you got arrested with?"

"Yup!"

"Have you talked to him about this?"

"No. But he's already suggested it to me. There won't be any problem. He's got a house there. All I have to tell him is that I have a cousin who wants to lie low for a while, and he won't say anything."

"And what if he turns us in later?"

"Don't worry. We got busted together, and I still have info on him. Hood solidarity, bro."

"What's it like where he lives?"

"There's nothing there. A village. Nothing but old people. The sea. The sun. Fields and hills."

He thought about it, doodling with his finger in the bread-crumbs.

"They're way Catholic down there. They can't find out about Syria or any of that, because they'd flip."

"Well, what are you?"

"Me? What do you mean?"

"You're a fucking Catholic on your grandmother's side."

"What the hell are you talking about?"

"I remember when you first went totally nuts for religion. You pretend not to remember because you're ashamed. But you're pure Jesus from Grandma. Breton!"

He laughed. "Whatever."

He asked me for a cigarette, opened the window, and lit up. His chest rose with the first drag, and he asked:

"What about you?"

"Me? I'll deal with things here and then join you."

"No, but I mean, what will you do there?"

"Don't know; I'll see. I've got the car, and a little money set aside. Not much, but we can start a new life, or go somewhere else."

"Where?"

"Brazil, bro."

His eyes gleamed for a second like a kid with a big stick of cotton candy. Then he was lost in thought again.

"What about Dad, and Grandma?"

OLDER BROTHER

It was Sunday evening. My brother had been back for a week. And he already had to leave again. It was killing me. Because, at the end of the day, it wasn't really his fault. He was a good kid, a little naive, head in the clouds. He didn't know what he was doing. But you don't exist alone on this earth, and there were other people who wanted nothing more to do with him. He had to disappear. He had to go.

"How long does it take to get there? Portugal?"

"Twenty hours or so by car. Pack your bag; we'll leave tomorrow. I'm going to call Mickaël to get the key. We can't hang around here."

"Tomorrow? That's too soon."

"You're crazy, man! What do you want to do here?"

He raised his eyes to the ceiling and drew in a deep breath.

"Give me a cigarette."

After the first puff, he answered:

"Not before Wednesday. Come on, wait. I just got back. Give me a minute to breathe."

"Wednesday?"

"That's three days away."

"What about Dad?"

He sighed. "I need to go see Grandma first."

"Tomorrow's Monday and you can't. That's the only day they don't allow visitors. We'll go on Tuesday."

"Not until the day before we leave?"

"No choice. Should have thought of that before. And Pop?"

"Let it go. It'll only cause more problems."

I let it go.

On Monday I drove to earn a little more cash. Bring in a few more euros before we took off. My brother spent the whole day out walking. He said, "I need to say goodbye to my life here." I didn't dare say anything to him about it. He might as well enjoy himself a little bit, because he might never see this world again. It wasn't prudent, but with the baseball cap and bike I lent him, there was no way anyone would spot him. That's how I moved weed when I was younger.

On Tuesday we went to visit our grandmother. Her nursing home was in western Paris. The opposite side of town from where we lived. In a trendy suburb on the edge of a forest full of very tall, very old trees. It was an ancient manor house that had been turned into a nursing home. Very chic for an old lady who'd come from Aleppo half-ruined. It cost plenty, but Pop wanted only the best for her, and he put her there so she'd be well taken care of. First time anyone in the family had been allowed to a little luxury. For her to be ending her days in a swanky five-star establishment like this, well, it was bizarre. Of course it was. It had been one of Dad's ideas, after all.

Whenever I walk into a retirement home, I have to wonder if old people still have any sense of smell. Probably not, otherwise they'd have run away already. As soon as you step through the doors, an indefinable scent hits you like a wall. It doesn't smell dirty or bad, exactly; it's a mixture of camphor, sweat, old scabs, dead skin, rotten fingernails, bad breath, full beds, and disinfectant. Even after a year of visits, I hadn't gotten used to it.

At the reception desk, we said my brother was a cousin. No choice; the biggest risk was that Pop would find out about it, otherwise we didn't give a fuck about the staff there, and unless the cops had hidden microphones in the old people's beds, nobody here could possibly find out he was my brother. The receptionist asked him for some ID, and I braced myself for failure. He rummaged in his pockets and brought out a card from Pompidou Hospital. I glared at him to say, *What the fuck are you doing?* The girl started scribbling something in the visitors' book, and I saw that the name written on the card wasn't his. He smiled at me. *Don't worry.*

Grandma's room was on the third floor. Up an iron staircase, at the end of a dark, narrow hallway, behind a half-open door. The scene was surreal. A very old gentleman, tall and red-faced, broad-shouldered and elegant, was standing in front of the mirror in my grandma's room, finger in the air, talking to his reflection in the glass:

"In my school notebooks
On my desk and the trees
In the sand in the snow
I WRITE YOUR NAME!"

It sounded like something from elementary school, but I couldn't remember what it was.

"'Liberty,'" my brother whispered, "It's 'Liberty' by Paul Éluard. Remember when Dad badgered you into memorizing it?"

The old man turned around.

"Get the hell out of here. I'm not going to Germany."

"Pardon?"

"I said I'm not going to Germany. I have a family."

"Excuse me, sir, but I don't understand what you mean. We're looking for our grandmother, and this is her room."

He continued to rant threateningly at his double in the mirror.

"Stay there, Paul. Why are you leaving? You're afraid of Colonel Tixier. We're going to liberate France, but help me make him understand that working for him doesn't mean we're going Kraut-hunting."

"I think he's touched in the head," whispered my brother in my ear. "Must be an Alzheimer's patient."

"Answer me, Tixier!"

Suddenly, the man threw a punch at the mirror, which shattered into a sunburst. The old scoundrel might not have too many brain cells left, but he still had a mean right hook. His hand was all bloody.

"*Collabo!* Traitor!"

"Sir, don't move. I'm going to get help. Stay with him."

"Go on, lad. I'll deal with Tixier. He's a Nazi!"

At the front desk, the nursing assistant looked up at me slowly. I told him the old man had broken the mirror. He didn't seem too worried about it.

"Him again . . . Okay, I'm coming."

He moved like someone who was tired of everything, even himself.

"He's got Alzheimer's disease. Since he can walk, we transferred him to room 204, and, for your grandmother's comfort, we moved her down to room eighteen, here on the ground floor. That way it's easy for us to take her out."

Gray vinyl flooring, high-gloss white-painted walls, and one door after another: it was like a chicken coop for humans. We went into room eighteen without knocking. Quietly, we sat down on the bench next to her bed. Always the same ritual, for four years now. The war had ruined the old lady for good. No more words, her face expressionless. Just her eyes moving, observing the world around her. I didn't know what was keeping her alive. What was her reason for living? Personally, I don't believe you stay alive just for the sake of it. Without a reason, you just fade away. So if she was still alive, that had to mean that somewhere, deep down, there was still something giving her reason to hope.

We sat silently side by side, looking at her. I could feel my brother's knee quivering against my thigh. He looked sad, his hands folded in his lap. I tried to sneak a sideways glance at his eyes. Tears, or not? I think that if I'd seen him cry, I would have lost it too. For fuck's sake, our grandma was in this goddamned bed, lying on the white sheets, her face turned to the window, her gaze distant, waiting to die. The Japanese cherry tree outside the window was taller than the second floor. Maybe they were the same age. I took her hand. Immediately, she recognized the texture of my skin. Her fingers closed over mine. Her peasant's hand, the top soft and the palm hard, that skin, I'd known it forever. In the muscles of her fingers, I could feel the thousands of hours spent kneading dough, peeling vegetables, cooking, sewing, cleaning house, digging, sowing, planting, harvesting, loving, and smacking her children.

"*Jidda*, it's me," my brother said.

Her hand released mine. Slowly, she turned toward him. The first miracle: a smile. Then her eyelids, her lips, her chin perked up, her eyes grew moist, and I saw tears flow softly, silently, down her face and along her nose. She *was* still alive. She *could* still think. She had Alzheimer's, too, but there was still some part of her left. I'd visited her fifty, a hundred times, brought her strawberries and vanilla ice cream and bonbons, washed her and rubbed her feet, brushed her hair, told her about my day, my life, to stimulate her memory, her mind, but nothing. Until now we'd thought that, in her mind, everything had stayed back in Aleppo. She coughed and indicated to her glass of water. I motioned to my brother to take care of it. He leaned closer, delicately, stroked her forehead, then kissed it, before reaching for the glass of water and helping her to drink. Life is about balance; yesterday she was the one raising us, cleaning us up, feeding us, educating us, and now I was watching the other dog take care of her. She drank in little sips. We told her she needed to drink to stay alive, because old people stop being able to tell when they're thirsty. So now, to hold on to life, her lips clung to the glass like suckers. As if someone were going to steal it from her. She coughed again, then puckered her lips into a heart shape to give a kiss. My brother leaned closer to her, and she pressed her thin lips to his clean-shaven cheek.

"You . . . shaved . . . off . . . your . . . beard?"

Her voice came from the very depths of her lungs. A quavering voice, like a soft breeze. She'd asked the question in Arabic, to which my brother responded with a smile. She motioned for him to come closer. He leaned in again. During the five minutes that followed, I could hear snippets of Arabic, but without being able to tell what she was saying to him. When she finished, she gestured for him to sit down again, and without a glance at me, she turned her face back toward the Japanese cherry tree. It was 11:59 A.M. The caregivers would be coming at any minute to feed her. She fell a few months ago, and since then she hadn't been able to walk. So she was bedridden. Sometimes the staff put her in a wheelchair and took her for a walk in the park, but often she didn't want to be handled. A question of modesty, undoubtedly.

My telephone rang. It was Le Gwen. I left the room and answered in a whisper, my hand over my mouth for fear my brother would hear.

"Hello?"

"Hello! Where are you! What are you doing? You haven't called me back. Why didn't you come on Saturday? You need to come see me NOW. It's incredibly important."

"Why 'incredibly?'"

"Extremely urgent. Why are you whispering?"

"I'm visiting my . . ."

What a fucking idiot I was. If he ever looked at the security camera footage, or the visitors' log, he'd see that I wasn't alone. And he'd trace it back to us . . .

"Where are you?"

"At the movies."

"Come as soon as you can. After the movie, if possible."

"Okay, I'll see what I can do."

Shit. Anyway, we were leaving soon. In my grandma's room, a nursing assistant was feeding her.

"Who was that?"

"Nothing. A buddy of mine."

"Why'd you tell him you were at the movies?"

"So he wouldn't hassle me."

"I heard you whispering, okay? You a secret agent now, or what?"

"You're an idiot. I just didn't want to disturb the old people."

The aide was spooning food between our grandmother's worn lips. Like a little child, she smiled as she ate. Mouthful after mouthful, her eyelids drooped, and soon she couldn't keep her eyes open.

"Eating really tires her out. She'll be asleep soon."

The old lady didn't open her eyes again. We left. In the car, my brother was in his own little world, but I could tell he was really back home now, among us. Put back on track through some magic trick that only my grandmother could perform. He stared out the window silently, speechless, a faint smile on his lips. What had she said to him, to make him grow years older in just a few minutes? My dad berated his old lady when the kid brother left. He blamed her for teaching us about Islam when we were kids. What he didn't understand, though, is that, deep down, my brother didn't become passionate about Islam because of Grandma, or because Mom died. That had nothing to do with it. He's a mystic, and he had his first real mystical experience in Brittany, when we were staying with our other grandmother, Mamie Malo. It was better that someone at home had taught us about religion, anyway, because otherwise we'd have learned about it on the streets, with the pressure of the ghetto. And you know where people who learn on the streets end up.

I was fifteen, and my brother was thirteen. We'd gone to visit our maternal grandmother, the *Bretonne*. We didn't see her very much, and it wasn't easy to love her, really, because she was too different from us. We were from Bobigny, we played soccer in the street, we stole bikes and scooters, and our supreme insults were *Go fuck yourself* and *Shitty Frenchman*. That summer we were staying with her in Saint-Malo, and we had to act like everything was fine, because we couldn't make our mother's old lady sad. She was nice, and she loved us. Every Christmas and on our birthdays, she sent cards and gifts. So, one day that summer, in Saint-Malo, we were at a newsstand with her, and when we got to the register, my brother put a magazine down on top of my grandmother's newspaper and my soccer magazine: *The World of Religions: God, the Cosmos, and Infinity*. I remember because it cost at least thirty francs. Grandma bought it without batting an eyelash, because it was reading material, whereas I had to beg her, elaborately, for a twenty-franc pair of Brazilian flip-flops the day before. Anyway. For days after that, it was like my brother was hypnotized. I could see his pupils frenetically scanning the lines of text, one after the other. At the beach, at the café, at home, in the car. He devoured the thing maybe five or six times, until he knew it by heart. He stood looking silently out to sea, his gaze on the horizon, watching the motion of the waves.

"Did you see that girl over there?"

"Fuck, it's huge."

"What are you talking about?"

"The universe."

"You're an idiot. Look at all these girls. The little English ones, and everything. Why are you talking about the stars, dummy?"

One weekend we left for our grandmother's hometown, to spend the rest of the vacation there. It was a tiny village between Brest and Saint-Brieuc. Two hundred people, a *crêperie*, and a church. The priest was a childhood friend of our grandma's. Maybe they'd even had a love affair once. He was an old guy but not too old, and nice, with a round face, who whispered his words like they'd fall out of his mouth if he pushed them too hard. Entering the churchyard, the first thing we saw was a huge Japanese telescope. Now that I think back on it, the priest must have really been sick of this little ass-backward Breton town to buy himself a telescope. He told us you could see the stars much better out here than in Paris. With his finger, he pointed out the evening star.

"That's Venus. He didn't put it there for no reason."

"He? Who?"

"God the Almighty, my son. Everything has a purpose. There are no coincidences."

"Even me?"

"Yes, my son. Doing good is our main purpose."

At that exact moment, I saw my younger brother's eyes change. They became glassy, like when he was reading his magazine. In the evenings, our grandma let us go and look at the stars with the priest. My brother asked thousands of questions. He talked about time, and infinity especially, and he insisted that the priest give him answers, and the priest talked about the apostles and Jesus and the Gospel as best he could. The kid brother said:

"But I don't understand. If God can do anything, can he create a planet, or not?"

The priest flashed his knowledgeable peasant's smile before replying that he himself wasn't God, with His ability to answer every question.

"And the Big Bang, was that really God? Because if it was, what was there before that?"

My eyelids were drooping. I left. The kid brother came home half an hour later. I couldn't sleep; I was thinking about Mom. He gazed out the window, still looking at the stars.

"I don't know why we're here, really. It doesn't make sense. Why did God create us?"

"Dunno, man. You're getting on my nerves with your weird questions. Go to sleep, okay?"

"We really found God a long time ago, He's infinity. And He's everywhere. You can't really know what infinity is."

"Is your mouth infinite too?"

"Come on, listen to me for five minutes. You look at space, right? What if you come to the end of it, and there's a wall. But if you climb to the top of the wall and look over it, there will be something else there. If you jump over to the other side of the wall and keep moving, you'll find another wall. You can climb that one, too, and there'll be another one, further on, and so on. There's no end. It's endless, the universe. Infinite."

I'll admit, he surprised me. I started thinking about his idea of the wall, and the fact that space is infinite, and it gave me a headache. I was in bed under the covers, but I felt like I was falling through space, falling off a building, about to die. Except that it was endless. My heart pounded and I clutched at my quilt, but I couldn't slow myself down. Then, gradually, I stopped in front of a sort of yellow, red, and blue star, like a ball of energy. I think I was at the beginning of the universe. When I remember that, I think it wasn't the ganja that turned me half-brain-dead; I already was, and the weed only made it all worse. Later, maybe about five o'clock in the morning, I woke up when a rooster crowed. My brother's bedside lamp was still on. I could hardly open my eyes, but in the snippet of an image that did manage to reach my corneas, I saw him reading a book.

"Hey, why aren't you asleep?"

"Leave me alone. I'm reading."

"You're turning into Dad now, with your books. Nerd."

"Come on, go back to sleep. Leave me alone."

So I went back off into my own little world, my head on the pillow and in the clouds. With Mom. That night, she told me

206 · MAHIR GUVEN

to take care of my kid brother, because he didn't know what he was doing; he was too young, and too curious about everything. Hungry for the world, for people, books, things. Then she was gone again, with her cigarette in her hand. She flew off the balcony and away. And I saw my old man crying in the living room.

In the morning, the sun's rays tickled my eyelids, and I woke up. The clock read 10:15 A.M. My brother was sleeping on his back with the book open, covering his face: the Chouraqui Bible. Had the priest given it to him? That was the first thing I asked him when he came down to the kitchen for breakfast. It was almost noon.

"He lent it to me."

He annoyed me for the rest of the vacation. He spent his time going to see the priest, to ask him questions. The old guy must have been happy to have recruited a new follower, because there weren't many people in France going the Jesus route anymore. My brother lost himself in the New Testament, talking about it with the old priest for hours. I went with him at first, but I got tired of it pretty quickly; I don't know, it wasn't from our era. But the kid dove headfirst into it; he remembered everything, every passage, every story, the prophets, Jesus, God, Abraham, the myths, the tribes, the apostles, the baptisms, the saints. God was everywhere. In the heart of every man, and in every part of life. The plants, animals, sea, waves. The rest of the vacation was a bunch of crap. I was all alone, because the kid had his head in the clouds and didn't want to do anything. I ended up helping my grandmother in the kitchen, waiting patiently for the end of summer, when the old man would come to get us, and we'd go back to Bobigny, and school and soccer would start up again, and we'd be with the neighborhood family, with our kind of people again, before my brother turned into some kind of Catholic superman.

After the nursing home, I dropped my younger brother off at the apartment. I didn't know what to think anymore; my brother's return, my grandma talking again—it should have made me happy, but nothing comes for free in this life, and even miracles have a price. The bill for all this shit was the collapse of my world. The only path now was to run away. I wanted to get the hell out of here as fast as possible, take him to Portugal, and then come back and quietly bring my life here to a close: shut down my business properly, sell my furniture, empty out the apartment, maybe sell my car, collect what a bunch of different people owed me, party with Mehmet and the others until dawn. Without telling them I was leaving, of course, so as not to raise suspicion.

Le Gwen was waiting for me. I left the car in the parking lot and walked to the station on foot. On the second floor, he greeted me in a cloud of cigarette smoke, with dark circles under his eyes and new lines in his face.

"Was the movie any good?"

He caught me by surprise, I must admit. I jumped like a bomb had gone off. I'd forgotten what I told him on the phone.

"Yeah."

"Who were you with?"

"My girl."

"Your grandmother?"

"What do you mean? I was with my girl."

"But I thought you were getting sick of the fat one."

"No, it's serious."

"Ah."

He sighed.

"Got nothing to say to me?" he asked.

Silence. Doubt, in the beginning, is a tiny drop of water.

"Like what?"

"Like, what you were doing this afternoon?"

"Huh?"

"Where were you this afternoon?"

"At the movies."

"What did you see?"

"Uh . . . the thing . . . the one with . . ."

I couldn't remember what was playing right now. He answered for me.

"*Liar Liar*? With Jim Carrey?"

I couldn't keep from smiling, because he was trying to be tough, but it was just pathetic. Just like me, he spent his time lying. He wasn't in a joking mood today. He slammed his fist down on the table.

"Why are you lying?"

Doubt is a leaky faucet. Drop by drop, doubt hollows out the soil, digs its path in the ground.

"Why're you so desperate for me to be lying? I went to see *Mad Max*."

He lit a third cigarette.

"Okay, listen. Stop the lies. I had your phone tracked. First, you were at your grandmother's nursing home. And second, there was another phone there, another number in your name."

Doubt is intimate. It's in the deepest part of you, a candle you light next to the big book that is your brain. Doubt starts with a flame, burning the corner of a page.

"I was with a buddy of mine."

"Why are you lying? Who were you with?"

"Mehmet."

I shouldn't have lied. He could check that by having Mehmet's phone traced.

"Doesn't he have his restaurant to run?"

"We went to pray for my grandma."

"And why does he have a phone in your name?"

"I gave him a SIM card."

"Why?"

"It was an emergency. He just needed one because he lost his phone, so I lent him one until he could get a new number."

"Sure, yeah, because you're just that kind of guy, right?"

"Hey, we've been friends since elementary school, okay? Calm down."

Le Gwen was being a weird bastard that day. I couldn't figure out if he knew. If he was tracking me, then he must. He was bouncing all over the place, but he was in control of the situation. He was capable of telling a lie to lure you out of your hiding place, and then squeeze you like a lemon. Sometimes firm and authoritarian, sometimes warm and jokey. The hard part was knowing when he was playing the cop role and when he was being himself. In the end, whatever happened, he'd put you through the blender, and you'd end up a smoothie. He'd done the same thing when I got arrested. He was a pro.

"Your brother used to work at Pompidou Hospital, didn't he?"

"Yeah. So?"

"So, my friend, I've got a big problem. A big, big problem. A huge problem with your brother."

"Like what?"

I felt like I was burning up. The heat started in my cheeks and spread out to my ears; sweat trickled down my back. I tried to focus. Fuck. I was walking a balance beam, and Hurricane Le Gwen was blowing. I just had to get through this one bad moment. Someone must have seen my brother and ratted him out. He must have had us followed. But I had to keep my mouth shut. Without proof, what he said didn't mean anything; just a cop's word.

"What are you talking about?"

In the city, every street kid worth his salt lies as well as any cheating husband. Lying isn't about yes or no; it's about saying nothing, which drives the cops crazy.

"I'm not going to beat around the bush. There's been a theft at Pompidou Hospital."

"Yeah, I saw that in *Le Parisien*."

"Oh, yeah? And why did that interest you?"

He was sticking to his guns. But so was I. And mine were bigger. Well, I think so. Not sure.

"I read the paper every morning."

"What for?"

"Hey, come on, dude, what do you want? Take a vacation, okay? I just came for my license."

Suddenly, he was screaming.

"Fuck your license, and fuck your fucking life. Stop lying to me, asshole! Your brother! Your fucking brother, Goddammit!"

Doubt is a black wave that crashes over your certainties, submerges them, and finally takes over the reins of your spirit.

"What about my brother?"

I played dumb. Even when doubt ascends the throne, there are still a few members of the resistance left to fight. You have to keep them alive, because doubt can be an error in judgment. In this case, your soldiers have to retake power very fast, to clear up the doubt.

"The theft at Pompidou Hospital. They found fingerprints. Your brother's."

Doubt is a shadow swirling around you, an idea hovering over you, whispering in your ear.

"That's normal; he used to work there."

"Do you think I'm stupid? That was three years ago, his fingerprints would have been wiped away by now. And there's another big problem, and that's what was stolen. Acetone, caustic soda, potassium, chlorine. In large quantities. Access to the storeroom is through an armored door via security badge. The night of the theft, only one person went in, with a badge that wasn't in your brother's name. But see, the last time that badge was used in the hospital was three years ago. Before your brother left."

What was the truth? Was what he was saying true? Was he lying? Maybe someone had snitched, and he was sounding me out? Fucking Le Gwen. What should I do now? I denied everything, and defended my turf like a vicious dog. Barking no to each of his questions. No, I don't know anything. No, I haven't seen my brother. No, I was mistaken at the bus station. No, *rien, rien de rien, non, je ne regrette rien*. I regret nothing. Not hiding him, and not helping him get away.

Life in Raqqa was harder than it had been in Al-Bab. In Al-Bab, it wasn't ISIS that controlled things but Blondbeard's organization. Occasionally, we had to go to the capital to buy medicine and supplies, or visit patients who had been transferred to the general hospital. In the past few months, the Russians had started bombarding Raqqa; the bridge across the Euphrates was gone now, so we had to make an hour-long detour north to cross. A nightmare. Half the city was destroyed and deserted, and in the other half, in the rich areas, ISIS members had moved into the abandoned mansions.

I loved passing through the French quarter. It did me good to hear my own language. There were always kids playing soccer in the street. The children of guys from back home. Their parents were living their dream. Creating a nation. Living in the Holy Land. You could recognize the French people immediately. Tracksuits. Nikes. Soccer jerseys. *Kamis* over it all. Sunglasses and everything. Always had style. I'd stop to say hello. While we were shooting the shit, they never failed to ask me what the hell I was doing in Al-Bab. I always dodged the question. They kept to themselves, which was normal, because they couldn't speak much Arabic, which didn't exactly help them assimilate. Plus, the truth was, they were snobs about Syrians. The reality was that the Syrians who stayed behind in Cham were the most backward ones, the hicks, the ones who didn't have the resources to leave: no car, no money, no family abroad. And they really were extremely poor. They were pitiful to look at: no teeth, their clothes in rags. The French people here spoke down to them, aiming veiled insults at them, treating them like ignorant peasants. Guys from the hood, acting like colonialists. Anyway.

The guy who sold us medicine and explosives to manufacture artillery shells was named Abou Fatima. Every time we visited him I had to endure his sermons. "Shave your mustache and let your beard grow. That's an order from the Prophet." My beard was long enough now that in France I'd be seen as a jihadist. But in Raqqa, it was too short, almost reckless. I didn't want to shave my mustache like the Salafists. It made my jaw look too big. "By God the glorious, if you don't shave it, no medicine for you, and no explosives either. You wait and see how your emir likes that." So, that day, I shaved it right then and there. It made my face look bizarre, like the frame of a truck. I looked like a fighter now; all I needed to do to complete the ensemble was learn to fire a gun. We drove the loaded pickup back toward Al-Bab. The road was crowded with fighters and residents of the towns retaken by Bashar's army, streaming toward Raqqa. Soon there wouldn't be enough room there for all of them.

After the capture of the tower, I decided to do my *muaskar*. My military training. I wanted to be a munitions specialist. So, for weeks, after work, I went to the warehouse next to the wedding hall for lessons. It was a huge space where a dozen people manufactured shells, rockets, and bombs for the combatants. Five metalworkers were busy producing empty ammunition. It was noisier than hell. Hammers, drills, sanders, turning out lovely warheads all day long. Of all sizes. For the largest ones, they used empty propane tanks. My job was to make the powder mixtures that would serve as an explosive charge. The formulas were given in a manual in English, French, and Arabic. Often ammonium nitrate, plus nuts, bolts, screws, and nails.

Blondbeard had created the workshop so we wouldn't have to buy munitions in Aleppo anymore. Since the start of the war, several small businesses had changed their production to focus on heavy weapons. The guy in charge of our operation was called Yasser. He had a mustache and very dark skin; you would have thought he was Pakistani. He had the right to shave his beard without getting hassled for it, because without him, there'd be no more ammunition. His left arm ended in a bandaged stump. Bedrettin and I were the ones who'd operated on him. He'd lost a hand—well, half his arm—because of one of his own grenades. They had the defect of exploding at temperatures over ninety-five degrees Fahrenheit, which is what happened while he was giving a demonstration to some combatants. Since then, the grenades were in fridges, and when the *mujahideen* went to the front, they carried them in coolers.

Yasser was in charge of the whole production. He was the former foreman of a factory in eastern Aleppo. Blondbeard had offered him a better salary to come here, and he'd had Yasser's old boss bumped off to be sure he would stay, and then helped himself to all of the other factory's tools. Manufacturing was concentrated on 82-mm and 120-mm shells, like the ones used by Bashar's men—except theirs came from Russia or North Korea. Kids would come help out in the warehouse after school. They'd go to dumps and collect aluminum. In exchange, they were given bread for their families. They also helped us fill the shells. The kids would bring buckets full of powder that we poured into the shells with a ladle and then tamped down with a rod, before screwing a head onto the top. We worked sitting on the floor, amid the empty shells and a pyramid of powder.

Yasser also taught me to make bombs. It was kind of like surgery, but easier. Little by little, I was given the responsibility of preparing explosive drones. These were Chinese devices bought in Turkey, with a range of three hundred to five hundred meters, depending on the weather. You could tape up to three hundred and fifty grams of explosives to each drone. Not much, but enough to injure or even kill enemies, or render a tank inoperable. We guided them with tablets or remote controls. Technically, they had three parts: an electric fuse, a priming explosive, and the main charge. Almost all bombs function that way. Yasser liked to come up with inventive new variants on the ignition system using watches, alarm clocks, and springs. I also learned to create human bombs. They were almost the easiest kind. Mostly you just load a vest with three to five kilos of powder, depending on who's wearing it. It can do a whole lot of damage. I learned everything. Everything I needed to be independent.

I put the whole plan together in my head. I went back to see Blondbeard and told him I wanted to avenge Syria and Muslims. Die as a martyr, so I could be with God. Die for my people. He tried to convince me that it was better for me to provide medical care, but I was determined. So he agreed. Life took another, unexpected turn. For a month, I formulated what I would do, and when I would do it. How to procure the munitions. I felt guilty for abandoning the hospital. Blondbeard recruited a doctor to replace me. A good guy. He told me I'd done excellent work despite my brief training. I thought of my mentors, Naeem in France, and Bedrettin in Syria. Other than Blondbeard, no one knew I was leaving. The operation was risky. For Blondbeard, too, because he would have to show the results to the higher-ups.

The hardest part was Leïla. I didn't know what would happen to her. And there were her little ones. Blondbeard and I agreed that he would look after her. I didn't want her to be sent back to a *madafa*. In reality, this wasn't Raqqa; the emir wouldn't have forced her to remarry, and she could have stayed in the house. I'd gotten used to her. It was good to live with someone. She'd taught me to make everything Dad used to cook. But she had to accept it. The important thing was my mission in France. My plan. To find my way. My path. My journey. And paradise.

32

OLDER BROTHER

I'd left my innocence for dead at the police station. An uppercut right in the truth. A right hook in the temple, and my innocence had fallen, stunned. In the ring, the referee started the countdown. "Ten, nine, eight . . ." In the stands, the crowd cried victory. "Seven, six, five, four, . . ." A complicated match, in which the past buzzed around me, like flies around shit. Or bees on flowers. Depending on which angle you looked from. My past? A tsunami. A tidal wave of problems, limitations, and mistakes, ready to demolish the meager foundations of my world. The only way out was to run. Far away, reducing and dropping what counted just a little or not at all. And then we'd have to detach ourselves from the earth's crust, shake off the dust of our problems and worries, and let them be washed away by the wave. And then we'd have to unroll our new life like a Syrian carpet. I meant it; this wasn't like snatching my towel away from a wave in Saint-Malo. The wave was maybe ten or fifteen years in prison. And in this world of the future with my brother, we hadn't yet found our place. We were just at the beginning of the journey. But we would look for it. When I thought about Pop, who had ditched his homeland for France and never gone back, the little voice in my head whispered: "You'll do the same thing." With my brother. I had to. Family before everything else.

When I opened the apartment door, my brother came out of his room. He asked me if I was okay; his face looked serious. He'd never have done that kind of thing in the past. Had he changed, or just gotten older? How had he spent the day? I didn't even think about it. His presence was like a mirage. He was there, which was incredible enough, but it felt as if he might disappear at any second. I thought I knew everything, but really I knew nothing. He'd told me some vague stuff, and I wanted to trust him. The Prophet said: "Help your brother, whether he is the oppressor or the oppressed. If he is the oppressor, prevent him from oppressing, and in this way you will help him." My brother was both: oppressor and oppressed. But I didn't want to think about all of that. I just acted, and that's all. I'm exactly like my old man that way. As soon as feelings come into the picture, I avoid, I leave, I run, I flee, I get the hell out of there. It prevents nasty surprises, unwelcome events, shifty gazes, disgrace, overly long explanations, sleepless nights, and whatever you might think of it, it's not a bad way of doing things, because time heals all wounds. On the balcony, I brought him a glass of sparkling water with mint leaves, a thing from the old country. I lit a cigarette to get the day out of my head and tried to see through his innocent, boyish expression. It made tears rush to my eyes. The memory of our childhood came back, and memories started bouncing around in my head at top speed, coming from every direction. There could be no doubt. None.

"It's bullshit!"

"Yeah, it's bullshit. You think repeating the same thing over and over like the loudspeaker in a metro station's going to change anything? I've spent years praying for this fucking planet, and men just keep on killing each other. Heaven is nothing but a promise."

He didn't know what I was talking about. Le Gwen, and all that. I couldn't answer him. It was beyond my strength. My hand shook, and I wanted to cry. He'd ruined everything. Everything. I'd avoided prison by adjusting my conscience a little. He won the jackpot, a terrorist rap sheet in the making, and had come back to make sure I'd reap the benefit of it. My desire to talk about it had vanished like my libido at the sight of a cross-dresser. Just then, a delivery truck arrived at the butcher shop on the ground floor of my building, and I took advantage of the noise to stick my head over the balcony so I wouldn't have to look at him. What if he lied as well as I did? We were Pop's sons, after all, and if there was one thing he'd taught us perfectly, it was to blend in with the crowd. I tried to imagine how this situation would unfold in a normal family. One of your loved ones comes back from Syria, even though all of France hates jihadists, Salafists, and anything even remotely related to them. He doesn't tell you anything, or only a very small part of the truth. He doesn't call his father, and hides away like a rat in his brother's house all day, because he thinks he'll go to prison if anyone sees him. Did he kill people in Syria? Since his return, I'd been searching for a killer's glint in his eyes. What was behind his sad, teary eyes? A wife and kids left behind over there? Fear of the future? Mom's death? Or the hundreds of people he'd killed, decapitated? And then there's a cop telling you his fingerprints were found in the medical storeroom of a hospital where they keep products that can be used to make explosives. But I knew this cop as well as if he were my own father. Conclusion: it was a lie to test me, to try to worm something out of me.

"What did you and Dad do when I left?"

I watched the cars going past on the street below. The concerto of horns, the engine noise, and the insults coming from the drivers' seats bombarded my ears. The butcher on the ground floor was heaving carcasses around while cursing at his apprentice. My second cigarette was smoking between my fingertips. The city oozed despondency and the fatigue of a long day of work. There was a sense of nostalgia in the air for a time when everything was okay. I refocused on my brother, who was waiting for an answer. He'd gotten reaccustomed to my silences, my rhythm, my way of doing things. It's how dreamers and ganja-smokers operate.

"We waited for you, like dogs, for days. We thought you were dead. Pop scoured the Yellow Pages, he called all the hospitals, all the police stations, his whole taxi-driver network. I kept thinking about all the trouble we'd gotten into in the past, my stuff with weed, my little side gigs, all our messes. I smoked all my worries away. I didn't want you to be dead. Just for you to be happy. For life to go well. Then we got your e-mail. From an unknown address. Pop wanted to beat the shit out of you. He screamed even louder that day than when Mom died. I was out on the balcony smoking cigarettes then, too, just like her. We never believed you were in Mali. From the beginning, we knew you'd gone back to the old country. I couldn't sleep at night, I kept picturing you cutting heads off, back there in the homeland, in Palmyra. Did you know our village is called Tadmor? That's not a joke. Tadmor in Syria, that's where Palmyra is. Thank goodness the old lady got out. Then I thought about our cousins, and I hoped you hadn't killed them. Even if they were only cousins in a photo, it's still family. That would have destroyed Dad. I sat by the window every night, leaning out under the stars, so I wouldn't have to hear him crying, just killing joint after joint, like with Big Moha when my leg was broken. The old man cried so much for six months, I forgot he was capable of smiling. Did you think of that before you left, asshole? The only thing I wanted to do was punch your teeth in. Grab you and handcuff you and gag you and beat you until you apologized. You had no right! Because you had something to lose, not like those other lowlifes. I watched every video I could find on the Internet about those desert rats. Those sons of bitches. The cops called me in. Someone must have snitched. There was a lot of talk about you around the hood. I didn't have this job yet. Still doing my little pieces of business here and there with Moha's gang and Sevran's guys and Mickaël. Transporting weed, some-times, and coke. Had to make money somehow. At least it made me think about something else, passed the time. People asked where you were, and I had to lie. I said you were sick, or you were in Brittany, and then I started saying you'd been transferred. But nobody believed it, because your phone was out of service. And then people kept coming up to me and asking for your new number. It was like the walls were talking about Cham. I started snooping around in your past. First with Pharaon at the mosque in Aubervilliers, and then with Kamel. People were suspicious of me, it was weird. Something didn't add up, but I couldn't figure out what. They told me they'd had nothing to do with your departure. I started hanging around with them, to try to find out more. And I actually ended up liking them. They were right about a lot of things. They just went too far with it. Then I tried to reconstruct your life, from the moment I broke my leg to the day you left. Imagine retracing ten years of a life, like in a movie. Image after image. First your friends from soccer, and then middle school and high school, and the ones from the neighborhood, and then nursing school, and the mosque. I went everywhere except Brittany, because Mamie Malo was dead, and the rest of them were never really family. The priest, the stars, the Bible, the Quran, and all your bullshit. You had to make everything complicated. You couldn't just do what everyone else does. Pray on Fridays, hoping for better things, and otherwise just do the best you could every day with your job. Respect what's important in life."

He didn't have the face of a person who could rob Pompidou Hospital. Impossible. He'd barely left the house. And where would he have stored it all? The truth was, it was my brother or Le Gwen. Family, or justice. I couldn't tell any-more if my brother was lying. I wanted to believe in family. There was no way my little brother could be a liar; all you had to do was look at him to see that. His shoulders were hunched, his chin quivering, his teeth chattering. He bent his head so I wouldn't see him crying. Cheeks wet with tears of guilt, wiped away with the back of his hand. Feelings never lie.

"Look me in the eye like a man. Like your father's son. And then, one day, there was the video. You could see your face, surrounded by beardos. Your big, stupid French face. Everyone started talking about you after that, everywhere. Half the city congratulated me discreetly and the other half avoided us. I won't even mention the old people who came by to lecture us or tell us how sorry they were for us. The cops summoned both me and Dad again. Even though the police were only looking into it, to Pop you were already guilty. Too late. It was worse than if you'd stabbed him. Going back to his home country, to make war. He tore apart all his own memories looking for the reason you left. You son of a bitch. I've fucked up too, but I've never betrayed the family. I kept making deliveries with Sevran's guys, hiding the weed in the trunk of my car. Driving fast, early in the morning, when the cops and everyone else were asleep. Four thirty, five in the morning. I got pulled over for speeding a few times, but you know me, I got out of it in a snap. And then, one day, it got out of hand. The highway was closed for construction. I didn't have time to look at the map, I just took the first exit. It was the big car show near Orly. That place is as big as a city, a few square kilometers at least. Mickaël was behind me, in another car. He had the cargo, and I was making sure the coast was clear. Anyway, we went into the fairground thinking we'd just go out the other end. Except that with the terror alert level high the way it's been, there were cops and dogs everywhere. They arrested us, and the dogs sniffed out the shit. I'll spare you the details. The cops found the grass. Pop didn't know anything about it, because at the time I was renting a studio apartment with Mickaël, so that our families wouldn't get in trouble if we got busted. Luckily, it

was Mickaël who got charged with possession. I disappeared
for weeks. The old man thought I'd gotten myself killed too.
But then I reappeared. I would have gone down, but thanks to
a cop I managed to stay out of the shit.

"Now you're going to stay calm and sit down and listen to
me. I didn't have a choice. Do you hear me? I didn't have a
choice. That was my only choice, right there. It's the path I
chose. With all the bullshit your friends had been up to in
France, the cops were recruiting a ton of people. And I happened to run into a good guy. A guy from the same place as us,
a Breton. Le Gwen. A decent guy who knows what he's doing.
He managed it so that my record with weed got wiped. But
nothing's free in this life. I became his bitch without ever suck-
ing him off. I put on my Muslim disguise and went to the
mosque, waiting patiently for the wind to come up and blow
back the curtains, so I could see what was behind them.   ˙

"Every week, there'd be some guy warning us that an attack
or bombings were about to happen. And in the end, there
ended up being three. They were fucking horrible. The night
Bataclan happened, I thought we were all done for, that we'd
all be packed off back to where we came from, crammed into
boats and planes. Goodbye, social security, iPhones, retirement, shopping malls, soccer, school, taxes, decent roads, cars,
and everything else this country has to offer. I was more afraid
than anyone else, except the others whose family members had
fucked off to the desert.

"Le Gwen helped me like a father. The apartment and the
job, too. He kept me from having a rap sheet, quietly, and that
opened a lot of doors for me. I became like a ghost, bro. There
are two of me now. The working stiff in the suit who drives
people around, and the whore with my eyes and ears wide
open. In the end, I realized that Le Gwen didn't give a shit
about me. He wanted me to whore myself out for him, and I
worked my ass off so he wouldn't abandon me. Supposedly so

they'd be lenient if you came back. You know Malik from Bondy? The day his brother came back, they locked him up before he could blink. No questions asked. Since then, I haven't trusted them. That's why I told you not to move. Yeah, I'm a snitch for the cops. No choice, otherwise I'd be up the river for five or six years. But, for you, I didn't tell them anything. They don't know anything. We'll go away together. No choice, anyway—rent in France is too expensive. Portugal or South America, Brazil. Brazil, bro, pretty girls in Rio."

He listened to it all, and his tears had dried. In his mind, just like in mine, snitching for the cops wasn't a life choice; it was a forbidden path. Worse than Cham. Almost as bad as being a pedophile.

"When did you go see for the last time?"

I hesitated. But I felt like I could trust him.

"This afternoon."

I had lost control of my tongue on that balcony. Too many words. Just a few words too many. One word. One single word was enough. Because a word will always be more powerful than an idea. It's the vehicle for it. I'm the driver. Without words, ideas can't travel. And God knows words are powerful, so powerful that ideas have to submit to them. Words are dangerous. Just a few little letters stuck together can send you to prison or to heaven or to hell.

33
OLDER BROTHER

There was only a quarter moon shining. On the balcony, beneath a night sky full of stars, I looked out at the concrete plain filled with buildings and highways. What were the stars? Why were they there? A tear leaked out. Shit. It slid down my nose. My brother hadn't seen it. Phew.

Autumn was talking to me, in the murmur of the wind and the quivering of the branches: "I am the last defense against the winter, and soon I'll be gone. Be strong until spring comes." A second tear escaped. Then a third. A fourth. Soon, ten, twenty, thirty.

Behind me, the kid brother was flipping through the channels. He got up to piss. There was a literary show on. On the screen, a presenter in a suit, with longish hair, good-looking, with eyes that were mischievous and almost wicked, was distributing questions, thank yous, and smiles to the guests. He had a book in his hand and was accompanying each of his remarks with deliberate hand gestures. Then he'd open the book, perch his glasses on the end of his nose, and lean his head back slightly so he could focus. "*Death on the Installment Plan*—Louis-Ferdinand Céline," the title and author of the book. "Here we are, alone again. It's all so slow, so heavy, so sad . . . Soon, I will be old. And this will finally be over . . ." The journalist sighed with admiration. "And this will finally be over . . . and this will finally be over." He didn't add anything else, just looked questioningly at the panel of writers. Silence.

The sentence kept running through my head. *And this will*

finally be over . . . I relit the joint. My brain rewrote the phrase: *Soon I will be dead, and this will finally be over.* Beyond the railing, there were six floors of emptiness. Hold the ledge with one hand, put one leg over, then the other. Hold myself straight, firm, dignified. Then let go. Without saying goodbye. Fall, fall, fall. It would definitely be better. From up here, my little brother would see a body crushed on the ground, head shattered, in a pool of blood. The police would be here within fifteen minutes. What would he do then? Stay for me and get handed over to the police, or save his own skin? I'd failed at my life; he'd failed at his. Maybe he'd chosen to succeed in his death?

34

OLDER BROTHER

I didn't know which one to drive out: doubt, or my brother. What Le Gwen said was impossible. Leaning against the railing of the balcony, my brother had stayed silent. Finding out I was a snitch for the cops had blown him away. He said it was bizarre to hear me admit it. I didn't know if it was a question or a comment. I was kind of like the dad myself now, and I didn't need to justify myself or have pissing contests with anyone anymore. Anxiety had taken control of his tongue; he wouldn't drop the subject, kept firing questions at me. Why? When? What? How? And every time, he saw how I answered with no guilt about what I'd done. Finally, he accepted it and put his hand on my shoulder, as if to thank me. His mind was somewhere else tonight. He asked questions without listening to the answers. There was something else going on in his head. In twenty-four hours, we'd be on the road to Portugal.

"What are you thinking about?"

"Nothing."

"Quit lying. You're not even listening to my answers. I can see it. Is it Portugal?"

"Nah, forget it."

He asked me if I had any family photos. I had only one album. The one from the only time we'd gone to a summer resort together. Dad had given us both disposable cameras. The first picture was one I'd taken in the parking lot. Pop and my brother were standing together in front of the car. The old man looked angry, as usual, but it was his happy-angry face, and the kid brother was smiling as if Mom were still alive. Turning the pages, we lost ourselves in our teenage memories. That vacation was the only time I ever went fishing. I'd just turned fourteen years old, and my brother was twelve. It was at a camp with mountain-biking and canoeing lessons, not far from Rennes, on the banks of the Vilaine River. The old man had found the place through the taxi drivers' union. One afternoon I was sitting on the riverbank with one of the instructors and my brother. The guy couldn't have been more than twenty. He was holding the only fishing pole in the whole camp. He'd already filled a bucket with all kinds of fish, but he wouldn't let us try even once, and just kept reeling in the trophies and holding them up to brag. We'd found two long branches to use as poles and tied fishing line to the ends of them. And we waited. For hours. I looked up at the sky, begging heaven to send me just one fish, even a tiny one, so I could experience the joy of fishing, too. Nothing. Even back then, I was questioning whether God was really on our side, or the side of the assholes. I mean, because it always seems like we, the people on the side of justice, suffer more. All this is to say that after three hours, my bladder was about to burst, because we'd each guzzled down a bottle of Coke. I was so afraid of missing a fish that I held in my pee to watch the river. But, finally, I couldn't hold it anymore, and I found a huge oak tree that was twice as tall as our apartment building. I still remember that because I compared the size of my dick to the size of the tree and thought about how we really were nothing in the universe. I still get that weird image in my head even now, whenever I'm fucking a girl. I picture a woman with a huge tree trunk between her legs.

Anyway, at the exact moment I started pissing I heard my brother yelling, "Come here, you're getting a bite! Hurry, come back!" I was aiming at the little spots formed by the tree bark, and, unfortunately, once I start pissing I can't stop. I still tried to cut off the stream by clenching everything, but it was unstoppable, like a geyser. The kid brother yelled for me again, but my bladder was too full. There was so much it hurt to empty it. I pissed a stream, a whole river even. It flowed from between my legs and right toward the river. A shiver of pleasure and pride ran through me, but I was already thinking about the fish again, and after I finished, I ran back toward the fishing pole, dodging between the tents. I got there just in time to see my brother grabbing the branch and pulling out the fish, which wriggled on the end of the line. I wanted to grab the fish and pull out the fishhook, but the fucking thing slipped between my hands. We put it in the bucket, and my brother took out the hook. It was an ugly catfish. I was happy and disappointed at the same time. Happy because we'd finally succeeded. But disappointed because I'd missed everything for the sake of a pee. My brother was the luckiest man in the world. The catfish was his double. His double, because you can never hold on to a fish; it always slips out of your hands. And a cat, because it's an asshole that comes and rubs against you when it's hungry or wants to be petted, and then fucks off immediately when it wants to do its own thing.

We'd come to the end of the photo album, tripping out on a few photos. We'd made some French friends back then. We started remembering the names that went with the faces: Nicolas, François, Pierre, Paul, Alexandre. Stupidly, I think both of us were wondering about stuff like, "If I'd paid attention in school, if I hadn't spent so much time hanging out outside, if I hadn't smoked so much pot, if I'd spent less time in mosques, if I'd listened to Dad, if the highway exit hadn't been closed on the day the police nabbed me, if I hadn't gone to Syria, if Mom hadn't died." Ifs, and more ifs. Life is the sum of our ifs. And then there was nothing left to say. I mean, there was a lot, really, but it took courage, and that wasn't my thing.

But my brother, he was a warrior. He started talking about Mom's funeral, and our Breton grandmother, and our Syrian one. And, little by little, the rest came out, all our shared memories: the problems in cousin Ismaïl's marriage to Assa, the black chick; the disappearance of Rainman the big shot; Mehmet; soccer. The hours ticked by, and in the air there was a feeling like that at the end of war and the beginning of peace. Gabbing, smoking cigarettes on the balcony, moving to the living room, standing and gabbing, smoking more cigarettes, and then more, and my gums bled with each one.

My brother talked, talked, talked, as if his mouth had been taped shut for ten years. But still, his gaze kept dropping to his feet. In fact, we hadn't talked like this since were teenagers, before each one of us went his own way. What is growing up? Making choices, experiencing the consequences? What is getting older? Understanding that there's nothing but choices. You take one path, or another, it doesn't matter much; eventually, we all end up doing the same thing: giving up the ghost. As he talked, I was lost in my own thoughts. As lost as the weed could make me. I had to be, because all this talking was well and good, but after a war, you have to rebuild everything. The English teacher used to say: "Stop speaking and crying, just work." For the "speaking" part, we knew we were going to Portugal. I'd told Mickaël that one of my buddies was going to hide out at his place for a while. He'd given me the keys and I'd made a copy for my brother. First I'd go and get him settled in, and then come back. Get everything in order here, and join him again. Hoping he wouldn't disappear.

"What about Dad?"

Once again, no answer. I don't know why he didn't want to see Pop. There were only a few hours left, so I tried one last time.

"You're going to leave without seeing the old man?"

He hugged me tightly, and we went to bed. For me, it was

just a short round trip. All our problems would end with simple solutions. He'd come back illegally, and now he was leaving again the same way. A quick stop back here to see that his life in France was over and he had to go somewhere else. Me, I was just the driver. The other possibility was to turn my brother in to the police. That did cross my mind. Would it be simpler? In this night, where all cats were gray and the moon was high, Mary Jane and I weighed the pros and cons of this whole shitty mess. Selling my brother out would mean years and years of sleepless nights, friends who hated me, and Pop disowning me. It would be my death sentence. Because after that, what would be left? The pride of having been honest? The car, and ten hours a day being ordered around by a mobile phone? Fill the fridge, fuck the girlfriend, summer vacation in Spain or winter vacation in Thailand, offer up a few prayers at the mosque to make yourself believe you're one of the good guys. The only choice, my only choice, our only choice, our way out, was the road to Portugal. Smell the air and breathe, think, leave again, and take a new path. To death. All paths lead to death. So it's best to choose the most comfortable one.

In bed, my eyes closed, thoughts whizzed through my head like they were on a road without speed-traps. Too fast. Impossible to grasp on to any one of them. What if the police raided the building in the night and found us? Street noise drifted through the window, splitting the silence, hammering at my ears, snuffing out my courage. Sweat, sweat, sweat. I tried to pin my worries down to make them shut up. But they slipped away when I came after them. Like Mohammad Ali versus Frazier, eighth, ninth, tenth round . . . In the eleventh round, I finally understood. I understood everything. We needed to keep our heads above water, not make waves, glide across the surface, across life, so we wouldn't sink. Then, someday, if God willed it, there would be peace in France and we could come back. To do what? Dunno, but it was our homeland. No point in pretending otherwise.

Rusted-out factories, high-rise projects, twisted faces, missing teeth, buddies in prison, stolen cars, scooter races, Afghan hash bars, baggies of coke, religious beardos with wives sealed up in burqas, friendly imams, sons of bitches, the atmosphere of a kebab joint, the smell of onions, oil, and harissa, nights that never bring any answers, hookers and girls who are virgins in the pussy but not the ass, the others who get their hymens sewn back together before the wedding, the bastards with orange Police armbands, blue-white-and-red badges, snitches, liars, junkies with bloodshot eyes—we'd miss all of it. Even with a dream life on the beach, surrounded by nice round asses and big fake tits and tanned skin, cocktails, sunglasses, money, Colgate smiles, villas, coconut palms, and flip-flops, poor or not, the past would come back, and we'd want to wrap our arms around it and hold it tight, like I dreamed of doing with Mom every morning before I went down into the mines.

In round twelve, exhausted, I closed my eyes. I was at the wheel of my car, my little brother was looking at the map. We were in outer space. To our right, the moon called out a goodbye. All around us, it was immense, beautiful, infinite, a deep black canvas with stars gleaming mysteriously. I floored the gas pedal toward Saturn, and we parked the car on Titan. No life here. Too cold. Not for us. It would take thousands of years to adapt to it. We left and roamed through space in every direction. I opened my eyes again when I thought I heard the apartment door click shut. The sun was beating down on my face. I was back on Earth, my eyelids crusted together, and I hardly had the strength to open them. It was 9:17 A.M. I got up, pissed, made coffee. Sitting out on the balcony, my feet on the table, I woke up gently, along with the city. We were leaving that evening and would drive through the night. Less traffic.

That way we'd cross the Spanish border in the early hours, when there'd be fewer border checks, because in the evenings, there were kids driving drunk, and cops pulling drivers over for breathalyzer tests.

Only one more day to kill, and I wasn't going to spend it hanging out at home. There wasn't going to be any more cash coming in and we'd need plenty soon, so I wanted to work for a few hours this morning, to get money for the road trip, at least. Plus, if the cops hassled me, it would be a kind of alibi. I showered, brushed my teeth, put on my suit and white shirt, and fixed my tie. Seriously, anyone in real life would have said, whether they have blue, black, brown, or green eyes, white, black, or yellow skin, that it wasn't a chauffeur in the mirror but a man to be respected. I slipped my feet into my polished shoes and then checked my bag: ID, check; license, check; keys . . . where were they? They were usually either in my bag or in the drawer of the cabinet in the entry. They weren't in the drawer, either. I must have left them in the car. I went down to the parking garage. Surprise, surprise; my car was gone, too. I checked the lower level of the garage just in case, then went back over every square centimeter of the whole place twice. The car wasn't there. There had been a couple of times in the past when, stoned, I parked the car on the street to avoid smashing into the corner of the garage entrance. I went out to the street, looked around a little, but my memory wasn't failing me today; I remembered driving back here after my visit to Le Gwen yesterday. I went back up to the apartment. My brother still wasn't up. Maybe somebody from our hood had swiped the car. There were always old grudges being revived around here. Or maybe someone from the building had found the key in the door and taken the car. On the very same day we were leaving for Portugal. Wouldn't you know it.

I went to wake up my brother. In his room, everything was

neat and tidy. The bed was made. His suitcase was gone. And so was he. There was a note on the bed.

> I've taken the car. Don't move until I call you. Don't turn on the TV. Don't do anything. It's very important. If I haven't called you by one this afternoon, go to Mickaël's.
> Don't worry.
>
> Your brother.

I pulled out my phone. The voicemail said he was unavailable. What good was the mobile I'd bought him? Zero. I called back. Fifteen times. Twenty. Twenty-five. Nothing. Just the voicemail. My brother had left. Gone.

Doubt. It's a guy who grabs you by the shoulders and shakes you like a soda machine. And the guy is you. The first doubt is self-doubt: the fear of having been wrong without being able to provide either the proof or the reason. Doubt is a series of questions without answers, which feed off one another and eat away at you, down to the bone. Doubt is the ultimate test. When you have to act, it hits out at your confidence, at the truth, at the habits and actions of daily life. You go forward with your mind quivering, confused, the doubt nibbling away at your freedom of thought and movement. Doubt is unstable ground, dangerous, slippery, deadly.

10:47 A.M. I called his number back. Voicemail.

10:48 A.M. Voicemail.

10:49 A.M. Voicemail. I left a message. "Okay, where the hell are you? Call me back."

10:55 A.M. Voicemail. "You fucking bastard. Call me back."

10:57 A.M. Voicemail. "You're freaking me out. If you get this message, call me back right away."

11:01 A.M. Voicemail.

I paced the living room in circles, rereading his note every five minutes.

I've taken the car. Don't move until I call you. Don't turn on the TV. Don't do anything. It's very important. If I haven't called you by this afternoon, go to Mickaël's.

Don't worry.

Your brother.

He'd used his best handwriting. The letters were nice and round. He'd written it carefully. No chicken scratch. And that made it even more infuriating. I stretched out on the sofa and closed my eyes to try to calm down, because doubt had been gnawing at me since yesterday, since the conversation with Le Gwen and all that business about fingerprints.

11:13 A.M.

I turned on the TV, flipping from channel to channel. Nothing. I was going out of my mind.

11:21 A.M.

I called the old man.

"Hello? *Ibni*? You okay?"

"Hi. Yeah, I'm okay, are you?"

"Fine. I'm on my way to the taxi drivers' protest."

I hung up.

11:22 A.M.

My dad called back several times. I didn't touch the phone. Finally I texted him saying I'd call back. He answered: *OK. There's problem?*

11:25 A.M.

I looked up my brother's Internet history on the laptop. Nothing. He'd deleted the whole thing.

11:28 A.M.

I took out the *Bridge on the River Kwai* DVD case.

11:29 A.M.

I started crumbling the weed.

11:30 A.M.

I licked a cigarette to remove the paper strip and empty the tobacco into the palm of my hand.

11:31 A.M.

The tobacco and the pot were mixed. I put it in a rolling paper.

11:32 A.M.

The joint was rolled. I lit it.

11:33 A.M.

I'd gotten a buzz, but I was still on the earthly plane.

11:35 A.M.

I continued dragging on the joint, the remote in my hand, switching from one channel to the next.

11:38 A.M.

I spent three minutes stuck on a twenty-four-hour news channel. A report about Islamist places and *taqqiya*. The art of hiding, concealing, covering up. I started flipping channels. The fucking fingerprints.

11:40 A.M.

My heart clenched. My mind was racing. He had lied to me, the bastard. Why was his room so neat? I tried to convince myself it was because we were leaving that night, but I couldn't make myself believe it.

11:42 A.M.

I searched his room. Lifted up the mattress. Rummaged through the armoire. Nothing. The rest of the apartment, nothing. No hint. I cried out and kicked the armoire. The door cracked.

11:43 A.M.

A police siren. Was it for me?

11:44 A.M.

The siren receded into the distance.

11:45 A.M.

I called him again. Voicemail. "Where are you? What are you doing? I'm panicking, man. Call me back right away."

I screamed out with rage. Screamed, because he'd fucked me. It was too easy. He'd come back just like that, without saying anything. Without explaining himself. Too naive. His head had been messed up for ten years. Me, I thought I'd won the lottery. That I could get him back with no consequences. You don't have to be a girl to believe in Prince Charming.

A ghost. Gone without a word. Just "don't worry." And that "don't worry" was exactly what was making me worry so much. I kept pacing. I was losing my mind. I was trembling. I begged the darkness. Who could I call? Mehmet? Too late.

12:12 P.M. I didn't know what to do.

Piece by piece, I went back over everything in my mind. The bus he got off of, which came from Germany, and what Mehmet told me. The story in the paper about the theft at Pompidou Hospital. And the fake hospital ID he showed the receptionist at the nursing home. And the fucking finger-prints! The fingerprints. Why hadn't I believed Le Gwen, dammit? *Taqqiya*! It had to be *taqqiya*! I grabbed my phone and called the lawyer.

"I told you," he said.

"What do I do now?"

"Go to the police. Tell them everything. File a complaint about the car. You have to protect yourself. Otherwise, you're an accomplice. You have to be convincing so they believe you didn't know anything."

"But I didn't know anything!"

"Maybe, but that's not what's important. What's important now isn't the truth; it's to create a truth, the right truth. And that truth is that they believe you don't know anything. So go, now."

"What if I don't go?"

"Then get yourself the fuck away from here! Go somewhere far away, far, far away, and disappear. For good."

12:19 P.M. Go where? And how? Without a car? And what if my brother told the truth? I didn't know, I didn't know anymore. Nobody would believe me, but who knew him as well as me? Doubt! It was a beautiful day outside. I went down to the street and lit what remained of the joint. People kept turning to look at me because the weed must have stunk. There was a pretty brunette, fortyish, with little kids on the sidewalk across the street. Next to her was a double-parked police car; a female cop and a male cop coming out of a kebab place. I don't know what they were saying, but they looked happy to be talking about it. I started walking.

12:25 P.M. My brother had written, *If I haven't called you by one this afternoon, go to Mickaël's.*

Did that mean go to Portugal?

My feet were walking of their own accord. One after the other, they pulled me down the street, my hands in my pockets. The leaves on the trees were turning orange; autumn was beginning. Tenon Hospital was on my right. Beautiful buildings on the left. People coming and going, living their lives. We were in a free country. It had taken me a long time to understand that. And even though we didn't have the life we'd dreamed of, we couldn't hate it. Too easy. I walked back up the street, cars going by. At the Pelleport metro station, taxis were lined up. Poor people having a hard time of it.

I sat down on a bench and took out my phone to connect to the driving app. After five minutes, I had an assignment. I canceled it and then logged off. The end of a world. On the street around me, the atmosphere had changed in only a few minutes. Bizarre. People walked fast, panicked, stopping to look at their phones and then starting to walk again with quick steps, looking around, anxious, as if evil were circulating in the streets. It felt like a war was beginning. People ducked into shops quickly, into buildings, cafes, or came out of them on their way to somewhere else. In five minutes, almost all the pedestrians and cars had vanished.

12:34 P.M. The street was empty, and I was still on my bench. Not so much as a cat around. My phone vibrated several times. They were news alerts.

"Attack warning: car explosion in Paris."

The beginning of my end.

37
YOUNGER BROTHER

I set foot on German soil almost two months ago. Blondbeard had gotten me a Syrian passport. The three others arrived together two weeks later. Enough time to prepare for our arrival in Paris. It wasn't actually that complicated, but we had to be patient. Wait for the perfect moment, on the perfect day. I monitored the news on the Internet. Step by step, I went over my plan. Where to do it? When to do it? How to get there? How and where to set up the explosives? With what materials? Where could I get them without being noticed? A month beforehand, everything was ready. I waited for the right time and then took the bus to Paris. The others followed a few days later.

On D-Day, I took the car and we headed for Paris. It was a sunny day. Beautiful. People were having lunch outside. Perfect for a massacre. Maybe one or two hundred deaths. In the car, I didn't even dare look at them anymore. I wore jeans, a button-down shirt, a nice jacket, to blend in, just in case anything went haywire. I started the car. Once we turned off the beltway, we took the road that ran alongside the Seine. It felt like the end. I tried to control my shaking. The four Kalashnikovs were on the floor in the back seat, under the others' feet. I prayed that the police wouldn't stop us.

I ran to the closest café. On TV, the newscaster was giving the first bulletins. A car had exploded in Paris. For now, the channel didn't have any more information. People had taken refuge in the café. I looked at my phone every thirty seconds. I was nauseated, my skin was crawling, and I was boiling hot. My shirt was soaked and stuck to my back. The first images came through. The newscaster was talking about a Japanese car, a black one, but they didn't know yet if there were victims or passengers inside. A reporter was there, where it had happened; there was no live feed, but you could hear her describing the scene. I was about to faint. My car was black and Japanese. For a second, I tried to reassure myself, because there are a ton of cars like that, especially private hires. But the doubt flooded back almost instantly, punching me in the gut. I went to splash some cold water on my face in the bathroom, to try to calm down. Life was over, the other dog was dead. No more future, nothing, exploded, no time to think about whether to cry or not. My brother was in a thousand pieces. I lifted my head from the bathroom sink, and in the mirror my reflection spoke to me:

"I'm afraid of losing you."

I took a step backward. Stunned, I spit. The gob of spit stuck to the mirror. I was hallucinating, like in Chad.

The muffled voice of the newscaster filtered through the bathroom door.

"The explosion appears to have taken place near the Gare de Lyon."

Dead, gone, goodbye. And my dad? A life for nothing. His wife dead; me, on the run, the other son in a thousand pieces. We wouldn't even be able to bury him. When the reporters showed up at Pop's place and the media circus rang his doorbell, he'd kill them with rage. And he'd go to prison. Our race was cursed. We were made to serve others and disappear. We were good for nothing. Useless. Fucked from the very first generation. This country gave us everything, and all we wanted to do was fuck it in the ass. In the end, everyone lost.

12:41 P.M. My phone vibrated. I looked at the guy in the mirror. He was the same age as me, handsome like me, wearing a dark suit and white shirt like me, his skin pale and blue like mine, his hair brushed back and tied in a ponytail. Like me. Why had this guy's brother blown himself up? And why had this guy been so determined to believe in his brother from day one? This time it was too much. I started crying like a girl. The guy in the mirror knocked on the glass.

"What are you doing, you fucking fag? Be a man. Get the hell away from here! You going to let yourself be locked up like a pedophile? Do they call you Pilot or not?"

12:44 P.M. My phone vibrated again. I tried to think but everything was happening too fast. I couldn't concentrate. Someone knocked on the bathroom door.

"You okay in there?"

"Yeah. Sorry, I'm having a little problem."

I heard the man laugh.

12:46 P.M. The phone vibrated again. This was it; the calls would be nonstop now. Reporters? Had they given out my car's registration number on TV? I had to get out of here.

12:47 P.M. My phone wouldn't stop. It was vibrating constantly.

12:48 P.M. I opened the bathroom door. The café was packed. Everyone was staring, mesmerized, at the TV screen. I threaded my way through the crowd toward the front door. The boss called out after me.

"Sir, on the news they're advising people to stay where they are."

I nodded at him.

12:50 P.M. Phone still vibrating.

12:51 P.M. I had to get to Bobigny, take Dad's car and get away. I looked at my phone. Nineteen missed calls. From my brother!

12:52 P.M. The phone vibrated again. My brother again. I was going crazy. *Little brother*, it said on the screen. It wasn't possible. I answered it.

"Hello? Shit, what are you doing? It's number six, come to the crossbar."

It was him. I wasn't crazy. Six was his number on the soccer team. The crossbar? The Lilas soccer field.

"You're at Lilas?"

He told me in Syrian Arabic not to talk on the telephone, asked me to confirm that I'd understood, and hung up.

39
Younger Brother

Near the Cité de la mode, that big green piece-of-shit building across the Seine from the Bercy metro stop, I got out of the car on the quay, pretending I needed a piss. I walked about twenty meters away from the car. The phone was in my underpants. In Syria, I'd learned how to ignite a charge using a telephone. You connect a cable to the jack outlet, and when it rings, it'll explode. There are ways of delaying the explosion. For example, the electric signal sent to the telephone during the call could set off a timer. Apart from that, everything's the same: a primary charge ignites and detonates the main, secondary charge. The second I took out my phone, the three others in the car turned back into human beings. With a father and a mother, a family, a life. The Seine flowed next to me. I wanted to throw the phone in the water and take off running. Maybe they would have gunned me down. I thought of you. And Dad. And Mom. And Grandma. And life. I didn't have a choice anymore. I'd have to disappear. It was the only way to escape them. No other choice. I'd have to die with them. Glimpses of their lives flashed before my eyes; I saw them as kids, playing with their parents. Then at school. The dreams they'd had. I imagined the funerals. The families, broken, destroyed. And all of that kept me from acting, paralyzing me. I wasn't born to kill. I treated people; I repaired lives and living people. It was me or them. And I thought of you, of us. With your plans for Portugal. You'd already decided we would go. It might have been an idea only, but whatever happened, I knew you'd do it. And every time I thought about all that, I told myself this would be only one moment in time. A test. That I'd forget one day. It would take time, but at the end of the day we wouldn't get caught. Not Dad. Or you. Grandma? I hadn't figured her into the plans. I'd forgotten her. Down the drain. Whatever we might think, she was already dead in that place full of old people waiting to die.

The phone was in my hand. Pressing the Call button meant killing three men and disappearing, as far as the world was concerned. Dead on paper. Officially. I could have tossed a "go fuck yourselves!" at them before blowing them up, but I wasn't killing them only for that. It was for me. To save my own ass, to live in peace. So that Blondbeard would think I was dead, so he'd never look for me, and so France would think I was in Syria, or dead. And I would come back, maybe in thirty years, when everyone would have forgotten the whole thing. My mind and heart blank and empty, virginal, in my country. I'd convinced Blondbeard I wanted to blow up France. It was the only way I could get out of the hell of Cham. There was no other way out. Otherwise, they'd think you were going to report them, and they'd kill you. I screwed them over. But I had to make it extreme so they wouldn't suspect me. Make them think I was dead. That I'd fucked the whole thing up.

The car exploded, and in the flames there were three fewer lives, and my freedom reborn. I was behind a big concrete post. Paralyzed by the scene in front of me. It would have been easy to cry. The hardest part wasn't pressing the button but living with the deaths afterward. No time, no choice. My family and I were what mattered. I became a robot. I ran along the quayside. There was nobody there, except for a security guard who had no idea what had happened. Then everything blurred together in my head. I was drenched in sweat. There were sirens all around me, everywhere, crisscrossing the city. Panic filled the air. People smelled it and hid. And you, my goddamned brother, my fuck-ing goddamned brother. I reached the underground parking garage where I'd parked your car. Panicking. My legs were trembling; I'd run like a dog. My chest burned, and I tasted blood. I thought I was going to die right there. That it was over. Some son of a bitch had tried to drive his American 4x4 into the parking garage, but he'd gone the wrong way, down the exit ramp, and his overly large car had gotten jammed against the ceiling. Stuck, brother. There was a tow truck, cops, people gawking, the whole shebang. I'd left my suitcase and papers in the car—everything we needed to leave. I don't know how, but everything came together lightning-fast in my head. If I left your suitcase with everything in it, they could trace it back to you—and me—quickly. So I slipped discreetly into the parking garage. The police were just local ones. I walked casually past them and then back out with the suit-case, papers, and bags. At first I wanted to go back to the apartment, get you, and get the hell out of there. But when I got there, you were gone. So I called you. No answer. Then I told myself I couldn't wait there because the cops might show up at any moment. And within a few seconds my brain came up with a solution. The soccer field.

40

OLDER BROTHER

I n the vacant lot, the goal we'd always used when we pretended to be famous soccer players still stood between the rows of buildings. How many penalty kicks had we aimed at the crossbar? Hours and hours' worth of them, in our beat-up shoes and sweaty jerseys, following in the footsteps of our Brazilian idols, Ronaldo, Romário, Bebeto. I walked across the dusty ground in my leather jacket, my steps firm, more determined than they'd ever been. There was no one around. I puckered my lips and whistled like I used to do back in the day, when I'd come home at night and signal him to open the door for me. The answer came from behind a bush. His Greek-god curls appear between the branches. He put his hand on my forearm, cleared his throat, and gasped out a few words. The kind that, like in a good movie, turn the whole story upside down.

"It wasn't your car."

Marble. I froze like a marble statue. Like when Mom died. Laugh or cry, scream, rip his head off, punch him, strangle him, kill him and kill myself. I grabbed him by the collar and cursed at him in whispers. Tears, nerves, rage, it was all boiling inside me, and yet I held it all back, because family and the survival instinct outweighed any problems. We were both swimming in the same shit. If we went down, it would be together. To get out of this we'd have to dog-paddle like migrants when the lifeboats arrive. So, after the cursing and the questions and the heart palpitations and the trembling hands and glaring daggers at him, I put my anger aside. It was up to me to make an effort at peace. That's how life is: you only recognize peace when you've been through wars that rip your heart out. He was huddled up like a beaten child, eyes red as a junkie's, face struck with guilt. I trembled uncontrollably as my phone vibrated nonstop with calls from my dad. There was a side of me that felt sorry for him, but, in the silence, I also saw the face of an executioner. I managed to calm him down. This was no time to screw things up. We went to find the car in the underground parking garage. It was five hundred meters from the house. A baseball cap jammed down on his head, my brother kept close to the walls. The 4x4 and the city cops were gone. The coast was clear.

41
OLDER BROTHER

On the highway, like two zombies, gazes fixed on the space between the white lines painted on the asphalt, we ate up the kilometers like a Somalian in a butcher shop on an evening during Ramadan. In my head, everything was okay, and not okay at all. It came and went. Life or death? A jerk of the wheel and we'd be off the road, the car flipped, blood everywhere, and all our problems would be over. "Accident on the highway. Two dead," a friend of mine would read tomorrow at the café, in the right hand column of a paper or on his smartphone. Impossible to think much at the moment; our heads were empty, our synapses barely firing. We were like robots, programmed to survive. To make sure their loved ones survived. My little brother, despite the tears and the fear and the death, was in the same state of mind. Fraternal instinct; otherwise he wouldn't be here. Each with our hand in the other's shorts, protecting his balls in a cowboy grip. We stopped the car before the moon went down. We'd reached the Cévennes Mountains. Eyes ringed with dark circles, brains fried with exhaustion, neither one of us spoke. He stretched, sighed, suppressed his tears one last time, and asked me if we should get off the highway. I started driving again and took the first exit. It was a country road. He had me slow down and stop. In the night, in the moonlight, his face was blue. We were at the end of the world. His mouth opened, and he began telling me the whole story, starting with his departure from France, up to that day. The guy is crazy.

Totally insane. Abnormal. Touched in the head. But he's my brother, and he saved himself. Life is hard. It's a pitiful thing to say, but I'm not ashamed. Otherwise, why is it always preferable to death?

I'm behind the wheel, still and always. Eleven hours a day. It's not work, it's learning the best way to pass the time. There are the customers. There's the radio, the programs, the hosts. And then there's the paper. The words. The notebook. The pen. Between fares, I park my car on a street corner, lean my seat back, and write. Sometimes one word, often a few lines, occasionally several pages. It nourishes me. I fill the page with anything and everything. Just as it comes. Raw. With my heart open. The most important thing isn't doing stuff perfectly; it's just doing it. Because with time, it feeds into itself, it gets better. Good things take time. And a little bit of love.

My brother's name is Hakim. It means "the just, the wise, the fair," or "the doctor." Someone who labors to do good. But I don't think we have the same definition. Life goes on. Despite everything. Without him, but with his spirit. No idea where he is. Maybe in Cham. Maybe in heaven. Maybe somewhere else. Since the night I dreamed of him at the Gare de Bagnolet, my nights have been filled with storms of thoughts. And if you're reading these lines, it's not thanks to me so much as it is to the grand waltz danced by my neurons, courtesy of ganja. I was dreaming. I'm insane, but conscious of everything. Putting on a suit and getting behind a steering wheel, that makes a man. Lookout by day, watchman by night. The spirit of the world whispering the sounds of life in your ears. My name is Azad. That's my first name. Back home, it means "free". And I am free. Not in life, but in my head. The mind is like the universe; it has no borders, and you can expand it endlessly. All you have to do invent, and reinvent, and you can create a world out of nothing much. A notebook, a pen, and a computer.

A guy got into the back seat of my car the other day. Fifty-five, maybe sixty years old, I'd say. Thinning hair. Gray at the temples. Elegantly mismatched jacket and pants. A sort of English gentleman, the kind you'd never suspect of any crime whatsoever, the kind who wouldn't hurt a fly and does only good in the world. It was a nice fare; he lived quite a ways away, in Hauts-de-Seine. It was late in the evening and raining, felt like a scene out of *Taxi Driver*. I imagined the guy's life. His wife, kids, job, etc. He seemed easygoing, the kind of customer who wouldn't give you a hard time, who'd say hello and thanks and goodbye and "have a nice day," who'd smile at you. Perfect. After a few minutes, he took out a book. I couldn't see the title in the rearview mirror; it was just a couple centimeters too low. I don't know if he could see the weird head movements I had to make, trying to figure it out. I didn't usually ask customers questions, but this time my curiosity won out. "*Battling Siki*," answered the man. "It's about boxing. I edited it, and I'm rereading it now because I have to talk about it on the radio." It was the story of the first black French boxer, originally from Senegal, a genius in the ring. In the 1920s, in the world championship match, he KO'd the reigning champion, Georges Carpentier, in the sixth round. The referee disqualified him and refused to name him the winner. The crowd screamed for almost twenty minutes and put pressure on the referee, who reversed his decision. The boxer emigrated to the United States and led a life of glitz and glamor, and then, one night, somebody shot him twice in the back and killed him. The story interested me so much that he gave me the book.

Editor. I'd discovered a profession. For the rest of the drive he told me about his job, and I told him about mine. And after that it was just a crazy set of coincidences, a lightning strike, as happens sometimes in life. A tsunami of good vibes you just have to throw your surfboard on and ride out as long as you can. We exchanged cards and, like a lot of old people discovering social media, he added me on Facebook.

A few days later, on an evening when my mind was off on some gaseous planet, between Saturn and Jupiter, maybe on Titan or Europa, my tongue sticky, my eyes half-closed, words starting resonating in my ears, and I wrote something from deep down in my gut.

My brother was my partner in street fights driven by the kind of adolescent energy where I had less confidence in the solidity of my punches than in the speed of my legs to get me out of there. He was the wild nights that ended at noon the next day without a *centime* in my pocket and lungs full of tobacco, begging the employee at the McDonalds at the end of line 5 for a cheeseburger. He was my feet lined up behind the penalty mark, confident as Che Guevara that the ball would kiss the net. He was the heroic match of Double Z against Brazil in 2006, the kilometers run instead of paying cab fare, the hours spent hanging out at shopping strips, in front of the kebab place at the Pablo Picasso metro stop, skimping, plotting, gossiping, talking shit, scheming, dodging, dreaming, lying, imagining. The adrenaline of the first scooter races. Then the victories, and the euros won on car races. My brother was the one who opened the door for me when the moon was high and my brain was foggy and the old man was snoring like a brass band. He was the man who followed me everywhere all the time, my eye always on him, because he didn't have a father or a mother, and I thought I was his only beacon. Right behind me, from the police station to the movie theater, a head shorter and so baby-faced he didn't even need to shave. In the evenings, his young teenage eyes ravenous when he discovered girls, and his horse-cock when he got his first pieces of ass. Me, the young hoodlum commander, lover of cars and pretty girls, a joint smoking between my fingers, and him, the smart kid and faithful lieutenant, nose in a book, reading and rereading the story of the prophets, his idols. My brother was a man who found his path making others' lives better. A soft heart wounded by the distress of the world. Yesterday he would have prayed for Abbé Pierre; today it's for Syria and Palestine, and the day after tomorrow he'd have been running off toward someone else's tears. That's how my brother was. My missing ball. My other half. Dead or alive, he's with me, everywhere, always, every minute, in every move I make, every word. He didn't go wrong. Nobody goes wrong. He chose a path. A simple path. And he could have taken another one. It was his choice. In the end, he'll turn around and see that they all lead to heaven or the grave. My greatest lesson in humanity is my brother.

After I wrote that, the man from the taxi got in touch with me. "I can feel something boiling in your blood, demanding to be expressed. You want to write a book?" His blue eyes were moist, gentle, understanding. This wasn't the expression of a queer looking to get some; it was the look of a dreamer, someone who thought we could still change the world, put out the fires that burn your wings and your dreams. It was the look I would have liked to see from my dad the day I failed my exams, the day I chucked everything and joined the army, the day I came back with that damned sickness in my head. And the day my brother left.

So I told him everything. Everything, from childhood up to now. My brother, me, Mom, the old man, and Zahié, my grandmother. Everything you've read in this book. And then, as I was stripping my memories bare in search of an idea, he held up his hand like a priest, cutting me off, requesting the floor.

"What if your brother came back?"